HARD FIRE

J. B. TURNER

HARD FIRE

A **JON REZNICK** THRILLER

Published by Thomas & Mercer, Seattle

www.apub.com

Amazon, the Amazon logo, and Thomas & Mercer are trademarks of Amazon.com, Inc., or its affiliates.

ISBN-13: 9781542030069
ISBN-10: 1542030064

Cover design by @blacksheep-uk.com

Printed in the United States of America

HARD FIRE

HARD FIRE

One

The sky darkened over the north Maine woods.

Jon Reznick sat wrapped up on the deck of his lakefront log cabin, nursing a single malt. A fine mist had settled over Allagash Lake. Yellow-bellied flycatchers, ospreys, and grouse swooped low over the cold water.

It was the last night of a two-week-long vacation. He had found his place of true solitude. Hiking, trout fishing, and swimming in the freezing water. Enjoying the great outdoors. He cherished the peace and wild beauty of nature in all its glory, from the endless trails through the woods to the sound of the pristine water washing over the rocks to moss and fallen branches across the shoreline. It was a sanctuary. A place he could quiet his mind. Quiet the white noise in his head. A place where flashbacks and dark memories didn't intrude. A place to stare out over the water and forget. He understood the need for veterans to be alone.

He needed time to decompress. A time to clear his head. A time to drift away. A time to read biographies. Military history. American history. He also reread Thoreau's *The Maine Woods*, the copy his father had given him when he was a boy.

Reznick breathed in the cool air. He loved the backwoods. A place that appeared not to have changed. It was still nature in the raw. The winters were brutal, but the land remained untainted. Unspoiled.

His father had taught him to hunt, shoot, and kill. His own mother's bloodline was Scottish. Her ancestors had been forced off the land during the Highland Clearances. They had found refuge in Canada. Then they crossed the border into Maine. Reznick was descended from these poachers, lumberjacks, trappers, and renegades. He felt at home in the wilderness.

It was once said that Maine's earliest European settlers were "children of a hard country." It was true. It took a lot of character, brutal toughness, and sheer stubbornness to survive, let alone flourish. The hardships, deprivation, and dangers from wild animals were all around. But those settlers soon learned that the way to survive was to use the bounty at their disposal. The fish, the wildlife, the birds, the wood to build—it was all around them.

They learned.

Reznick's gaze now wandered to the edge of his deck. Resting against a wooden pillar was his trusty Nosler long-range carbon hunting rifle. He had hunted his share of moose, deer, and grouse over the years. Lately, he carried the rifle on his hikes to protect himself against bears.

Despite enjoying disconnecting when he arrived in a pristine part of the country, his hunter instincts, honed as he had learned to shoot as a boy and perfected when he joined Delta, meant he could sense danger. It was second nature. And those instincts had served him well.

Reznick enjoyed the simple life. He looked up at the billions of stars in the inky black sky. A shooting star streaked over the mountains.

He closed his eyes, enveloped by memories. He just wanted to forget.

Late the following afternoon, he finished packing all his belongings into his truck. He had a six-hour drive back to his hometown of Rockland. He looked forward to getting back to civilization after a time away. But his journey stopped almost as soon as it started, delayed for a few hours after a lumber truck overturned on a narrow road.

Reznick could only sit and wait in line, glad he had made some sandwiches and had hot coffee in a flask.

When he finally got back to Rockland, it was the dead of night, not a soul in sight.

Jon Reznick yawned as he drove his truck through the deserted streets. The radio played low, a Tom Petty number from way back when. The traffic light up ahead turned red. Reznick pulled up and relaxed, eager to get back home after nine hours on the road.

His mind drifted as he sat at the traffic light. He couldn't wait to get the fire lit, maybe have a nightcap after the long drive.

The light changed to green.

His cell phone rang.

Reznick groaned. He resented whoever the hell was calling in the middle of the night, even if he was already awake.

"Yeah, Reznick speaking."

"Jon, it's Sam Ripley."

It took a few moments for the name to register. "What the hell, man?" He hadn't heard from his old friend, a Black Hawk pilot, for years. "Where you calling from?"

"I'm in Gibraltar, working."

"That explains the time."

"Shit, I just realized the time. Man, sorry."

"It's OK. I'm driving. What you doing in Gibraltar? You working with the Brits?"

"It's a NATO training exercise. I was drafted in to mentor some of their rookie pilots. Getting to show how the Black Hawk works and handles."

Reznick knew Ripley from numerous Delta operations. He was an elite "night stalker" helicopter pilot, the youngest pilot in the Army's 160th Special Operations Aviation Regiment, Airborne (SOAR-A). And Delta always insisted that Ripley take them on their missions. Ripley was also superbright, and he was a history buff.

"Good for you, man."

"Listen, I'm coming home in a couple weeks. You want to meet up? A bit out of the blue, I guess. But I was just scrolling through the names from the old days. I realized I hadn't seen you in a long while."

Reznick glanced in his rearview mirror. The lights of a black cargo van. "Sounds good. Send me a text."

"Not a problem. I'll give you a call when I get back."

Reznick ended the conversation, eyes fixed on the approaching van. He noted the slow speed of the vehicle. He drove on and looked again in his rearview mirror. Silhouetted figures in the vehicle.

The van began to overtake him. He turned and stared out his side window at the occupants. The two men's faces were invisible behind ski masks.

Reznick's senses came alive. He drew his eyes back to the road and kept a steady thirty miles per hour. He followed the van through the downtown streets and onto the back roads leading out of town. He called 911.

"Masked men, sir?" the female dispatcher said as if not believing what she was hearing. "Are you sure about that? Right now?"

"I'm tailing them. It's a cargo van, black. I didn't get the plates."

"Sir, what sort of masks?"

"What sort of masks? Ski masks. Their faces were concealed."

"I must caution you not to engage. We have officers on their way. I would advise you to back off right now."

Reznick ended the call. He kept driving. It was suspicious, to say the least, that the men were wearing full face coverings in a car, at night. The only explanation was that they wanted to conceal their identity. But that posed the question *Why would they want to conceal their identity?* Who from? Were they about to commit a crime? Had they just committed a crime? There were barely any cameras in Rockland, mostly inside stores, pointed at the register.

He decided to keep on their tail.

Reznick accelerated. A few moments later, he got close enough to read the van's license plate. He called it in to the 911 dispatcher.

"Please do not engage, sir. I repeat: these men could be armed and dangerous."

Reznick ignored the repeated requests from the dispatcher. He followed them onto the road to Thomaston. The van accelerated faster and faster as they headed north on Oyster River Road. Over the bridge. Suddenly, the cargo van lights switched off. The night spread out black in front of the van.

Reznick headed along the dark road. Seconds passed until he realized he had lost sight of the van.

"Fuck!"

He searched for locations they might be able to dump the vehicle. He was now seven miles from Rockland, headed for the small town of Warren. He checked his rearview, expecting the cops to appear. It was still just him.

Suddenly, farther up the road, his headlights illuminated a silhouetted figure.

Reznick hit the brakes and screeched to a juddering halt. There was the black van, a man standing beside it. He pointed a rifle straight at Reznick's truck. *Fuck.* He ducked down in his seat. Then the truck got raked by gunfire. Reznick crouched lower as the bullets shattered the windshield, shards of glass raining on his face.

He stayed low, reached over, and cracked the door open.

More gunfire. He dove out of his truck and spread-eagled in the long grass. He crawled to the rear of the vehicle, worried the fuel tank was going to explode.

Reznick breathed hard as he got his bearings. He quickly popped open the tailgate. He reached in and pulled out the Nosler hunting rifle.

He got back in the long grass and crawled forward.

The man fired off a quick burst of bullets into the trees, narrowly missing Reznick.

Reznick rapidly zeroed the sights on his rifle. He was about one hundred yards away. Then he took aim. He squeezed the trigger. The noise echoed into the dark skies. He took one shot.

The man went down screaming, clutching his shoulder, writhing in agony on the ground.

Suddenly, lights still off, the van sped away.

Reznick aimed at the vehicle's silhouette and fired off a rapid succession of shots. He heard bullets piercing the van's rear. But a moment later it was out of sight.

He was breathing roughly as he got to his feet. He walked slowly toward the man, still writhing and moaning on the ground.

The man reached out for the semiautomatic a few feet from him.

Reznick took out his Beretta from his shoulder holster and shot the man's kneecaps. A howling scream split the night air. He kicked the AR-15 out of reach and stood over the bleeding man. He bent down and held his Beretta over the man's temple. "Who are you?"

The masked man had tears in his eyes. "I ain't gonna tell you shit," he drawled.

Reznick reached into the man's jacket and pulled out a cell phone. He ripped off the man's mask. "What the fuck are you doing masked up?"

"Go fuck yourself."

Reznick pressed the heel of his boot into the bloody wound on the man's shoulder. "Why are you passing through? Who sent you? You sound like you're a long way from home."

The man scrunched up his eyes and screamed. "Motherfucker!"

"Wrong answer, shitkicker. You either give me the answer or you will die. Now, try again. Who are you?"

The man began to shake. "You need to get me to a hospital. I'm bleeding out."

"So be it."

"Don't leave me here, man. I need to get to a hospital."

"So, talk!"

"I'm just a bit of muscle."

Reznick studied the tattoos around the man's neck, protruding from his shirt. "Look like jailhouse tats."

"Man, I'm bleeding out! You got to get me an ambulance. I don't want to die in the road like a dog."

"Who sent you?"

"I was told I had to disarm and beat up an old guy. That's all I was told. I was given the guy's name."

"Who?"

"An old fella. White guy. Up here in Maine."

"Name?"

"Eastland. Bill fucking Eastland!"

Reznick felt his blood run cold. He gazed down at the wretched bastard, fear etched into his face, tears in his eyes. "Eastland?"

The man moaned. "Are you fucking deaf? I'm bleeding out!"

Reznick felt as if he had been hit by a truck. He was a friend of Eastland. A very close friend. The man who was previously the chief of the Rockland police until he had retired. A man who had fought in Vietnam with Reznick's father. "Who were the guys in the van with you?"

"I don't know any fucking more! Go fuck yourself!"

Reznick put the man's cell phone in his pocket. He looked down, feeling nothing but rage. He kicked the man once hard in the side of the head. The tattooed man passed out cold, his blood pooling on the road.

His mind on fire, thoughts careering around his head, Reznick walked back to his bullet-ridden truck. The windshield shot out, glass all over the seat and floor. He wrapped his hand in a rag and brushed it off. He switched on the ignition. It was working. The bullets hadn't hit the engine. He slid back into the seat as he turned the headlights on.

Reznick called Eastland's home phone as he pulled away, the sound of screeching tires echoing as he did a sharp U-turn and accelerated back toward Rockland. He called his old friend's cell phone. It rang and rang. No answer. No voice mail. "Fuck it!" He drove faster as he approached the far edge of town, fearful of the scene he would encounter. The cold wind whipped through the missing windshield, buffeting his face.

He pressed his foot to the gas. "Come on, come on, come on!"

Reznick pushed the truck to go faster. A police cruiser finally sped past him, going the other way. He turned a bend into Rockland. Down the deserted Main Street, then onto the smaller roads.

He saw the house, Stars and Stripes flying from a first-floor window.

Reznick screeched to a halt. He rang the bell and rapped at the door. Nothing. He peered through the window. The interior was cloaked in darkness. He went around the back and pressed his face to the window.

He saw a woman lying on the floor of the kitchen. It was Bill's wife, Elspeth. And she was moving.

Reznick kicked in the back door and rushed in. He crouched down beside her, holding her bloodied hand. Her face was swollen. "Elspeth, what the hell happened? Where's Bill?"

"He's dead. He's upstairs."

Reznick felt sick as his mind went into free fall. "Oh my God. Elspeth, who killed him?"

Elspeth's warm blood on his cold hands. "Men in masks. They beat him up bad. Pistol-whipped him. They killed my husband."

Reznick cradled the back of her head as he called 911. It rang and rang. "Stay with me, Elspeth! Help is on the way!"

The voice of a dispatcher: "Are you the same gentleman who called earlier?"

"Yes! We need an ambulance. And cops." Reznick's mind raced as he gave the Eastlands' address. "Did you get that?"

"Sir, we have paramedics three miles away. It won't be long."

"Three miles? Tell them to hurry!"

"Sir, we're doing the best we can."

Reznick put down the cell phone. He clasped Elspeth's hand tight as he peered into her rheumy, sad eyes. "Hang in there, Elspeth! Do you hear me?"

Her eyes became lifeless. Elspeth Eastland went limp in his arms as she gasped her last breath.

Two

The Gulfstream crossed into American airspace off the Eastern Seaboard of mid-coast Maine at 0404 hours. It had originated in Lyons, France.

FBI Assistant Director Martha Meyerstein had managed four hours of uninterrupted sleep but spent the back half of the flight with her reading light on. She couldn't get back to sleep, so she ordered a strong coffee as she caught up on some paperwork.

Meyerstein was the most senior member of a US delegation fifteen-strong attending a high-level meeting between American law enforcement agencies and Interpol. The conference was aimed at forging closer ties to counter transnational organized crime, targeting Russian, Mexican, and Asian gangs.

The FBI's closest international partners were the British. Meyerstein heard from those in Britain's National Crime Agency, who talked about the threats they faced in London, everything from Bengali machete gangs to Somali street thugs, from Nigerian fraudsters to Russian hit squads, among others. It was fascinating for Meyerstein to get insight on the different organized crime threats in different countries. They sat in meetings to discuss organized crime in the Western Hemisphere, mostly centered on countries like El Salvador, Guatemala, Mexico, Colombia, Peru, and Bolivia, and mostly pertaining to drug-smuggling operations. Meyerstein provided information on the traditional Italian-American Mafia, still strong in New York and New Jersey.

Meyerstein's gaze wandered around the cabin. She saw representatives of the State Department and the Department of Justice, as well as various police chiefs. Most were sleeping after the exhausting week.

Her cell phone vibrated on her table, and she winced and answered out of habit, realizing that she had accidentally left her phone turned on during the flight.

"Meyerstein speaking."

"Ma'am, sorry to bother you." The voice of Jorge Martinez from the FBI's Strategic Information and Operations Center on the fifth floor of the Hoover Building. It was the law enforcement agency's 24-7 global command and communications center and contained six crisis action team rooms, five operations areas, briefing areas, and conference rooms. "I've got a name you might be familiar with. It was just flagged for your attention as urgent."

"What name?"

"Jon Reznick."

Meyerstein's heart sank. "Are you kidding me? What now?"

"He's been involved in a situation."

Meyerstein asked, "Is he OK?"

"He's fine, apart from a few grazes and abrasions."

"What happened?"

Martinez quickly outlined what had happened, from the pursuit to finding Bill and Elspeth Eastland's bodies, and concluding with "The guy he shot is now fighting for his life."

Meyerstein felt her mood dip as she thought of the ramifications of Reznick's actions. The last thing she needed was for Reznick to get embroiled in a rogue or renegade operation. He seemed to have become prone to embarking on high-risk situations since she'd first met him. "Is the guy going to die?"

"We're still waiting for a medical update. The Boston field office has sent a team up and is keeping tabs on this. Just thought you'd want to know."

"Where did this happen?"

Martinez related the sketchy details of the location of the shooting.

"Reznick's home turf?"

"Yes, ma'am."

Meyerstein took a few moments to compose herself. "Where is Reznick at this moment?"

"This is where it gets complicated. Rockland's sheriff's department is about to interview him."

"We need to shut this down. Police departments are notoriously leaky. Keep me up to date."

"Got it, ma'am."

"One final thing. You better let the Director know."

"Ma'am, I have him on the line as we speak. Can I put you through?"

Meyerstein closed her eyes. It was the last thing she needed. "Of course."

A few moments later, FBI Director Bill O'Donoghue was on the line. "What the hell am I hearing, Martha?"

"I just heard about it myself, Bill."

"Now listen to me very closely. I want you to find out what happened. And I want Reznick on a tighter leash. This is unacceptable. Totally unacceptable."

"Bill, let's not jump to conclusions. We don't know the full story. It sounds to me like self-defense."

"Sort it out, Martha. Get up to Rockland and speak to him. We're under press scrutiny night and day. The last thing the FBI needs is to have it revealed that Reznick has worked for us in the past. I swear to God, he will be the death of me."

Meyerstein had been looking forward to getting back home and seeing her children again. That would have to wait.

Three

Reznick nursed a cold coffee as he sat in a windowless police interview room in Rockland. Sitting opposite him was Tom Cain, Knox County sheriff's investigator, as well as his deputy, Brad Cheevers. He knew Tom well. He was a decent guy. A Rockland boy through and through. But Cheevers, in his late twenties, was new to the town.

Cain checked the papers in front of him before he stared at Reznick. "Do you need medical attention, Jon?"

Reznick shook his head.

"I can see a few cuts on your face and hands."

"I'll clean up later."

"Very well. You know why you're here?"

"Tom, do you want to get to the point?"

"We've got two people dead, Jon. And one fighting for his life."

"Just to clarify, the two people dead are good friends of mine. Bill Eastland and his wife, Elspeth."

Cain nodded as he checked the notes in front of him.

"Do you want to talk us through what happened again?"

"I've told you guys what I know already."

"Tell me again. Go through it from the start."

Reznick sighed. He knew they were making sure his story stacked up, no anomalies in the different versions. He again patiently recalled exactly what had happened from the moment he saw the masked men in the van to the moment he shot one of them. Then the sequence of events as he rushed to Eastland's home.

Cheevers shook his head, eyes dead. "That is a lot to take in, Jon."

"Are you finding it difficult to keep up?"

Cheevers sneered at him. "Don't get smart with me. You have a lot of explaining to do. Why didn't you just call it in? Talk me through that again."

"I did call it in. Check the dispatcher's conversation."

"I have. And I can't understand why you disobeyed her instruction not to follow the van."

"I called it in. But as a good citizen, I wanted to track them down until the police arrived. The problem is, they didn't until it was too late."

Cheevers exchanged a knowing look with Cain. "You shot one of the men despite being told not to follow. That strikes me as someone spoiling for a fight. What do you think?"

"The van pulled up sharply. Its headlights were off. It was dark. I saw a guy pointing what looked like a semiautomatic. Then he starts shooting. At me. I didn't start this."

Cheevers scribbled notes. "Why didn't you just take cover?"

"The guy was shooting up my truck. I had to get the hell out of the vehicle."

"You didn't answer my question. Why didn't you just take cover?"

"My life was in danger. I needed to defend myself."

"No matter what?"

"No matter what."

"Jon, you went after those guys knowing full well they were armed."

"I'm trained to deal with stuff like that. It's self-defense."

"The whole situation could have been avoided, could it not?" Cheevers asked, needling him.

15

"A group of masked men driving through my small town in the dead of night might have been headed to kill someone else for all I knew. I did the responsible thing."

"Jon, that's bullshit."

"They had already killed Eastland and his wife. Do you think those guys would have been apprehended if I hadn't taken action?"

Cain interjected, "You're making wild assumptions. We don't know how it would have worked out."

"I didn't want to find out. They needed to be stopped, but they started a fight."

Cheevers's pupils were like pinpricks. "We uphold the law, Jon. You're not the law."

"They teach you that at college, Brad?"

Cheevers flushed. Cain shook his head. "Let's all back up for a few moments. Jon, tell me where you've been this last week."

"I've already given you that, Tom."

"I'm simply trying to piece together everyone's movements."

Reznick told them again that he had been on vacation at his cabin up in the north Maine woods.

Cheevers shook his head. "So, no one can verify where you were?"

"Well, if I'm in my cabin up in the woods, in the middle of goddamn nowhere, that's right. That's kind of the point."

"Let's go back to the early hours of this morning," Cheevers said. "Just so I'm clear on this. You're just driving back into town, minding your own business?"

"How many times? That's exactly right. It was a long drive. Then I saw the guys in the masks in the van."

"You went after them. You hunted them down."

"You're being melodramatic, Brad. I followed them. Nothing more, nothing less."

"Despite not knowing what they were involved in."

Reznick wondered whose side Cheevers was on. "We seem to be going around in circles, guys. Who the hell drives around in their van in the dead of night wearing ski masks? Do you know anybody who does that?"

"Jon, you are not law enforcement," Cheevers said.

"I never said I was."

"I know you've consulted with the FBI before. Were you playing at being a special agent, Jon?"

Reznick glared across the table at Cheevers. "Listen, son. Your college-boy humor is wearing thin. Do you think it's appropriate to wisecrack only hours after a retired Rockland police chief and his wife were beaten to death in cold blood on your watch? You disgust me. You know, Cheevers, if you actually knew how to fire your weapon once in a while, you might remember the purpose of it."

Cheevers flushed again and seethed.

Cain interrupted. "We're just playing devil's advocate, Jon. Let's get back on track. I want to know more about your motivation. You were the one that shot that guy. We only have your word for how that all went down."

"A few miles outside the town, they switched off their lights. Then it all happened."

"Why do you think they turned off their lights?"

"So I couldn't pursue them, I believe."

"Then what?"

"I saw the silhouette of a guy with a rifle standing in the road. That's how it started. He began the confrontation. I've told you that two or three times now. He began the shooting. AR-15 or a pretty good imitation. I managed to get out of my truck—and remember, the guy's pointing a semiautomatic at me. So, I got my rifle from the truck, took aim, and defended myself."

Cheevers said, "That's not how it works. You should not have pursued that van. You had no evidence, at the time, of wrongdoing.

They might have suspected you were following them, and they were defending themselves. Forensics will report their findings. And then we can start to get to the bottom of this."

Reznick leaned closer across the table. "Did he have an ID on him?"

"We're still trying to establish who he was."

"What about the tattoos?"

Cheevers leaned forward, hands clasped. "Tell me, slowly, how you got from a road outside the other side of Rockland, near Thomaston, and back to Bill Eastland's house if your truck was shot up."

"With difficulty. Glass was everywhere. But I wiped it off the seat."

"How did you know it was Eastland who was the victim?"

"The guy I shot gave me the name of the person they had killed."

"Voluntarily? He gave up that information?"

"I guess he had a guilty conscience."

"Don't fuck with me, Jon. Did you torture this guy? Is that how you got that information?"

Reznick folded his arms.

"We have a hunting rifle bullet they dug out of his shoulder," Cain said. "But also a bullet hole in each of the guy's knees. A 9mm slug, the hospital says. So, it appears you kneecapped this guy at point-blank range. Did you kneecap him to get that information?"

"I was defending myself, Tom."

"And you just so happened to hit him right in the knees?" Cain scribbled some notes on a legal pad in front of him. "He was defenseless on the ground."

"I made him defenseless."

"Listen, Jon, we don't know who these guys are. That's true. But I can say that the gang tattoos this guy has, we know they're not people to be messed with. You need to be aware of that."

"Are you saying these people might come after me?"

"That's exactly what I'm saying."

Four

It was a short walk back to Reznick's home on the outskirts of Rockland.

He struggled to take in the brutal killings of Bill and Elspeth. He headed out to his deck overlooking Penobscot Bay and sat down, dejected. He needed time to be alone. Time to process the events.

He felt shattered. Rockland, his hometown, was his sanctuary. A place where he felt safe. A place where he wasn't the trained killer. The assassin. He could relax and be himself. He could live.

Reznick couldn't wrap his head around this level of violence in his quiet town. Towns of eight thousand people didn't have these sorts of slayings, especially with the victims being the ex–police chief and his wife. Eastland was more than an ex-cop. He was one of the good guys. A tough guy, for sure. But he was fair. Even-handed. But what wasn't widely known was that Eastland also had a big heart. Not many knew that side of him. Reznick did.

Eastland and his wife had set up a charity that had supported dozens of homeless veterans in the Rockland area over the years. Men who were down on their luck. Hungry. Without a dime. Bill made sure they got a roof over their head. He fundraised hard for veterans—hundreds of thousands over the decades. The charity eventually bought a small five-bedroom residential facility on the outskirts of town.

Rockland would miss Eastland, that was for sure.

Reznick remembered Eastland teaching him some fly-fishing techniques when he was a boy as his father sank a few cold ones.

Eastland and Reznick's father were both Vietnam vets. Tough. Uncompromising. Men's men. But they were also hardworking family men. Loyal, no-bullshit men.

Reznick's mind drifted back to trips to DC when he was a boy. His father took him every year. They would see all the monuments. But the main focus was the Vietnam Memorial. The solemnity was painful to watch. His father would touch the black granite wall and weep. The names of the soldiers, now dead, he had served along-side. Eastland, despite being a vet, never went. He once confided in Reznick that he didn't want the memories flooding back. It was Eastland's way of coping. He tried to forget.

Reznick understood that. He didn't want reminders of Fallujah, Iraq, Afghanistan, the blistering heat, the dust storms, the stinking mess, dead animals in stagnant water, flies all around. Bloated bodies floating down the Tigris, victims of torture. Eyes gouged out. He didn't want any reminder of that. His way of coping was not to talk about it. He just left it there. The dark memories had receded over the years. But occasionally, if he met up with old Delta buddies, the flashbacks to Iraq would return with a vengeance, haunting him like ghosts from his past.y

Reznick preferred to focus on happier memories. He thought back to all the times he and Eastland had enjoyed digging into fish tacos and craft beers in the Rock Harbor Pub on Main Street. The uproarious laughter. The grizzled old guy, his beer belly and cold stare, the fire still raging inside. The more Eastland drank, though, the darker his eyes got. The more hooded.

Reznick had heard all the tales, from both his father and Eastland. The fights in back alleys with sailors on shore leave, drinking until they blacked out on the street, finding their money and wallets had been taken from them. The whorehouses, the sadness, the drunken euphoria. But also the story of Reznick's father with his Army revolver in his mouth one morning. Eastland confided that he was haunted by distant screams from their comrades, dying alone in the jungle. The Vietnamese children, fighting alongside the Vietcong, shot by their rifles. He remembered Eastland telling him that was the turning point for them both. When they realized they had shot kids dead. It haunted both his father and Eastland. All their days.

The tough cop, sweating profusely after a day drinking at a bar in Rockland. The same guy who had hugged Reznick tight after he returned from his first tour of Iraq, wide-eyed, crazed, unable to tell the world what he had witnessed. What he had done. Eastland knew. His father knew. None of it was good. They knew the signs only too well.

Reznick recognized it too. He had seen it in his own father. He knew how to deal with it. Quietly cajoling. He could see when Eastland took a dislike to a patron in the bar. A perfectly acceptable guy with a goatee, or a kid wearing flip-flops. Eastland seemed to take offense at hipsters, men with man bags, or men who dyed their hair. It sent him wild. He was seriously old school. But Eastland also hated wannabe troublemakers. Reznick remembered the time Eastland had squared up to a biker who was staring him down at the Myrtle Street Tavern. The biker didn't like his odds when Eastland walked over and grabbed him by the throat, squeezing until the guy began to cry.

Reznick had to gently calm Eastland down. The target of his ire would inevitably apologize, even if they weren't in the wrong. Bill had that kind of command.

Reznick wondered whether Eastland had been targeted for retribution by some punk he had locked up or whose ass he had kicked.

The more he thought about that, though, the more implausible it seemed. That a guy would turn up, out of the blue, years later, with a few friends, masked up, and beat Bill and Elspeth to death? It didn't seem probable or plausible.

Reznick thought it bore all the hallmarks of a professional execution. Gangland in its ferocity. To send a message. He sensed there was far more to this than met the eye. He had seen the work of the death squads—both Shia and Sunni—operating in Iraq. And they were ruthless. Off the charts.

While the killing of Eastland and his wife was not on that level of barbarism, it was possible there might have been a tit-for-tat retribution element to it. Had Eastland gotten on someone's bad side? Maybe a powerful person with heavy-duty friends. Maybe an organization.

But Reznick couldn't figure out who could feel such savage hatred toward Eastland.

The masked gunman Reznick had shot sounded like he was from the Deep South. A long, long way from Rockland. It couldn't have been a coincidence that the guy turned up at Eastland's door. That meant he had to have been sent. So, the question remained: Sent by who? And more to the point, why?

The more he thought about it, the more questions piled up. All Reznick was left with were questions. And a gnawing emptiness inside. Eastland had taken Reznick under his wing when his father passed away. When he returned from Iraq, Eastland saw the way Reznick was. He was the one Reznick approached to talk quietly with about his feelings. The rage which was boiling up. The same man Reznick had spoken to when his wife died on 9/11. He had trusted Eastland with his life.

Reznick snapped back to the present. He needed to have a clear head. He couldn't let this go. He needed to figure out what he was going to do. The police knew far more about the attackers than they were letting on. He knew from countless discussions with Eastland over the years that the police always kept so much information to themselves as their investigations progressed. It might be kept from the relatives of the victim, the media, or from the perpetrators, so they didn't get a heads-up that the police were closing in.

For Reznick, the double killing was deeply personal. He sensed they were outsiders. He couldn't prove it. And the ferocity—and killing Elspeth as well—was beyond the pale.

He got up from his seat and scrambled down to the cove. The smell of the salty air. The sound of the waves crashing off the rocks. He gazed out over the water. He remembered Eastland sitting down in the sand with him, chugging beers, talking about football, the Red Sox, and everything in between. He seemed to enjoy taking an hour or two every couple of weeks and talking freely to Reznick, without his wife to censor him. But in all the years he had known Eastland, his friend had never mentioned being in trouble or fearing for his life. He imagined that if Eastland was in trouble, he would have confided in Reznick.

Did Eastland have something to hide? A darker side Jon didn't know about?

The prison tattoos might be a clue. Was the gunman who had fired at him part of an organized gang? Had Eastland put the guy away years ago? Was there bad blood?

According to Sheriff's Investigator Tom Cain, the guy who had shot at Reznick was fighting for his life in the hospital. Would finding out that guy's identity unlock the mystery? He needed to know more. So much more. Who was the guy? Who were his associates, in and out of prison? Where exactly was he from?

Reznick got in his car and took the ten-minute drive to Rockport. He pulled up outside the Pen Bay Medical Center. He headed to the emergency room.

A nurse approached him. "Excuse me, can I help?"

"A guy was shot in the middle of the night, just outside Rockland. I'm inquiring what his condition is."

"Have you got a name?"

"I don't know his name. I just want to know if he's OK."

The nurse smiled. "No gunshot patients here for at least two weeks. Sorry I can't help."

Reznick thanked the nurse and drove back to Rockland. He realized he needed to call a guy who might be able to get the information. But he didn't want to leave a digital trace.

He pulled up at the Greyhound stop adjacent to the Rockland Ferry Terminal. He headed across to the public pay phone. He picked up and dialed a number he hadn't called in a while. He loaded up the pay phone with three dollars in change.

"Yeah, who's this?" The voice of Trevelle Williams, reclusive ex-NSA-contractor-turned-hacker.

"It's Reznick."

"Man, where the hell have you been?"

"Here and there."

"Last time I saw you was when you were in Mallorca, right?"

Reznick smiled. "That's right. And thanks again."

"Interesting you're calling from a public pay phone. You thinking you might be under surveillance?"

"I just wanted to take extra precautions."

"I thought your cell phone had all the encryption in the world? I devised it, so trust me."

"I know . . ."

"Don't tell me. You're old school."

"Kind of. But I don't want to attract heat for you or me, leaving a digital trail of any kind to my cell phone."

"What do you want, my friend?"

Reznick saw a fisherman he knew, a regular at the Myrtle. He acknowledged the guy, who waved back at him. "I shot a guy last night outside Rockland."

"What?"

"Cops have the details."

"Are you OK?"

"I'm fine. I shot one man, who was admitted to the hospital. I don't know which one. Knox County Sheriff's Department is leading on this. But I don't know for how long. I suspect the FBI will be taking this over."

"Suspects crossing state lines?"

"Possibly."

"You want to give me details?"

Reznick retold the story.

"Jon, I'm sorry about Eastland and his wife. That's awful."

"It is what it is, man. I want to find out who did this."

"Copy that."

"The guy in the hospital. I want to know more about him."

"Which hospitals could it be?"

"It might be Maine Medical Center in Portland, I'm not sure. It happened around three o'clock in the morning. I spoke to a dispatcher."

The sound of tapping in the background as if Trevelle were frantically entering the details into his computer. "Not much to go on."

"I know. But I hope you can access a database or two, whether police, hospital . . . who knows, maybe the FBI? See if there is anything on this guy. I believe he had prison gang tattoos on his neck."

"You really aren't giving me much, man."

"I know. This is important."

"I'll do what I can."

Five

It was a fleapit motel in Biloxi, but it was three blocks from the beach.

Dwayne McLellan stared out the dirty window at dark clouds rolling in off the Gulf, throat parched. His T-shirt stuck to his back. "Goddamn air-conditioning broken still?"

Connell could only stare at the floor. "They're going to fix it soon."

"Who's going to fix it soon?"

"The maintenance guy. I called reception."

"I'm sweating my nuts off here. I've been inside for fucking years. And now that I'm finally free, I can't enjoy some relaxation in a civilized environment. It must be one hundred and ten fucking degrees in here, I swear to God."

"They'll fix it, I said. The guy had three other rooms to fix. It's a routine problem."

Connell's tone of voice irritated something deep inside McLellan. "What did you say?"

"I said they'll fix it."

"You keep on saying that."

The door opened. Draxler, the distinctive *ABT* initials tattooed across his throat, walked in with a grocery bag of cold cans of beer, bottles of Jack Daniels, and cans of Coke. He slammed the door shut and emptied the bag onto the unmade bed.

McLellan leaned over and picked up a can of cold Mexican lager, cracked it open, and took a large gulp. "Nice."

"Straight out of the refrigerator. First one you've had in a while, right?"

"Damn straight." He lit up a cigarette and watched the smoke drift across the room to Connell. "What do you say, Stevie?"

"I ain't saying anything, man."

McLellan took a couple more large gulps of beer. He glared at Connell, whose very presence was annoying him. Intensely. He had never met the guy until he got out seventy-two hours earlier. But something about the way Connell spoke, the hesitancy, ticked him off. He sounded as if he was scared. It was almost like Connell was out of his comfort zone, hanging out with Dwayne and his AB crew. "I don't like being kept waiting. We kept our side of the bargain. When we getting our money, Stevie?"

"I'm picking it up in half an hour."

"Is that right, huh?"

Connell shrugged. "Yeah, I told you that already."

"Where?"

"Room at the Star Casino."

"What if you run off with the money?"

Connell gave a nervous laugh. "Are you kidding me? I wouldn't do that."

"Wouldn't you?"

Draxler smiled across at Connell. "Dwayne's just yanking your chain, man. Relax."

McLellan gulped down the rest of the beer. "What about Jimmy's share?"

"I'll make sure I pick that up too," Connell said. "Don't worry."

"The money goes to his wife, right?" McLellan said.

"Damn straight."

McLellan dragged hard on his cigarette and watched the blue smoke waft out of the window. He stared long and hard at Connell. The guy was heavyset like a tattooed bodybuilder. "Where you serve your time?"

"Florida?"

"Raiford?"

Connell shook his head. "Correctional facility. Miami."

McLellan grinned as he inhaled deeply. "Bunch of pussies down there."

Draxler laughed. "Man, he's just busting your balls. He's messing with you."

Connell shifted in his seat. "What's your problem, man?"

"You know how long I was inside for?" McLellan said.

Connell shook his head.

"Since I was twenty-two."

"Long time."

"Fucking right it's a long time. A long, long time." McLellan crushed his cigarette in the ashtray on the armrest. "You know what doing serious time does to a man?"

Connell remained quiet as if afraid to say the wrong thing.

"You become mean. You know what I'm talking about, Stevie?"

"You've got to stand up for yourself."

"Damn straight. So, listen, Steve Connell, where you from? I mean originally."

"Why do you want to know that?"

"It's not a national secret, I'm assuming, Stevie."

"No, of course not."

"So, where you from?"

"I was brought up in a small town. You wouldn't know it."

"Try me."

"Anniston, Alabama."

"Nope, never heard of it."

Draxler sniggered as he poured a Jack Daniels and Coke into a chipped cup.

"Not many people have heard of it," Connell said. "It's a small, small town. Not much going on."

McLellan stuck his chin up at Connell. "How does it feel knowing you were in on a kill job like that up in Maine?"

"It's fine."

"You ever been on a job like that before? Be honest."

Connell shook his head. "Don't believe I have. I don't ask questions."

"That's very good."

"The papers say the guy you killed was a seventy-nine-year-old retired cop."

McLellan grinned. "Holy shit, that's a bonus, huh?"

Connell nodded, his eyes on the floor.

"A goddamn cop and his wife. It's a double bonus!"

Draxler laughed as he knocked back another bourbon and Coke. "Serves the fuckers right."

McLellan leaned closer to Connell. "You better fucking believe it."

"Can't imagine it would be too much for a guy like you. I mean, having the balls to go in and do them."

McLellan locked eyes on Connell until the Alabama boy averted his gaze. "What do you mean, a guy like me?"

A silence opened up between them for a few awkward moments. "I just mean a guy that does what has to be done. You've done serious time. You know what I mean."

McLellan studied the tattoos on Connell's right forearm. Shamrocks, swastikas, and lightning bolts with the initials in red, *AB*. "Nice selection of tats, man."

"Thanks."

"You with the Brand?"

"What?"

"AB. You know what that stands for, right?"

Connell shrugged. "They're just tattoos."

Draxler looked at his feet and smiled.

"You ever shank anyone, Steve?"

"No. I'm just a driver. I'm not really the muscle side of things."

"So, are you part of the Aryan Brotherhood?"

"I'm an associate. I deal dope for them. Give them information if they need it."

"So, you're not Aryan Brotherhood?"

"Technically, no. I hang around with them."

"Is that right?"

"Yeah, but the crew I usually hang with is the Southern Brotherhood in Alabama."

"Word to the wise, son. Cover up your tattoos while you're around me. I've seen men get shanked on the yard in broad daylight for less." McLellan took off his top and showed off his selection of Aryan Brotherhood of Texas tattoos. "We're a separate crew from the AB who are big in California, just so you know. I got these in Leavenworth. You've got to earn this. The hard way. You know what I mean by that?"

Connell cleared his throat, clearly feeling uncomfortable. "I think so."

Draxler shook his head as if unimpressed.

"I mean," McLellan said, "if there's a name in the hat, and you're picked, you have to kill the motherfucker. It could be a Mexican in the yard. A Black gangbanger. An MS13 fucker on your shower block. If you're picked, you take the fucker down. No questions asked."

"I didn't mean any disrespect."

McLellan stared coldly at Connell.

"I'll put on a shirt."

"A word to the wise, Alabama boy. Don't ever show them again. Not around me. Not now. Not ever."

Connell nodded.

"Got it?"

"Got it."

McLellan lit up another cigarette. "I've spent twelve years inside, and I'm spending time in a fucking room with you. You don't know the first thing about what that symbolizes. It means you fucking earned it. It's not a fucking game."

Draxler opened a can of beer and chugged it in a few huge gulps. "Wow, that's nice. Hits the spot."

Connell smiled.

"You not having a drink, Steve?"

"I don't drink anymore. I need to drive wherever you guys want. That's what I do."

McLellan opened up another can of beer as he dragged on his cigarette. "Those guys who hired us paid big. They must be big shots, wanting that guy and his wife to be iced like that."

Connell nodded. "I guess."

"What did they do?"

"Who?"

"What did the dead guy do to piss off these big shots?"

Connell shrugged. "I don't know if they're big shots or not. They don't talk much. But as far as I know, you got the name because you were being released, and because you were in the neighborhood in Maine, they thought you might oblige."

"Always happy to oblige. I mean who doesn't need money, right, Draxler?"

Draxler spat at Connell. "Absolutely fucking right. Listen, Steve, how do we know we can trust you? I've never worked with you before. How do I know you're going to come back here with our money?"

"I guess you've got to trust me."

McLellan looked at Draxler. "I know you, man, right?"

"Sure you do. We did time in Leavenworth. Serious time."

McLellan turned to look at Connell. "We know each other. Have for years. We both spent a year in an underground cell. You imagine that? Pure solitary confinement. And trust me, if you can withstand that psychological torture, you can stand a lot."

"What are you trying to say?"

"What I'm trying to say is, there is trust between me and Drax. A bond. Blood in, blood out. We're in it for keeps."

"I respect that."

"I know you do. And that's why when you go to collect the money, my friend Drax will accompany you. That alright?"

"No, it's not alright. The guy said I had to come alone."

McLellan crouched down beside Connell and whispered in his ear. "New rules. Drax will be with you. And if anything goes down, Drax will be there to make sure everything is cool."

Connell went quiet for a few moments. "OK, I guess that's fine."

"You ain't gonna try and fuck over the Brotherhood, are you?"

"Never, man. That's not what I do."

McLellan cocked his head. "Drax, you go with little Steve. Keep a close eye on him."

Draxler got to his feet and finished the rest of the beer. "Be my pleasure."

"Get my money. And then we split."

Six

The headlights appeared on the dirt road leading to Reznick's waterfront home.

Sitting on the front porch, Reznick was already holding his Beretta, a glass of Scotch at his side. He watched the vehicle get closer. It could be the cops, he figured. But when the SUV slowed down and turned, he recognized the profile of the woman inside. It was FBI Assistant Director Martha Meyerstein.

A Fed in the front passenger seat got out and opened her door.

Reznick tucked his gun into his waistband and stood. "I was wondering when you'd turn up."

Meyerstein smiled. She approached him but didn't embrace him. This was business.

"You want to come inside?"

"I don't mind if I do, thanks."

"What about your friends?"

Meyerstein shook her head. "They're going to be staying at a nice place on Main Street."

"250 Main?"

"That's the one."

"Very smart."

Meyerstein turned and signaled to the Feds. "I'll see you guys later."

The one who had opened the door acknowledged her and got back in the vehicle. The SUV turned around and headed back the way it came.

Reznick watched as the vehicle edged down the dirt road, leaving clouds of dust in its wake. He walked her through the house and out onto the back deck. "I was expecting you." He pointed to a comfortable chair beside a table. "Take the weight off. Can I fix you a drink?"

"Whatever you're having."

"Single malt?"

"Sounds good."

Reznick fixed their drinks and handed Meyerstein her glass. "There you go."

Meyerstein swirled the Scotch around the tumbler and inhaled the aroma.

Reznick raised his glass. "Slainte."

"What does that mean?"

"'Good health' in Gaelic."

Meyerstein sipped her drink, taking a few moments to savor the flavors. "Where did you learn that?"

"Guy in the SAS."

Meyerstein smiled. "The guy in Mallorca? Mac?"

"That's the one."

"Have you heard from him?"

"Last I heard, he's back in Cala San Vicente. So, all good."

Meyerstein sighed long and hard as she gazed out over the water. "I'm sorry about Bill Eastland and his wife. I know you were very close to him."

"Yeah, I was. Big, big shock."

"I'm going to be honest with you, Jon. And I need to speak frankly. I'm sure you understand."

Reznick shrugged.

"You're a good man. I know you care about your daughter very much. You're a loyal person. But I'm concerned the killings of Bill Eastland and his wife could trigger you to take the law into your own hands. I know what you'll be thinking. I know what presses your buttons."

"You do?"

"You want to find the people responsible."

Reznick sipped his Scotch, warming his belly.

"I'm worried you're going to go down an all-too-familiar route on this. A route that could get you killed. That's why I'm here to warn you. You need to let this go."

Reznick sat in silence as he closed his eyes.

"No one is immortal, Jon. I don't want to lose you. I want you to live. The FBI is working with local and state police to track down those responsible. And I will make sure everything possible is done to bring those people to justice. That's my promise to you."

"I want to help." Meyerstein shook her head. "You either take me on board, or I go it alone."

"You're not making it easy for me."

"Let me in. I can help."

"I came to tell you that this is strictly an FBI-led investigation. We *will* find those responsible. But we can't have any outside interference. None whatsoever."

"I've helped you in the past. I can help you again."

"Not this time."

"Why not?"

"Things have changed."

"Meaning?"

"We're more risk averse, shall we say."

"I appreciate you coming to speak to me face-to-face. But listen to me. I can't sit back and let this go. This happened in my hometown. Eastland meant a lot to me. To the town. So, this is personal."

"That's the problem, Jon. The FBI isn't interested in helping you deal with personal issues. It's about upholding the law."

Reznick was quiet as he considered Meyerstein's hardline position.

"What have you got so far?"

"I can't reveal that, Jon."

"My take on it? This has a different feel from the run-of-the-mill stuff. This is organized."

Meyerstein sipped her drink, displaying her best poker face.

"There's a heavy-duty element here. This was not a random attack. It wasn't a home invasion. This has the feel of organized crime."

"I deal with organized crime, among other things. We've got this."

"But how far will you go to find the people who did this?"

Meyerstein shifted in her seat.

"I mean not only catch the people who did this, but the people who ordered it."

"You're getting ahead of yourself. This very well might be someone from Eastland's past that has a long-standing grudge. It happens."

Reznick shook his head. "I don't dispute that. But it wouldn't explain why they killed his wife. That indicates a willingness to be ruthless. Crazies. Not people with grudges. But hired psychopaths."

"Jon, come on, you have no way of knowing that."

"I know how to deal with unpleasant stuff. Unpleasant people. Sometimes they don't play nice. I understand that. And I can deal with that, trust me."

"Let it go, Jon. Let us do our job."

"Bill Eastland and me go way back. He was synonymous with Rockland. The town. Its people. This house we're sitting in now—my father built this with his bare hands with the help of Bill Eastland. He didn't get a fancy architect. He drew up plans himself. All the wood and materials he sourced himself from the surrounding area."

"You've never told me that before. Your father built this home?"

"There was nothing here before. Just a bit of scrubland overlooking the sea. He bought it with money he saved when he was overseas. And he put it all into the house. Bill Eastland worked every weekend, with my father, to build this house. He policed this town for over thirty years. He was a good man. And he didn't deserve to die like a dog."

Meyerstein went quiet for a few moments as if trying to calibrate her answer. "I understand that connection, Jon. I just don't want you getting hurt."

"You already said that. Why are you so convinced I'm going to get hurt? What exactly do you know? Do you know who did this?"

Meyerstein put down her glass. "I've never lied to you, and I'm not about to start now."

"You know more about this than you're saying, don't you?"

"Don't get involved. For all our sakes, do not get involved. That's all I'm saying."

Seven

It was after midnight when Draxler and Connell returned to the sweat-drenched motel room in Biloxi. Connell, red-faced, carried a case of beer.

McLellan searched their glazed eyes. He dragged hard on his cigarette. "Where the fuck you guys been?"

Connell smiled. "Getting laid and getting high."

"Well, good for you. Did you get the money?"

Draxler threw him a wad of bills wrapped in an elastic band. "Count it. Twenty big ones."

"What about Jimmy's share?"

Draxler handed it over.

McLellan crushed the cigarette in the ashtray, then counted out the bills in the second bundle. "This is for Jimmy's widow and her kids, do you hear me? This is Jimmy's twenty."

Draxler said, "Where she live?"

"Rosa? She lives in Midland, not far from me. I'll drop it off."

"That's pretty shitty, man," Draxler said. "Jimmy was one of us to the end, man. Here's the thing. What if Rosa talks to the cops?"

"She ain't gonna talk. I know her brothers. They'll make sure she doesn't say a word."

Draxler grinned. "Well, I'm gonna take a shower. And then I'm gonna split."

Connell smiled and lit up a cigarette. He sat on a chair opposite McLellan. "You look really pissed, man. Are you OK?"

McLellan peered at Connell. "What took you guys so long?"

"Like I said, we got loaded. What can I say?"

"I'm sitting here, like some nobody, waiting for you to get me my money? I don't like being kept waiting. Do I look like a patient man to you?"

Connell reached into the bag and lobbed a cold can of beer toward him.

McLellan caught it and put it down on the table beside him. "Where did you score?"

"A room at the casino."

"A couple of chicks?"

"Three, actually."

McLellan dismissed him. "Listen to me. When Drax is out of the shower, me and him are going to split."

"Where you guys going?"

"None of your business."

Connell finished his beer. He pulled out a bag of coke from his jeans. He sprinkled some on the table. He kneeled down and took a credit card from his back pocket. Then he chopped up the drug into raggedy white lines. He rolled up a fifty-dollar bill, bent over, and snorted one of them. He flushed red and smiled. "Motherfucker, real nice stuff."

McLellan curled his lip at Connell.

"You want a toot, man?"

"Not for me."

"Are you sure?"

"Beer and whiskey is my thing."

"You don't know what you're missing." He inhaled a second line. "Listen, I'd really love to go with you guys across to Texas. Like a road trip."

McLellan finished his beer. "A road trip? We don't do road trips."

"We could hang out."

"You're talking to the wrong guy. Besides, why would you want to hang out with us? What if we don't want to hang out with you?"

"Your choice, man. I just thought we could help each other out. I know a few guys in Texas. Easy money."

"Doing what?"

"Muscle on holdups at liquor stores, drugstores."

"If I want to do a holdup, I'll do a holdup. I don't need to hang out with some shitkicker who wants a tough guy to back them up."

Connell looked away.

"There's something about you, Steve. I don't know what it is."

"What do you mean?"

"Who are you? I don't know anything about you."

"I told you, I come from a small town in Alabama."

"Usually I only use people I trust with my life. When I look at you, I'm not sure you've got what it takes."

"What do you mean?"

"Would you kill a man if you had to?"

"I'll do what I have to do."

McLellan smiled. He could smell the fear emanating from every pore of Connell. He sensed a scared small-town drug dealer who was in over his head with a real crew.

"I hang with you guys. It'll be fun."

"Here's the thing, Steve. We're not a fun crowd, if you haven't already noticed. If you run with us, you need two things."

"What's that?"

40

"You need to keep your fucking mouth shut, and you need to follow orders."

"That's not a problem, man. I can follow orders. And I ain't saying anything to anyone, trust me."

McLellan was enjoying putting the fear of God into Connell. "And another thing, don't ever let me see those fucking AB tattoos again, do you hear me?"

"I got it. I've covered them up."

"That's good. That's real good."

Connell sniffed hard. "I want to be part of your group, Dwayne."

"See, there you go again. You don't just get to be part of the AB or our crew."

"I want to join."

"You want to be a prospect?"

Connell shrugged. "Sure, why not."

"Do you know what it takes to be a prospect? First, you follow orders. Second, when—not if—we say you have to kill someone, you have to kill someone. Period."

"I understand."

"You think you've got what it takes?"

"I think I do."

McLellan leaned closer. "If you're a prospect, it's not about flashing tattoos. It's about earning respect from others. From us. You have to show raw, brutal courage. You have to be tough as fuck. You don't back down. You have to kill without mercy. Blood in, blood out. That's how potential prospects have to make their bones."

"I can do that."

McLellan stared long and hard at Connell. "Let me ask you this. You ever been in a prison yard and shanked a shot caller from another gang? Maybe a Black. Maybe another white guy. You ever done that?"

"No, I have not."

"In the yard, you can't hide. Man, no place to hide under the sun. There's only God watching over you. There ain't nothing else like it. It's an honor to do the work of the Brotherhood."

"That's heavy-duty stuff."

"If you want to be considered a prospect, you've got to be able to do that. And without hesitation."

Draxler emerged from the shower, billows of steam following him. Rubbing his hair, topless, jeans and boots on. "You ready to roll soon?"

McLellan cocked his head toward Connell. "Steve here thinks he might be a prospect."

Draxler nodded. "Maybe. He seems eager."

"But is he a killer, Drax? That's what I want to know."

Draxler shrugged. "I guess we can find out."

McLellan smiled as he got to his feet. "Time to split. We got a long drive to Texas."

It was mile after mile of withered, bone-dry pines as they headed deeper into the woods of southern Mississippi.

McLellan drove fast, down old roads, farther and farther away from the coast. He once knew a girl from around about this part of the state. She rented a trailer deep in the woods. She drove to Biloxi to work in the casinos at night. And at dawn, she drove home to the trailer. It was an area just outside Saucier.

He stopped at a gas station.

McLellan turned to Draxler. "I've got to make a call."

"Do what you gotta do, man."

Connell gulped down the rest of a can of beer. "I got to take a leak."

McLellan eyed the kid from Alabama. "Five minutes, then we're out of here."

Connell got out of the car, hitched up his jeans, and headed to the bathroom adjacent to the gas station.

McLellan filled up the tank and paid in cash. Then he headed outside and walked over to the pay phone. He called the number he knew by heart. The shot caller inside Leavenworth.

"Who's this?" The gravelly voice of Michael "Mad Dog" Gilligan.

"We did the job up north. We're nearly home."

"Good work."

"We didn't all make it."

"What do you mean?"

"Jimmy got shot. Had to leave him behind."

"What happened?"

"Some crazy fuck followed us in his truck. Jimmy got out and blasted the guy's truck. But the guy shot him down. I don't know if Jimmy's dead or alive. We had to leave him."

"It is what it is, man."

"Look, we're gonna split."

"Do what you have to do. One final thing."

"What?"

"A name has gone in the hat."

"Whose?"

"Connell."

"Are you sure? The guy on the crew?"

"He's no good. We got word that he owes money. A lot of money. Unpaid drug debt to an associate of ours. He's been dipping in the horse money."

McLellan contemplated what he had just been told. *Horse* was prison slang for heroin. He watched as Connell, the stupid fuck, returned to the car. The guy was grinning like the Cheshire cat. The poor fucker was high off his ass, not knowing he was going to die. "Just so there's no misunderstanding, Connell's name is in the hat?"

"You got it. Once you do that, disappear."

The line went dead.

McLellan got back in the car. "Buckle up, you dumb fucks!" He drove on for another twenty miles, past the town of Saucier. His thoughts were plagued with the ominous conversation he'd had with Gilligan. *Connell's name is in the hat.* He needed to pass on the message. He needed to get this right. No ifs or buts. A name was in the hat. The guy was going to die. He turned to look at Connell, who kept his eyes straight ahead. "You OK, man?"

"I'm good. Where we going?"

"Just a slight detour to see a friend of mine. And then we can split. Listen, you want to be a prospect, right?"

"Sure."

"Well, we can talk about it when we get to this place. Maybe I've got you wrong."

"I can do whatever it is you want me to do."

McLellan ruffled Connell's hair. "You dumb fuck, are you sure you can handle this?"

"Trust me, I'm in, if you want me."

The car ate up the miles. Headlights picked out an opening in the trees. McLellan slowed down and took a left turn down the rutted dirt road.

Connell was chugging another beer. "Where the goddamn hell we going?"

"A friend of mine's got a trailer. It's the perfect place to lay low. No cameras watching us. We're going to rest up for a day or so, then split."

Connell grinned and turned around to look at Draxler. "You wanna get high?"

"Fucking right, I want to get high."

The headlights swept across the old retro trailer, no lights on, shrouded by pines.

McLellan pulled up as he kept the headlights on. "Give me a minute." He got out of the car and approached the trailer, knocked four times. No answer. He knocked another four times. Still nothing.

He tried the door. Locked.

McLellan was tempted to shoot the lock off. Instead, he headed back to the car and popped open the trunk. He saw a makeshift toolkit and a first aid kit. He reached into the box and pulled out a thin screwdriver. He went back to the trailer and thrust the screwdriver into the keyhole on the doorknob. He pushed it farther and farther. Then he twisted it hard.

Click.

The door was open.

McLellan popped his head inside. The smell of stale booze and old smoke. "Anyone home?"

Not a sound.

He headed back to the car and took the key out of the ignition. "Well, what are you guys waiting for?"

Eight

It was still dark when Reznick woke. He turned and saw Meyerstein sleeping. He got up and showered. Then he got dressed as quiet as he could and headed out of the house.

Reznick walked down the old dirt road into town, along fresh tire tracks from the SUV from the previous night. He headed down Samoset Road and angled toward the Rockland breakwater.

He stepped onto the granite slabs and walked toward the lighthouse. The water was like gray glass, not a ripple. He had lost count of the number of times he had walked here as a boy, accompanying his father, who loved nothing better than walking along the breakwater before the working day began. His father would gaze across Penobscot Bay as if in a trance. There was something about the peace all around. The sound of the water lapping against the breakwater. It was a balm to the soul.

Reznick fixed his eyes out over the dark waters. A burnt-orange sun peeked over the horizon, bathing the water in a tangerine glow. He had often headed down here with Eastland to talk while having a few beers.

Reznick realized he was going to go against Meyerstein's wishes. He had to. He turned and walked back along the breakwater to the harborside. He strode to the public pay phone and called his hacker friend.

It rang two times. "Morning, Trevelle, you got anything?"

"I got there, finally."

"Appreciate that."

"It took some time to get into a couple of systems. Cloud systems."

"So, you got a name?"

"Jimmy Adams. A former oilfield roughneck turned notoriously violent methamphetamine dealer. He's a mid-ranking psycho in the Aryan Brotherhood of Texas."

"Sounds like an interesting crew."

"He's a killer, Jon. He was released two years ago from Leavenworth."

"So, he headed up to Rockland, him and his friends, all the way from Texas, and they killed Bill Eastland and his wife?"

"That's him."

Reznick grimaced. "A guy like that doesn't fit the typical profile for serious crimes in this neck of the woods."

"What are you saying?"

"I'm saying someone hired this Jimmy Adams and his crew. It's a targeted killing. Tell me, has he got any distinguishing marks?"

"I'm looking at some of his tattoos on his mug shots. SS bolts across his chest and neck."

"Sounds like he's one of their crew, alright."

"Knifed a fellow inmate six years back. But his file says he's the go-to guy for AB-sanctioned hits across Texas and Florida. Mostly former members who run afoul of the leadership."

"Got an address?"

Williams gave an address in Midland, Texas.

Reznick scribbled down the details.

"Adams was also pretty tight with a couple of the leaders of the 211 Crew in Colorado when he served time there."

"Who the hell are they?"

"Racist prison gang. It appears 211 is a numeric code."

"What does it stand for?"

"Brotherhood of Aryan Alliance."

"I don't understand how these guys ended up here in Maine."

"Maybe Eastland's law enforcement past. Maybe he had a run-in with them and this was payback."

Reznick considered this, although he thought it was unlikely. "It's not impossible."

"You're not buying it?"

"The problem is, the killing of Bill Eastland doesn't fit that target profile. Anything else? What about associates of Adams?"

"Listen up, I do have some intel on them. Some nasty crazies he runs around with. There's a guy called Bernard Draxler. A serious Aryan Brotherhood of Texas dude. Spent time inside. Leavenworth. Described as highly dangerous."

"Address?"

Williams gave an address in Round Mountain, Texas, from ten years ago. "It's a tiny little town. It's about fifty miles northwest of Austin. It's not much, I know."

"It's something. And I appreciate that."

"One final thing: Draxler and Adams have connections to the Hell's Angels in Texas."

"Are there any biker clubhouses in his hometown?"

Williams tapped on his computer. "I can't see anything like that on the prison file I'm looking at."

"Former employer?"

"He used to work for his brother, Danny, a badged member of the Hell's Angels, who owns a motorcycle repair shop, Texas Chrome. Arrowhead Road, just outside his hometown."

Reznick added this to his notes. "That's something, I guess. I'd like more."

"Listen, I'll dig deeper on this. A lot deeper. But it will take time."

"I'll be in touch."

"You don't think these guys thought this up themselves, right?"

"Correct. Someone higher up the food chain ordered this. I need to find out who it was."

"Then what?"

"All bets are off."

Nine

The helicopter carrying Mort Feldman swooped low over the dark blue waters of Long Island Sound. He looked out the window at the sprawling estate by the sea, the largest waterfront estate on the coastline between Greenwich and New York City. They landed on a helipad on the property's manicured lawns.

Feldman breathed out long and hard as he took off his headset. He was always pleased to get back on firm ground. He wasn't a good flyer.

A bodyguard frisked Feldman as he stepped off the helipad. "No cell phones or iPads, strict orders."

"I understand."

The bodyguard ran a hand-held metal detector wand up and down over his suit and inside his briefcase. He turned and signaled to his colleague. "He's clean."

Feldman was escorted by two menacing-looking men wearing jeans and polo shirts into the house and through to the library.

He took a seat and placed his briefcase at his feet. After a few minutes, he started drumming his fingers. He couldn't even read his emails on his cell phone. He just sat as time dragged. He waited for nearly half an hour. It was par for the course. His client liked to keep him waiting. He wondered if he was being watched now. He knew the house was covered by electronic surveillance. He sensed there were eyes on him; he had felt it the moment he set foot inside the beautiful, sprawling home.

He had helped his client buy the achingly beautiful $110 million property through an offshore company Feldman had set up specifically for the purpose. Then a further $50 million was spent upgrading it. Renovating it. Decorating it. The finest Persian rugs. The most exquisite antiques in the drawing room. The most alluring decor. A couple of Jackson Pollocks on a wall, a couple of Van Gogh sketches, deep-pile carpets, Brazilian hardwood flooring. Air-conditioning experts were flown in from Florida, and on and on. His client didn't mind. He wanted the best. He got the best. He didn't give a fuck about the price. Truth be told, his client didn't give a fuck about anything or anyone. But his client at least seemed content.

The client adored his home. So besotted with the house was he that he had bought Feldman a rare George Daniels co-axial chronograph watch. It cost a cool six hundred fifty thousand dollars. One watch! It was insane extravagance, but hey, who was he to tell his client he didn't need or want it. So, he took the gift with good grace and a wide smile.

His client had lived on the property for more than five years. It was his refuge from New York.

Feldman's client had grown up dirt poor in the city. It was an impoverished upbringing in Bensonhurst from just after the Second World War. A world away from the gentrified Brooklyn of the present. His client had grown up the hard way. He worked on the docks as a kid. Then he got to know the union guys. He saw how to make money. He saw how protection rackets operated.

That's how it began for his client. He hustled for nickels and dimes. Then he got into the numbers racket. He saw more openings. He ran it all as a kid. He began to make money. More money than he ever imagined.

His client told him his life story when he asked Feldman to represent him. Feldman wanted to know everything there was to know about his client. He talked about the tight-knit Italian-American community. He began working for the Mob. Then he became a made man. A soldier. Then he was a feared capo. He learned to maim. Then kill. Sometimes both. It didn't matter to him. If someone had to be whacked, they got whacked. Sometimes he whacked close friends. It was the way it was.

Feldman listened in rapt amazement as his client told him all this. And more. But no one else. Not even Feldman's ex-wife knew. How could she?

The client appeared to have left his Mob roots behind. Feldman had been instrumental in turning the multimillionaire tough guy into a billionaire. He got his client involved in high finance, hedge funds, offshore companies, international trade, and so on. America, Europe, Asia, not to mention business dealings in the former Soviet bloc. He was, on the surface, legitimate. A spectacularly successful self-made man. His meteoric rise had been engineered by Feldman. He had helped his client forge links with biotech start-ups in Europe and Asia, looking for seed money. The client supplied money. And the contacts multiplied.

His client loved investing in high-risk stocks. He wanted stupendous returns. He employed fund managers from New York to Nantucket to make sure his investments were bringing in even more multiples.

Feldman watched as his client accumulated insane amounts of wealth. He was content to stay in the background. He had been raised in a safe, wealthy neighborhood, his home a townhouse in Lenox Hill. East Sixty-Fourth Street. His father, an affluent Jewish lawyer, had big clients. And it allowed Feldman to attend Dalton and then Yale. Then Harvard Law School. He had time and space and the financial wherewithal to prosper. By sharp contrast, his client had grown up with nothing. His client's father was an alcoholic longshoreman with a penchant for casual violence. His mother was a seamstress who earned virtually nothing for working nights in her kitchen, sewing buttons.

His client's greatest pride was providing for his mother. He bought her a beautiful home in Old Greenwich, not far from his gated estate.

A bodyguard entered and signaled for Feldman to follow him. "He'll see you now."

Feldman picked up his briefcase and headed across a long hallway, down some marble steps, and out into the huge gardens, overlooking Long Island Sound.

His client sat on a bloodred leather chair, smoking a cigarette, blowing smoke rings. "Sit down beside me, Mort. How the hell you doing?"

Feldman sat down as his client wafted cigarette smoke away from his face.

"Is that bothering you?"

"Not much," Feldman lied.

His client stubbed out the cigarette, exhaling the last of the smoke from the side of his mouth. "You know what I love about this place, Mort?"

Feldman shrugged. "Serenity?"

"That's the word—*serenity*. I love it. Peace, perfect peace."

"A lot quieter than Midtown Manhattan, let me tell you."

"I don't want to leave here. I'm loath to leave here."

"I know you are. But you have to leave here. Listen, tell you why I'm here. I've found you a new place. It's phenomenal."

"Where?"

"Arizona."

His client nodded as he looked around the grounds of his home, arms out wide. "And this good?"

"Wait till you see it. Exceptional. Twenty-five bedrooms, thirty bathrooms, a modern masterpiece of a house. Built three years ago. Helipad. And it's a bargain."

"How much?"

"Twenty million dollars. Sixteen-acre estate lot. Paradise Valley, on top of a mountain. You believe that?"

"Tell me about security."

"Guard gated."

"I'll need a security detail."

"It's all taken care of. I've arranged it. You will also have a new identity. New papers. No one will know. You're starting from scratch."

"And you've visited this place?"

"Last week. Private viewing. And I've already paid for it."

"Fuck. So, I own it?"

"No, a company I set up on your behalf owns it."

His client smiled. "So, we're set?"

"You're good to go."

His client got a wistful look in his eyes. "Seriously, I don't want to leave this place, Mort."

"I don't blame you. It's perfect."

His client looked out over the Sound.

"I know what you're going to embark on is huge for you. A huge step. I get it. But it's the right move under the circumstances. It means you keep one billion bucks in bank accounts in Switzerland, Bermuda, and Grand Cayman, and no one can touch you. It's all clean. And I have the legal agreement in place. Watertight."

"What about my mother?"

"She will be moved to a property three miles away from you. Different company will own it. It's secure. And beautiful. And you'll be close. Very close."

"What about my kids?"

"We have three other properties lined up for them, if they wish. You're all set."

"What the hell will I do with my time?"

"Golf?"

"Golf?"

"I'll get you membership at the ultra-exclusive Paradise Valley Country Club."

"I fucking hate golf."

Feldman laughed. "You'll learn to love it."

"What about you?"

"What about me?"

"Will you be staying in New York?"

"No one else will have me."

His client laughed. "You're a funny guy."

"You won't say that when you see your latest bill."

His client got quiet as if pondering the big move. "I'm not good with upheaval. I like order."

"I understand."

"A few weeks and I'm out of here?"

"A short journey to Westchester County Airport under the cover of darkness. Then Gulfstream down to Scottsdale. From Scottsdale, a chopper to your new home. Astonishing views, I swear to God."

"I didn't think it would end this way."

"It's not the end. Just a new beginning."

Ten

When Reznick returned home, Meyerstein was enjoying a cup of coffee, taking a call. He smiled as he cooked up some pancakes and toast for brunch.

Eventually, she finished the call.

"Good sleep?" Reznick said.

"Yes, thanks. Just checking in on the team. They're swinging by in an hour to pick me up."

"Well, you're not leaving here on an empty stomach."

Meyerstein sat at the breakfast bar as Reznick served up the brunch with more coffee and two glasses of freshly squeezed orange juice. "That's very nice of you."

"I don't get many visitors. At least ones with table manners. Enjoy."

Meyerstein began to carve up a pancake slathered in maple syrup, chewing slowly. "This is delicious. Who knew Jon Reznick could cook?"

"My dad used to make me these great pancakes, once a week, before school. Had to be Maine maple syrup or nothing."

"This is really good, let me tell you."

Reznick gulped his coffee, glad to get his caffeine fix.

"So, where did you get to before I woke up?"

"Clearing my head. Took a walk down by the harbor."

"Beautiful day out there."

Reznick was quiet for a few moments. "Yeah, it's lovely. Listen, Martha, I've been thinking about Bill Eastland."

"I don't want to talk about him. I'm sorry he's gone. But I don't want to talk about that. What I would like to talk about is you."

"Me? What about me?"

"I was talking to Lauren about you."

"What the hell were you talking to her about me for?"

"I'm worried about you, Jon. She's worried about you."

"Don't worry about me. I do just fine, thank you very much."

"Lauren told me about what happened the last time she was home."

"What are you talking about?"

"She said you were having nightmares. She heard you screaming at night. And she rushed into your bedroom. She was terrified to see you in such a state. You show all the symptoms of PTSD."

Reznick felt her steely gaze on him. "I don't see where you're going with this."

"We both believe you need psychological help. You don't sleep very much, and you have nightmares when you do. And you have a Dexedrine habit. These are all red flags. We want to help."

"You finished?"

Meyerstein smiled. "I want you to talk to a psychologist at the FBI. She's fantastic. She'll work through all those issues. It's nothing to be ashamed of."

"I don't want to talk about it."

"I think you could do with some support. You don't seem to rely on anyone. Everyone needs someone."

"I had Bill Eastland. Everyone in town knew him. He was always there. For anyone."

"But now he's gone. You don't have anyone to talk to."

"I don't want anyone. And I object to being lectured to."

"Jon, I only want what's best for you. So does Lauren. We care about you. A lot."

Reznick shrugged. "I just want answers. I want to know what happened to my friend. This happened in Rockland, for Christ's sake. Stuff like this doesn't happen here."

"Leave it to us, Jon. I promise we will find who is responsible. The best thing you can do is rest up." Meyerstein handed Reznick a business card. "Here's the number of the psychologist. She's based in DC. But I can have her fly up to meet you. Or maybe you can talk to her via Zoom."

Reznick shook his head and put the card in his pocket. "I'll be fine."

"Take a vacation. Get some sun. Maybe get down to Florida for a few weeks."

"I don't want any sun. I want answers."

The sound of a vehicle approaching the house.

Reznick glanced out the window. It was Sheriff's Investigator Tom Cain and a couple of deputies. "We got company."

He opened the front door.

Cain frowned at Reznick. "Put your hands behind your back, Jon."

"What?"

"Do what you're told. You're under arrest."

"Tom, what happened?"

"Charges finally came down. The alleged suspect died just over an hour ago."

Eleven

Shards of sunlight streamed through the dusty windows of the trailer nestled deep in the woods of southern Mississippi.

McLellan grimaced at his poker hand, a few hundred dollars on the table. He exchanged a knowing glance with Draxler, who gulped down some more beer as Connell snorted the last line of cocaine.

A fug of blue smoke enveloped them as they got loaded on cold beers and Scotch. The smell of sweat and ash lingered in the stale, humid air.

Connell sniffed hard, white residue of coke visible on the tip of his nose. He took off his shirt and dragged heartily on his cigarette. "What the hell happened to the air-conditioning? Feels like I'm frying alive."

McLellan's gaze was drawn to the shamrocks and lightning bolts and the *AB* tattoo.

Connell gulped his bottle of Heineken, sweat beading his forehead. "So, who's this trailer belong to, Dwayne? This a girlfriend of yours from way back?"

"She was a friend, let's leave it at that."

Connell smirked. "She due back soon?"

McLellan mugged hard at Connell as Draxler gazed out the windows as if bored. "I have no idea."

"I once knew a girl in Tuscaloosa," Connell said.

Draxler shook his head. "Complete shithole, Tuscaloosa."

Connell shrugged. "You been there?"

"Twice," Draxler said. "Fucking awful."

Connell looked annoyed. "Anyway, she lived in a trailer park on the edge of the city, just like this. Her daddy was mean to her. But I sorted him out real quick. Never bothered her again."

McLellan re-counted the hundreds of dollars on the table. He sat and listened as Connell ran his mouth. He had met the type before. The hanger-on. The wannabe. The nobody. He talked and talked. But he had never walked the walk. Not in the yard. He'd never felt the knot of tension knowing that a perfect stranger had to be knifed to death. In full view of everyone.

"Dwayne, you ever been to Tuscaloosa?" Connell asked.

McLellan shook his head.

"Let me tell you, the girls are something else. The college girls? Incredible."

McLellan lit up a cigarette and poured all three of them another large glass of Scotch. He looked at Draxler. "I want to make tracks, soon."

Connell yawned as he got up from his seat. "I'm gonna take a piss. You want to go right now?"

"Take your piss, man."

Connell went into the bathroom.

McLellan leaned across and whispered to Draxler. "His name's in the hat."

Draxler shrugged. "I got it."

"He's mine."

"Fair enough. Where we gonna take him?"

McLellan shrugged. "We're not gonna take him anywhere. We'll do it right here, right now."

Drax got up from his seat and shut the curtains as the sun streamed in. "Goddamn sun giving me a headache."

"You heard what I said?"

"I heard you, Dwayne. Relax."

Connell came back and sat down. "Are we moving, or are we going to play one final hand?"

Draxler sat down and smiled. "Sure, one final hand."

McLellan nodded. "Sounds good. Then we split." He looked around the trailer. "Nice place she has here."

"A woman's touch," Connell said. "All neat and tidy."

McLellan got up. "I'm going to nose around, see if she's got any cash lying around. Deal me in."

Connell grinned. "You bet, she'll have some hard cash stashed away. That's what they do."

McLellan opened drawers and cupboards as he looked around the trailer for any money or valuables he could find. He saw a nice chunky watch and put it in his pocket. He went into the kitchen and opened the small cupboard underneath the sink. He rummaged around. Cleaning chemicals, bleach, and dishcloths. His mind was racing as he thought about what he was going to do. He rummaged in a few more cupboards. Pots, pans, spices, packets of dry rice and pasta and cans of soup, tomato sauce, and salt, pepper, and cooking utensils. He looked in a cupboard and spotted what appeared to be a hair dryer. "What is all this shit?" On closer inspection he saw it was a kitchen blowtorch. He remembered seeing a TV chef using the device to sear fish for a barbecue.

McLellan turned and looked across at Connell's head. Running his mouth again, talking about girls, drugs, and the gangs of Alabama.

Draxler sat and nodded occasionally, as if listening.

McLellan caught Draxler's eye and nodded. He walked behind Connell, wrapped his huge left arm around the man's neck and squeezed tight. He exerted more and more pressure. Connell's face went red as he kicked out under the table.

McLellan picked him up and slammed him to the floor.

He stomped Connell repeatedly—ignoring the garbled screams—until his face was a bloody mess. He crushed his jawline and nose, a sickening crunching noise. He peered down at the bloody pulp of a face. Moans as Connell struggled to stay conscious.

Draxler grinned as he filmed the beating on his cell phone.

McLellan took out a penknife from his back pocket, kneeled on Connell's chest, and stabbed the knife repeatedly into the man's neck. One. Two. Three. Four. Five times. On and on he stabbed. He felt himself losing control. Losing his mind. He loved it. On and on and on. He stabbed twenty-two times. But still Connell was alive. Breathing. "You motherfucker!"

He got up and went over to the kitchen and picked up the blowtorch. He unlocked it. Ignited it.

McLellan walked over to the bloodied, moaning Connell, sprawled helpless on the ground, eyes pleading. "I told you to cover up your fucking tattoos in front of me, did I not?"

Connell moaned as blood streamed from his swollen, blackened eyes, his broken nose, and his mouth. He began to cry but was unable to move.

McLellan kneeled down hard on Connell's chest, left hand choking him again. He directed the blowtorch to the left forearm with the shamrocks. The smell of burning flesh as the screaming began. "Fucking disrespecting the AB, you piece of shit, huh?"

Connell passed out, unconscious.

McLellan burned the fucker's arm more and more until his skin caught fire. Blackened. He got up and went back to the kitchen and got some bleach. He poured it into Connell's bloody mouth as he gargled into consciousness. Suddenly his bleeding eyes were opened in full terror.

He poured the bleach onto Connell's eyes.

The screams echoed around the cabin.

McLellan rifled Connell's pockets. He pulled out approximately fifteen thousand dollars. He put it in his back pocket. Then he turned on the blowtorch again and aimed it at Connell's face.

The eyeballs ignited, flames erupting from Connell's skull.

Twelve

The cell felt cold and bare.

Reznick had been confined to the Knox County Jail for the weekend. He knew he was in serious trouble after the death of the shooter. He killed the time doing hundreds of push-ups, sit-ups, and mental exercises. He meditated. The bemused cops just watched as if studying some animal in the zoo.

It was Reznick's way of dealing with his situation. It enabled him to detach from his reality for a while. He needed to stay mentally strong. He had been in far worse places than the jail. He had hunkered down in open sewers on the outskirts of Baghdad. Now, that was unpleasant. By contrast, the Knox County Jail was the lap of luxury.

It was still dark on Monday morning when he was taken to the Knox County Courthouse for a private hearing. The judge rubbed his eyes, as if he wasn't a natural early riser, and listened to the charges, the top one being manslaughter.

The judge looked at him sternly. "I read about what happened. I have also received a few impressive letters. I can see from your record you are a man of impeccable character, Mr. Reznick. But what intrigued me most was a letter from an assistant director of the FBI, no less."

Reznick stood and listened respectfully.

"I've read about your work for our country. I've been shown details of your military service. I've been told a lot of it can't be released. Which I understand. I'm a veteran myself, Mr. Reznick. Vietnam. And I note from your file that your late father was a Vietnam vet."

Reznick nodded. "Yes sir, that's correct."

"I'm placing your bail at $50,000. I trust you will adhere to the conditions, sir."

"Yes, Your Honor. And thank you."

The judge took off his spectacles and leaned back in his seat as Reznick smiled. "Stay out of trouble."

Reznick went through the process of arranging for the bail and signing for his possessions, and as soon as he got outside he turned on his cell phone. It rang almost immediately.

"Where the hell you been, man?" It was Trevelle Williams, the recluse incredulous in his high-tech lair somewhere in Iowa.

"Long story. So, what've you got for me?"

"I have more information. And it's good intel on these Aryan Brotherhood of Texas psychos."

"What I'm trying to figure out at this stage is the motivation. Why was Bill Eastland targeted?"

Trevelle sighed. "It's sad, man. I almost don't want to tell you. You being his friend and all."

"Spit it out. Tell me what you know."

"Bill Eastland was a fuckup."

"I beg your pardon."

"I'm sorry to break it to you, man. He was a degenerate, hopeless gambling addict."

"Bill Eastland? Are you sure?"

"Positive."

"I know he liked a hand of poker."

"It's way more than a hand of poker. I've double- and tri-ple-checked credit agencies and debt management companies who had been chasing him."

"He was in debt?"

"He was more than in debt. He was technically bankrupt. A mountain of debt. He owed more than two million to a ton of creditors. Banks, loan sharks, casinos, you name it."

Reznick was shocked by the news. "Are you absolutely sure it's the same guy?"

"Jon, you don't know the half of it. He also liked the horses. He bet big on them. He had lost everything. The bank was in the pro-cess of repossessing his house. And pretty much everything in it."

Reznick closed his eyes. "I just can't believe this. Are you one hundred percent sure? Did you verify date of birth?"

"Jon, I checked and checked and checked again. It's your friend."

"I swear to God, in all the years I've known him, he never men-tioned debt. He was always helping out veterans in need. Christ, if I'd known, I would've helped him out any way I could."

Trevelle said, "He was in so deep, he couldn't get out, Jon. No one could help him with debts like that."

Reznick thought through the option of a creditor who'd had enough. "One of his creditors must have called in the debts. A loan shark. And Bill wasn't able to pay."

"Seems like it."

"Have you got anything else?"

"I do. I finally managed to access State Department and FBI databases."

"Seriously?"

"Deadly. I have no idea who's doing their coding or cyberse-curity. It's a mess."

"So, what have you got?"

"I used the photos they have of Bernard Draxler, who is a known associate of Jimmy Adams. My software has overlaid their data."

"You want to translate what you just said?"

"I got a real-time hit within the last twenty-four hours on Draxler. A casino in Biloxi."

"Mississippi?"

"Yup."

Reznick figured Draxler had been in on the operation in Rockland, but as it stood, there was nothing to link Draxler to Eastland's killing other than his connection to Adams.

"He very probably might be part of the crew," Trevelle said. "I don't know. He and Adams did time together."

"Who was with him at the casino?"

"This is where it gets interesting. The other guy is an anomaly. He's a typical low-level meth dealer from Alabama. Stephen Hanley Connell from Anniston, Alabama. He has drug-dealing links to biker gangs, although he's not in a gang."

"The Brotherhood?"

"Can't see any reference to that. He was jailed in Miami for dealing meth to college kids on spring break. Not much more on him."

"You've given me names and addresses already. Can you send it to me? End-to-end encryption, obviously. I'm going to look closer at that. What I want to hear from you, and I'll call you about this, is if any of these names ring a bell on your system. I'm talking police computers, supermarkets, whatever."

"You got it. Just wanted to say, Jon, for what it's worth, if this was me, I wouldn't be mixing with these cats. They're fucking crazy."

"Which raises another question: Who would send such animals to do hits? A loan shark? Because this sure as hell didn't originate from the Aryan Brotherhood. They're the triggermen on this, no doubt. But I need to get below all that. I need to find out who hired them."

"Jon, I'm serious, don't cross that line and head down there."

"Why?"

"I don't want you coming back in a goddamn box, that's why."

Thirteen

The seventh floor of the FBI headquarters in DC was where the most senior executives in the Hoover Building conducted their business.

Meyerstein headed down the carpeted corridor as she was escorted into a highly secured conference room. Two other senior FBI executives were already there, perusing her classified briefing paper on the Jon Reznick situation, but she was surprised to see a CIA officer at the table.

Rachel Crabtree had been assigned to a special project embedded within the FBI's National Security Branch. Meyerstein had only encountered her on a handful of occasions since she had been assigned two years earlier. Crabtree had her own office on the seventh floor, just down the hall from the FBI director. Cesar Mendoza, who worked with Meyerstein in the FBI's Organized Crime Group, looked up and smiled.

Meyerstein sat down and arranged her notes. "Apologies for my tardiness; my call went long."

Franklin Masson, who chaired these meetings, peered over his half-moon spectacles. "Good of you all to set aside this hour on such short notice," he said. "Rachel has asked to sit in on our meeting. I assume you don't have a problem with that."

"None at all," Meyerstein said.

"As you know, the Director is very keen to facilitate information-sharing at all levels within the intelligence community. Rachel has the highest level of clearance and free rein to ask questions."

"That's perfectly fine. I'm all for intelligence-sharing among our partners at Langley. Nice to have you here, Rachel."

"Nice to be here."

Meyerstein cleared her throat. "Let's get to it. This regards, as you know, our asset. He has been, to this point, a consultant on certain national security issues. I'm talking about Jon Reznick of Rockland, Maine. He has been highly effective, albeit unorthodox in his methods." She proceeded to give a detailed update on the timeline of the shooting of Jimmy Adams in Rockland and the subsequent fallout.

The three others, including Crabtree, took notes throughout and listened intently. Meyerstein explained how the situation had unraveled, potentially exposing in open court the involvement of Jon Reznick in FBI activities. It was something they were all keen to avoid.

Meyerstein also revealed that she had headed up to Rockland at the Director's behest. The purpose was to use her close working relationship with Reznick to ensure that the ex-Delta operator would not embark on a retribution spree after Eastland's killing. However, she conceded that Reznick's arrest in the presence of an FBI assistant director was not a good look.

"We are mindful," Meyerstein continued, "that there is a criminal investigation underway, but the purpose of this meeting is to try and close this case down before it becomes problematic. I know we've all got global terror cells and their activities, among a host of other issues. So, this might pale by comparison. But I would argue that it has the potential to be hugely damaging for the reputation of the FBI further down the road."

Rachel Crabtree frowned across the table.

"What's on your mind, Rachel?" Meyerstein asked.

"Is it OK to give my take on this?"

"By all means."

"I've got to say this makes for compelling reading, Martha."

Meyerstein shifted in her seat, suddenly uncomfortable.

"But with the greatest respect to you and everyone around the table, how has this been allowed to happen?"

"Do you mean on what protocol Reznick's expected to operate?"

"No, I mean, why was he brought in to assist the FBI in the first place? I knew Jon shortly after he was assigned to the CIA. But I'm surprised that he was allowed to operate alongside the FBI on American soil."

"It's complicated, for sure. But it was thanks to Jon that we foiled a bioterrorism attack on the Pentagon." Crabtree listened intently. "It happened because we needed to make a deal in regard to a government scientist, to get him to a secure place. We made a deal."

"Sorry to belabor the point, but why wasn't that a one-time thing? Why has he been used continually by the FBI for years?"

"We have sound reasons."

"Here's the thing, and sorry for being so brutally frank. This situation, in my eyes, is not tenable. If this got out—that the FBI was operating without authority, using this guy in whatever black-ops stunts he's pulling—you're looking for trouble."

"For the time being, we can say and prove that Jon Reznick is no longer working on our behalf."

"So, why is he causing us so many problems?"

Meyerstein took a few moments to compose herself. "Jon, in this instance, apprehended one of the gang responsible for killing a former chief of police in Rockland and his wife in cold blood."

"That's still to be established."

"Rachel, with respect, you're wrong. Jon Reznick stopped one of the gang in his tracks."

"I read the report."

"We believe the men are in a white supremacist gang. And they have crossed state lines. So, the FBI has a role."

"Jon Reznick isn't FBI, is he?"

"Not now, that's correct."

"So, he is a private citizen."

"Jon Reznick has served his country as a member of Delta Force with honor. And he has served the FBI in a classified capacity too. And the CIA on highly classified operations. He was given a Presidential Medal."

"The reality is, Martha, Jon Reznick is a cold-blooded killer. You know it, and now we have proof. On the streets of America, he is fighting this one-man war."

Meyerstein's gaze wandered around the three others at the table. She felt like she had just been humiliated and hung out to dry. The others sat in silence. "What do you think, gentlemen?"

Mendoza leaned back in his seat. "I think you need to ease up here, Rachel. Have you read the timeline of what happened from the sheriff's investigator in Rockland?"

"I read the summary."

"So, you didn't read the whole thing. Even a cursory glance at the chain of events shows that it was Reznick who saw the men in masks. He followed them at a discreet distance. He did not formally engage with them until he was forced to."

"According to who, exactly?"

Mendoza blinked slowly. "According to Jon Reznick's statement."

"You've kind of made my point for me, Cesar, if you don't mind."

"The chain of events is clear, unless you know different."

Crabtree sat in sullen silence and scribbled a note.

Mendoza cleared his throat. "Here at the FBI, we work in a collegial fashion. That's the way it's done. So, don't be starting arguments with Martha over how she runs her operations. Jon Reznick is part of our history. For better or worse. But we just don't want the world to know. Stuff happens. We deal with it. This is not the Agency. And we take responsibility when shit happens."

Crabtree seethed.

Mendoza continued: "Reznick followed the men at a safe distance. He called it in. The dispatcher at Rockland passed that on to a patrol car that was five miles away at the time. Then shots were fired at Reznick's truck. And he fired back. Self-defense, no question in my mind."

Meyerstein said, "Forensics has confirmed that bullets retrieved from Reznick's vehicle came from a modified AK-47 or a semiautomatic."

"That's right," Mendoza said. "And then we have Reznick taking cover. Retrieving his hunting rifle from the truck. And firing at the masked man, Jimmy Adams. So, let's cut out the tone and the accusations. We need to find out who committed this double murder."

Crabtree leafed through some papers. "I see here that Adams suffered a loss of blood from gunshots to the knee. Both knees. In addition to the rifle shot to the shoulder."

Meyerstein went quiet, as did Mendoza.

"So, correct me if I'm wrong, but that looks like excessive force in Reznick's alleged self-defense argument. And the 9mm bullets were from Reznick's Beretta, right?"

Meyerstein nodded.

"This is what I'm talking about."

Mendoza nodded. "Point taken. That said, Reznick was within his rights."

"To blow out the suspect's kneecaps when he was already incapacitated?"

"No jury is going to convict him on that."

Meyerstein put up her hand to silence the heated discussion. "If we can take a step back from this blow-by-blow account, Adams is Aryan Brotherhood of Texas. Do the field offices in Texas have this information?"

Mendoza nodded. "They've got it all. I was talking to Rodriguez from Dallas. They're up to speed. And they're putting out feelers to informants across the state. Relations, friends. We've got a lot of red flags. A group like the AB of Texas crazies being sent to mid-coast Maine, it's unprecedented. And it points to a possible organized crime nexus in the Southwest."

Meyerstein said, "The question that arises is: Where are these guys? We have a Mississippi connection—that's where we saw some casino images of a Texas AB associate, Bernard Draxler, and an Alabama drug dealer, Connell—small fry. The Jackson field office is working this angle. But listen, this is bigger than this crew. We need to speak to Draxler and any of the others."

Crabtree held up a picture of Bernard Draxler. "Wherever Adams goes, Draxler isn't usually far behind."

"There might be others," Mendoza said.

"Almost certainly," Meyerstein said. "Which brings us to the big question: Who hired them to kill Eastland and his wife?"

Crabtree said, "I've looked over some background on this guy, Bill Eastland."

Meyerstein was surprised she was taking such an active part in the investigation. "And?"

"And Eastland owed some casinos in Atlantic City and Vegas big bucks. But there were loan sharks, and he'd lost his house too. Was due to be repossessed."

"Who ordered the hit?" Meyerstein repeated. "We need to reach out to our high-level informants. We all have them. Someone knows something. I want the name of who's behind this."

Franklin Masson scribbled some notes. "Let's get back to it. We meet again in forty-eight hours. And let's try and cool it next time."

Fourteen

The call came at nightfall.

Reznick peered out at the dark waters of Penobscot Bay, down in the sandy cove. He took his cell phone out of his pocket.

"I got something, Reznick."

"I thought you were never going to call, Trevelle."

"It's taking me a heck of a lot longer than I imagined."

"What you got?"

"The two guys caught on the cameras at the casino in Biloxi, Draxler and Connell. We got a big development."

"Shoot."

"Stephen Hanley Connell, the meth dealer from Alabama, has been found dead."

"You sure? The same guy from the casino?"

"The very one."

"So, they're killing each other already?"

"Looks like it. Connell was found inside a trailer with multiple stab wounds and signs of torture."

"Where?"

"In the woods of south Mississippi. The police report said he had been *butchered*. Their word."

"Two things. Whose trailer is it, and an exact location?"

Williams gave the name of a croupier in Biloxi, Cherry Black.

"Who's she?"

"She rents the trailer. The nearest town is Saucier."

"Cherry Black, is that her real name?"

"Yup. Cherry Blossom Black. Prostitution charges a few years ago in Vegas, now dealing cards in Biloxi."

"Who discovered the body?"

"She did. She had been on vacation in Miami Beach with her friends. She drove back home. She found the trailer door open, then a decaying body inside. Helluva mess by all accounts. Blowflies laying their eggs in flesh wounds, you name it. Complete holy mess."

"I take it she's not living there anymore."

"I'm one step ahead of you. She's staying with her mother in Jackson." He gave the address to Reznick.

Reznick made a mental note of the details. "So, that's all we've got so far?"

"It's the best I can do. No idea where Draxler is or if there's anyone else involved."

"It's something. So, is this a local police matter in Mississippi?"

"So far. No indication of FBI involvement from the files I've accessed."

"Let me know if anything changes."

Fifteen

McLellan jolted awake in the back of the stolen car, a harsh morning sun streaming through the rear window. He squinted and shielded his eyes. "Where the fuck are we, Drax?"

"We're back home in Texas, my friend. Feels good, don't it?" Drax yawned. "Goddamn. I'm nearly falling asleep, man."

"My turn to take the wheel."

Drax pulled over, and McLellan slid into the driver's seat. "Don't go breaking the fucking speed limit."

"Don't you worry."

"I think we need to get rid of the car."

"I say we dump it in San Antonio."

McLellan drove for an hour until they hit a gas station off the freeway. He filled up and made a call from a pay phone as Drax slept.

"Who's this?" The voice of the shot caller.

"We're back in Texas. Not far from San Antonio. I want a safe place to crash."

"I'll call you back in five minutes."

McLellan stood around waiting impatiently in the broiling sun. Fifteen minutes later the phone rang.

"Yeah?" McLellan said.

"A town on the outskirts north of San Antonio. Hollywood Park."

"I've heard of it."

"You get to Bar 909, Blanco Road. It's open all the time. Ask for the owner, Rick. He's cool with us. He'll get you what you want."

"Appreciate that."

"Stay safe, bro. And stay in touch."

McLellan drove straight there. He pulled up an hour later. He woke Drax up, and they went inside, AC on maximum. It was empty, dark, football game replay on the TV. Rick, a former Bakersfield skinhead, handed him a cold beer and a key for a nearby apartment.

"You mind getting rid of the car outside?" McLellan handed over the keys.

"Not a problem, man. A friend of mine runs a towing company. He'll have it out of here within half an hour."

Rick drove McLellan and Draxler to a bleak apartment complex not far from the bar. "Number twenty-two, up the stairs, second floor. Nice and quiet. No one will bother you."

The two men crashed out in the apartment and slept for twenty hours straight.

The following morning, Rick picked them up and drove them to the main bus station in San Antonio. "Eight hours to Midland."

McLellan hugged the guy tight. "Appreciate that, bro. I won't forget."

Rick winked at him and shook Draxler's hand. "You'll be in Midland before you know it."

Sixteen

It was just after midnight when Reznick's plane touched down in Jackson, Mississippi. He caught a cab to a downtown hotel. He wasn't going to knock on the door of Cherry Black's house at such an ungodly hour. He would try in the morning. A stranger turning up at her door so late at night might unnerve her. But as it was, he was already playing catch-up, trying to get on the trail of Bernard Draxler and his crew.

Reznick was shown to his room. He unpacked his case and the backpack with his essentials—a change of clothes and his trusty 9mm Beretta. Twenty thousand dollars in cash he had sewn into his jacket for such emergencies, on top of the extra thousands he'd brought. He had no idea if he would need any of the items, but he always liked to come prepared.

His cell phone rang.

Reznick recognized the caller ID as Lauren's number.

"Hi, Dad, can you talk?"

"Of course. Everything OK?"

"I'm fine, Dad."

Reznick sensed tension in her voice. "Glad to hear it."

"Dad, I'm worried about you."

"Don't worry about me."

"But I do. I was talking to Martha. We're both worried."

"Did she ask you to talk to me?"

"Not in so many words. I just want you to think about where you're going, Dad. You need the FBI to investigate this. This isn't your job."

"Lauren, listen to me. I love you. I always will. But this is my business. What I get up to is up to me."

"Dad, I'm worried you're going to mess with some very dangerous people. People that could kill you."

"I can take care of myself. Listen, I appreciate your concern. And Martha's. But this is personal. I need answers."

"I just want you to be safe. I've got a bad feeling about this, Dad. The people who did this are incredibly dangerous."

"I'll keep that in mind, Lauren. Look, I've got to go. Take care of yourself. And tell Martha I said hi."

Reznick ended the call. He wasn't usually abrupt or sharp with his daughter. But the death of Eastland and his wife had shocked him to his core. As he had told Lauren, this was personal—and he needed answers, not a warning from the FBI.

Reznick showered and watched a late-night documentary on Iraq. He wished he had watched some escapist film on Netflix. But instead he saw once more the images of the American contractors hanging from that bridge in Fallujah. The searing footage still enraged Reznick. It brought it all back.

He popped a couple of sleeping pills, washed them down with water, and fell asleep within minutes.

The next morning, just after sunup, Reznick took a cab across town to where he hoped to find Cherry Black. The house was an old colonial. Neat front yard behind a chain-link fence.

Reznick walked up the garden path and knocked on the front door. The sound of shuffling feet inside. The door opened.

A silver-haired woman stood there, smoking a cigarette. "Yeah, what do you want?"

"Sorry to bother you, ma'am. I'm looking for Cherry Black."

"You a cop?"

Reznick smiled. "No, I'm not."

"So, what do you want with Cherry?"

"I'd like to speak to her."

"I gathered that. What about? You don't sound like you're from around here."

"I'm from Maine."

"Maine? What the hell are you doing down here, son?"

Reznick chuckled. He asked himself the same question. "I heard about what happened in Cherry's trailer. Up near Saucier."

The woman's face drained of color. "You said you weren't a cop."

"I'm not."

"You a reporter, snooping around? They've been here. I don't trust them not to twist that story. I told her not to get involved with reporters. Little snakes."

"Ma'am, I was hoping Cherry could help me."

"Cherry ain't helped anyone in her life. The only person she helps is herself. Selfish, goddamn fool of a girl. You a boyfriend of hers?"

"No, I'm not. Do you know where I can find Cherry?"

"Sure I do."

"I just want to ask her some questions. There was a double killing up in Maine. Both were friends of mine. I'm trying to figure out what happened."

"I'm sorry to hear that. Me shooting my mouth off. So, how on God's earth is Cherry going to know about that? She's never been to Maine. She's lived in the South her whole life."

"Ma'am, I believe one of the men who committed the crime stopped off at a casino in Biloxi. And the same man wound up dead in your daughter's trailer."

"What sort of bullshit story is that, son? Are you kidding me?"

"No, I'm not, ma'am."

The woman dragged heavy on her cigarette. "And you're definitely not a cop? And she's not in trouble?"

"No, she's not, ma'am. I'm just trying to piece together what happened."

"Ain't that the police's job?"

"It is. But the people who died up in Maine were close, personal friends of mine and my late father. The man was a veteran. His wife was a homemaker."

"God bless them." The woman cocked her head. "The all-day diner down the road. She's working there. Two hundred yards down yonder."

"The diner?"

"That's right. That girl, she'll be the death of me."

"Appreciate your time, ma'am."

"She's always been no good. I raised her well. But, only the Lord knows what He has in store for us."

Reznick turned and headed down the path. It was a two-minute walk to the diner. A handful of patrons inside, digging into grits, eggs, fries, and whatever else they could load onto their plates. He sat down at a booth and perused the breakfast menu.

"What can I get you, honey?" The nametag on the neat black uniform said "Cherry."

"Black coffee, toast, scrambled eggs."

The waitress scribbled down the order. "That all, honey?"

"I was hoping you could help me. I was just speaking to your mother."

The woman rolled her eyes. "Gimme a break. Are you a cop? I've had my fill of cops."

"I'm not a cop. I just want a minute of your time."

"What's this about?"

"A couple of friends of mine have died, up in Maine."

"What's that got to do with me?"

"Nothing. But I heard about what happened at that trailer of yours out in the woods."

"That was nothing to do with me. You from the insurance company?"

"Relax, Cherry. I'm not a cop or from the insurance company. All I know is that someone broke into your trailer. And a body was found."

"You sound like a cop."

Reznick showed his hands and smiled. "Trust me: not guilty."

"So, who the hell are you? Friends don't travel all the way down from goddamn Maine to Mississippi to find out who was responsible for some deaths."

"My name is Jon Reznick. I'm a veteran. My friend who died in Maine was a veteran. I just want to find out what happened. And I think his death is linked to the body of the man found in your trailer. Listen, I just have a few questions. That's all."

The waitress closed her eyes, hands on hips. "Never a goddamn break."

"Cherry, you could really help me out."

"I already answered all the cops' questions."

"I understand that. But I've got a few more questions. Five minutes, that's all."

Cherry shook her head and headed over to the counter, handing over Reznick's order to the cook. She served another couple of customers before she returned with Reznick's breakfast. "There's your breakfast." She topped up his coffee. "Anything else I can get you?"

Reznick slid ten hundred-dollar bills across the table. "This is yours."

The waitress surreptitiously took the money and slid it into a pocket of her uniform. "Seriously?"

"It's yours. Just a few questions, and I'm out of here."

She sat down opposite him. "What do you want to know?"

"Tell me about this trailer of yours."

"What can I say? It wasn't mine, that's for sure. I lived there rent free. Friend of mine owns it."

"The guy who was killed there, do you know him? His name was Steve Connell, from Alabama."

"Don't mean a thing to me."

"White supremacist drug dealer, by all accounts."

"It's Mississippi, honey."

"Someone brought Connell there. Maybe it was a falling-out among thieves."

"The police already asked about that."

"What exactly did they want to know?"

"Who it might have been. Who was involved."

Reznick took a gulp of his coffee. "Do you have any ideas?"

"I do."

"Did you give them names?"

"No, I did not."

"Do you mind me asking why?"

"Cops have never liked me. I was a teenage runaway. And I got into trouble. Was working the streets and the casinos. You know, for men."

"I get it. So, you never told the police who it was. Why not?"

"No one believes me. I'm scared they're going to connect me to this."

85

"Listen to me. Two of my friends died. I promise not to tell the cops. I just want to know."

Cherry closed her eyes, blinking back tears. "Boyfriend of mine from way back when. He used to visit. Fucking lunatic. But then he disappeared. Story of my life."

"A boyfriend."

"Ex-boyfriend."

"Does he have a name?"

"Dwayne."

Reznick nodded. "Last name?"

"McLellan. Dwayne McLellan. From out in West Texas. Wild. Jailbird. I thought he was exciting, if you can believe that."

"What else can you tell me?"

"He's originally from Lubbock. At least that's what he said. But he's crazy. Real fucking crazy."

"Why on earth didn't you tell the police about him?"

Cherry turned her attention out the diner window to the parking lot. "Like I said, I was concerned that I was going to get dragged into it. I'm no angel. I know that. But I wish to God I'd never met him."

"Can you tell me more?"

"Listen, mister, why the hell should I trust you?"

"I'm asking for a favor, one human being to another. That's all."

She brushed hair from her eyes. "He was a bastard. Stubbed cigarettes out on my stomach for fun. I was terrified of him. I'm glad he's out of my life." Tears welled in her eyes.

"That's tough, I'm sorry."

The waitress glanced around as another customer tried to get her attention. "Please don't mention my name to anyone. That's all I ask."

"You still scared he'll find you?"

"I made a lot of mistakes when I was younger. I'm trying to put all that behind me."

Reznick finished his coffee and thanked Cherry for her help. "I wish you all the best."

"A thousand bucks is a step in the right direction, right?"

Reznick smiled, left a fifty-dollar tip on top of the money he had already given her. "Take care of yourself and your mother. Is there a pay phone around here?"

The waitress pointed to the side of the diner. "Round the back. You want to borrow my cell phone?"

"I'm fine, thanks."

Reznick left the diner and walked around to the side. He called a number he had memorized.

"Yeah, who's this?" Trevelle asked.

"It's me."

"You're in the Deep South, I see."

"You better believe it. I got another name. Dwayne McLellan, originally from Lubbock, Texas. I think he's done some serious time in the past. I'd like to know where he might have headed. Haunts. And I need it now."

"I'll get back to you in the next fifteen minutes."

Williams was as good as his word.

"So, did you find out anything?"

"McLellan is a stone-cold lunatic."

"Where can I find him?"

"His last known address was in Odessa, Texas. But I see that house is now rented by a family of four. So, that's probably not going to be useful. But I was doing some cross-referencing and looking back on other addresses. And I see on the records that Jimmy Adams worked at a gas plant in Notrees, West Texas. It's an oilfield town. Workers mostly commute in from Odessa and Pecos and Midland. But there's practically no one living there."

"Go on."

"Listen to this. He shared a house with Dwayne McLellan, but remember, that was nearly twenty years ago. It's all I have."

"Notrees?"

"The middle of the desert. It's virtually scrubland. The address I have is 15 Third Street, just off State Highway 302."

"A handful of properties in the whole town?"

"A bit of a ghost town. It's right out in the desert, deepest West Texas. Dust and sand. There ain't nothing there."

"I'll be in touch." Reznick hung up and called a cab, which took him to Jackson International Airport. He booked a flight direct to Dallas. He was waiting to board when his cell phone rang.

"Jon, where the hell are you?" demanded Tom Cain.

"I'm taking care of some business. Loose ends, so to speak."

"Jon, listen to me. I'm outside your house now. The bail conditions are that you notify me if you leave the area. You have to be contactable."

Reznick grimaced. "You're speaking to me now."

"So, where are you?"

"I'm on my way home."

"You're due to appear in five days' time at a private hearing again."

"Do you want to email me the letter?"

"Jon, don't fuck around. I like you. And I know you. I've known you for a long time. The same as Bill Eastland. The killings have shattered the whole community. I get that. But don't try to play me for a fool."

"I hear what you're saying."

"Jon, the Feds have been in touch with me. They're considering you a flight risk."

"That's bullshit. I'm not running from anything. I'm free to leave the state, am I not?"

Cain sighed. "Yes, you are."

"Tom, you have my word. I'll be home for the hearing."

"One more thing. The funeral for Bill and Elspeth is the day after the hearing. I thought you'd want to know."

"Appreciate that."

"Jon, don't fuck this up. This is serious business."

Reznick ended the call. He hoped to get some shut-eye on the flight to Dallas. He began to think ahead. He would drive west on the interstate. Then into the heart of the endless Chihuahuan Desert.

Seventeen

Meyerstein felt frazzled as the meeting got underway in the seventh-floor conference room. She was annoyed to see Crabtree again.

Franklin Masson called the meeting to order. He looked around the table, his gaze fixed on Meyerstein. "Let's kick things off, Martha. Now, you know I am personally fond of Jon," he said. "This man's commitment to this country and on several classified investigations we have been involved in has been superlative. The one that springs to mind is the first one, in DC. The biological terror plot."

Meyerstein nodded. "I remember that well. And I appreciate your kind words about Jon. But this is business, right?"

"Absolutely. But I'm putting you on notice: this is your responsibility, and you need to get this straightened out. So, where the hell are we with this?"

Meyerstein's throat felt dry. She sipped some water. "Yeah, so, first, we now know Reznick is not in Rockland. We got a fix on him recently in Jackson, Mississippi."

Masson peered over his half-moon spectacles. "I'm assuming he picked up the scent of this Aryan Brotherhood crew after the murder in the trailer? And that's where Reznick is crossing a line with me. That's not his responsibility. Red line for me."

"Reznick is piecing this together," Meyerstein said. "He's not doing it all by himself. He's clearly getting technical assistance from somewhere. And I believe the guy we're looking for is Trevelle Williams. So, it's clearly interfering with an ongoing investigation. Interference from both of them."

Crabtree gave a patronizing smile. "Am I missing something here? Why don't we just pick up this Williams?"

"We would if we could find him," Masson said.

"We can't get a fix on him?"

Masson shook his head. "He was operating out of Iowa, but he's left the facility he was using recently."

"So, he dropped off the grid again?"

"Pretty much."

Crabtree shook her head. "So, why don't we arrest Jon Reznick?"

Masson shook his head. "Not a chance, Rachel. He was arrested in Rockland, and his hearing was private. But if he's arrested again, appears in a local court, and it gets out that he's known to the Feds and has actually worked for us, the shit will most certainly hit the fan. I can see leaks from the local cops. A shitstorm would ensue."

Meyerstein interrupted. "Jon's clearly trying to track down those he believes responsible. This Aryan Brotherhood of Texas hit squad. And that's where our main focus should be. Let's find them and stop Reznick from getting to them first."

Franklin checked his notes. "It's getting messy. These Brotherhood guys are already at each other's throats, and that's before Reznick appeared on the scene. I want to move away from that aspect, if you don't mind. During our last meeting, I asked everyone to go away and dig into who might have ordered this hit up in Maine. I know our field offices are working this problem." Franklin looked across at Cesar. "You work with the confidential informant coordinators. What are you hearing? Someone must know something."

Cesar pointed to the speaker in the middle of the table. "We've got a breakthrough."

Meyerstein smiled at Cesar. "Good work. What've we got?"

"I'm going to play an audio excerpt that we intercepted," Cesar said. "We caught a break. Cell phone conversation involving a low-level mobster by the name of Thomas Egan."

Meyerstein said, "How low level?"

"Well, he has connections to the Irish Mob in Boston and across the Northeast. But also the Italian Mafia. Egan and his crew distribute coke and meth across West Texas. So, the conversation was obtained via his cell phone. But we don't know exactly who he was speaking to."

Franklin nodded. "Play it."

Cesar pressed the remote in his hand. The audio started.

"Take care of a retired cop, goes by the name of Eastland. Out-of-state crew, no ties to us. Fucker owes a friend of ours a million-plus. You got a problem with that, Tommy?"

The audio abruptly ended. "So, this unknown caller," Cesar said, "perhaps from Boston or New York or Jersey, judging by the accent, is calling Thomas Egan. And it's spelled out in no uncertain terms. My take on this? This is what we've been looking for."

Masson scribbled some notes. "It's a very good starting point. Where was Egan when this took place?"

"Walmart parking lot in Midland, Texas."

Meyerstein leaned back in her seat. "So, there's the Texas connection right there. That's very good quality, Cesar. Have we run the conversation through voice recognition?"

"Nothing matches so far. We're still working on it."

Masson looked around the table. "This is a promising start. But I feel like we're chasing our tails. Reznick is in the South, maybe headed to Texas. Those Aryan Brotherhood nuts will be hiding out in a safe house. We need more. A hell of a lot more."

Crabtree said, "My take on this: I believe the priority has to be to intercept Jon Reznick. The bail conditions say he should not interfere with potential witnesses. He is jeopardizing our investigation. Am I right?"

Masson steepled his fingers. "What do you say, Martha?"

"I think you're right. I think it's important we get Jon Reznick back up north. He's killed one of these guys already. I don't think it's going to end there. But I know Jon, and I know how he works."

Masson grimaced. "OK, that'll do. We need to focus. We need to dig deeper, people. A lot more resources need to be deployed. We can talk budgets once this is all over. But I want this resolved. Who ordered the hit on Eastland? We need to dig into all our Italian Mafia contacts. We know Thomas Egan has links to them as well as the remnants of the Irish Mob. But we also know that the Italian Mafia has used the Aryan Brotherhood for hits in the past."

Crabtree said, "Why?"

"So there's no trail back to the Mafia. They contract out the killings. Egan is also real tight with a guy called Michael Gilligan, a psycho within the Aryan Brotherhood of Texas hierarchy. Get back to the confidential informant coordinators in Dallas, New York, every goddamn place. But as Rachel said, we need to find Reznick before this whole mess explodes in our face."

Eighteen

When Reznick landed in Dallas, he was acutely aware that the Feds would be using the surveillance cameras in and around major transport hubs to try and track him down. His details on the flight would have been flagged by the FBI or Homeland Security. He needed to keep one step ahead, even if it was something as rudimentary as a basic countersurveillance tactic.

He went to a gift shop and bought a Cowboys hat, Ray-Ban aviator shades, and a Lone Star T-shirt. He headed into the bathroom and locked one of the stalls. Reznick changed into his fresh T-shirt, put on the shades, and pulled the cap down low. He checked himself in the mirror. It wasn't fail-safe by any means. But it might give him a head start.

Reznick assumed they had tagged him the moment he arrived at the airport. The image would be scanned at the FBI's high-tech facility in West Virginia, using the Next Generation Identification System (NGIS). He knew it would take ten or fifteen minutes to process his image, maybe more. The agent in West Virginia would then have to liaise with the local FBI field office in Dallas. It would all take time. It would give him the window of opportunity he needed to avoid operatives or cops taking him into custody. If the FBI got their hands on him, they wouldn't care about his

Miranda rights or due process, and he might be detained for weeks or months as they investigated the case without his interference.

Reznick needed to stay sharp. If there were cameras trained on exits from the bathroom, they wouldn't register features partially obscured by sunglasses and a hat. But he knew the Feds would be closing in from the flight logs.

He headed for the exit, trying to blend into a large group of passengers pushing loaded airport trolleys to the doors.

Reznick went outside. A wall of heat hit him. He was in Texas, alright.

A cab pulled up beside him, and the window rolled down. "Hey. How ya doin'?"

Reznick opened the rear passenger door and took off his backpack. "I'm doing good."

"Where you going?"

"Truck stop outside Weatherford. There's a gas station adjacent to it. Just off I-20. You know it?"

The driver grinned as he looked in his rearview mirror. "Sure do. You just moved down here, son? You don't sound like you're from here."

"Got a job out in West Texas."

"Good for you, man. I moved here twenty years ago from New York."

"You miss it?"

"Fuck, no. Taxes, fucking weather, the crime, garbage everywhere. Couldn't stand it. You'll like it down here. People are real friendly."

"Good to know." Reznick sat back as the cab negotiated heavy traffic around the airport. It thinned out as they got on the freeway. They made small talk about the weather. Hurricanes, summer heat in Texas, and flooding.

Reznick was relieved to reach the truck stop. He wasn't fond of sustained conversations. He thanked the driver and slung his bag over his shoulder as he headed into the truck stop's diner. He sat down at a corner booth, eyes on the parking lot. He ordered a coffee and some pancakes with maple syrup.

The waitress returned with his order.

"You from around here, sweetie?"

"I'm traveling through."

"You ain't the only one. A lot of men working down here in Texas. You one of them?"

Reznick cut up the pancake and took a delicious mouthful. "Yeah, sort of."

"Well, enjoy yourself down here. Nice to have you."

"Thank you, appreciate that."

Reznick enjoyed the food. He had forgotten the last time he'd eaten. But what he needed was to get to West Texas without being stopped or recognized. He looked out the diner window. At the far end of the parking lot, he saw a grizzled, long-haired biker standing beside an old Harley, smoking a cigarette.

He drank his coffee as he casually observed the man checking his watch a few times, as if he was waiting for someone.

Reznick finished his meal, drank the rest of his coffee, and left fifty dollars for the meal, tip included.

"You want a refill?"

"Don't mind if I do. And please keep the change."

The waitress gazed at the fifty-dollar bill on the table. "Sir, that's a lot of money. You sure?"

"Yeah, quite sure."

The waitress topped up his coffee. She smiled as she tucked the money in her uniform pocket. "Real kind of you, thank you. You have a nice day."

"You too."

Reznick nursed his coffee for a few minutes as he kept watch on the guy dragging on his cigarette, standing by his bike. He doubted the guy was just having a break from a long ride. He saw the biker check his watch a couple more times. The guy was definitely waiting on someone.

Reznick picked up his backpack and slung it over his shoulder. He walked to the far side of the parking lot to the man beside the Harley. The sun glinted off the bike's gleaming chrome.

He approached the guy. "Sorry to bother you, bro. I was just in the diner, admiring your bike. She's a real beauty."

The man grinned. "Well, thank you. Appreciate that. I was hoping to sell her to a guy from Midland. Sounded real interested on the phone. But looks like he's a fucking no-show."

"Here's the thing. I would love a Harley. Always wanted one. But it's got to be a bike that's been well taken care of. So, I'd be interested."

"Seriously?"

"Yeah, I just never got around to it. One thing or another, you know how it is."

"Harley-Davidson is the best. It's American. Fantastic bikes. Heritage."

Reznick grinned as he snapped his fingers. "Heritage, yeah. There you go."

"So, you really interested?"

"Damn right, I'm interested. But what about the guy from Midland?"

"He's half an hour late. You're standing right here."

Reznick examined the underside of the bike's engine. "Tell me about this bike."

"Well, this here bike is a 2007 Sportster. Bit of a classic. Fifteen thousand miles on the clock."

"As low as that?"

"Yup. Runs great. I had it serviced one month ago. It's a very good bike."

"So, why are you selling it?"

"I got a brand-new one. Wife thinks I'm crazy." The guy shrugged as he lit up another cigarette. "What's she going to do, huh?"

"What were you hoping for?"

The man dragged slow on his cigarette, then exhaled the smoke through his nostrils. "Five thousand."

Reznick admired the bike. He took a wad of bills out of his pocket and counted them out. "Five thousand American dollars. In cash. We got a deal?"

The guy nodded as he laughed. "Cash? Damn right, we've got a deal."

Reznick handed the man the money and was given the keys and a helmet. He knew better than to ask for the title.

"What's your name?"

"Jon."

The man gripped Reznick's hand in a viselike grip. "Real nice doing business with you, Jon. You take good care of her."

"Nice doing business."

The man wandered off into the diner, shaking his head, no doubt about to enjoy a celebratory meal.

Reznick put on his helmet and fastened it tight. He started up the bike, revved it hard a few times. The engine growled low. He pulled away from the parking lot, got on the freeway. Then he headed due west.

Nineteen

The swanky restaurant was located on Park Avenue bang in the heart of Midtown Manhattan. It was tucked away on the street level of a modernist masterpiece of a building.

Feldman thought the brutalist concrete edifice was revolting. He pushed his aesthetic concerns to one side as he was escorted to the restaurant's private dining room. He saw Gordon T. Avery, the FBI's general counsel, mulling over the menu.

"Sorry I'm running a few minutes late," Feldman said. "Traffic's crazy."

Avery put down the menu and beamed. "Mort, so glad to finally meet you in person."

Feldman perused the wine list for a few minutes before he ordered a bottle of 2006 Dom Perignon. The waiter returned with the bottle, popped the cork, and poured a glass of chilled champagne for each of them.

"That's lovely," Avery said.

Feldman smiled. "I thought it was a perfect opportunity to celebrate."

"Couldn't agree more. So good we're able to cement this relationship between the Bureau and your client. This is a momentous occasion. I'm delighted we got there in the end."

Feldman raised his glass. "To good health."

Avery grinned. "I'll drink to that."

Feldman took a small sip of champagne as Avery took a large mouthful. "And before you ask, this is on my client."

The waiter took their lunch order and left them to make small talk for fifteen minutes. The weather, the Mets, the mayor, trash on the sidewalks, real estate hot spots.

The food was served, and Feldman and Avery both tucked into the Caprese starter.

"Delicious," Avery said. "This is so damn good."

"Better than the FBI canteen, I can imagine."

Avery laughed. "I used to work nearby about a decade ago, as you know. Haven't been in here since those days."

"Remind me, where did you work?"

"Worenstein and Faulds."

"Tough firm."

"Better believe it. They got their pound of flesh, don't worry about that. Making senior partner only precipitated my ulcer."

"The FBI can't have helped."

Avery laughed again. "Point taken." He lowered his voice as he leaned toward Feldman. "Anyway, Mort, I just wanted to give you a heads-up, face-to-face, like I promised."

"Sure, what's on your mind? The deal is done, after all."

"Signed and sealed—your client can go where he pleases, as and when he likes."

Feldman had made sure the contract specified that point. "Good to know."

"The thing is, and I'm a great believer in being open, I'm hearing a few whispers, which may or may not affect your client."

"A few whispers . . . coming from where?"

"The seventh floor."

"Do they specifically relate to my client?"

"They do. You see, there have been some unforeseen circumstances."

Feldman furrowed his brow. "I'm not sure I follow you."

Avery leaned even closer. "The FBI and the New York field office, along with Boston Feds, are trying to track down some Aryan Brotherhood crew who murdered an ex-police chief and his wife up in Maine."

Feldman's stomach knotted tight. He picked up his napkin and dabbed the corners of his mouth. He sensed where the conversation was headed. "I read about that in the *Times*."

"Here's the thing. The problem is, a friend of the police chief has gone after them. He shot one of them. And he's a bit of a renegade, former Special Forces hard case. Delta. The guy worked for the CIA. And he's good. I mean, very, very good."

Feldman shifted in his seat. "You think this is my client's doing?"

"I don't know. Maybe. There might be a connection to one of the five families."

"Has my client got anything to worry about?"

"It's fluid. But the thing is, this guy, this renegade, he's also worked for the FBI in the past. Which is problematic in its own way."

"Is this widely known?"

Avery hemmed and hawed. "It's a very touchy subject in the Bureau."

"I can imagine."

"So, this hothead is after the people he believes are responsible for the murder of the police chief and his wife. That's all I know."

"And he might target my client?"

"It's a possibility."

Feldman made a mental note. "Do you have a name for this Special Forces guy?"

"I can't divulge that."

"Where is he now?"

"Not exactly sure. Mississippi, last I heard. Bottom line? It would be in your client's best interest to take security precautions."

"I'll pass that on, but the FBI needs to find this nutcase and shut the whole thing down."

"Don't worry, we intend to. I just thought it common courtesy for you to hear from me, face-to-face, that I've got an eye on the big picture, and our special project with your client is safe."

Feldman considered his half-empty glass of champagne. He searched for how the FBI could believe his client might have been responsible for ordering the killings in Maine. "The FBI has no solid leads linking the killings to my client."

"I believe one or two people in the Bureau are looking into the possibility."

"You must have an inkling whether or not my client might be linked to this."

Avery finished off his champagne in one long gulp. He leaned close. "Does the name Joe mean anything?"

"It's a pretty common name."

"True."

Feldman recognized the name only too well. His client had spoken in person to a man he knew only as Joe a month earlier. He was a street fixer for his client. A guy who got things done. Feldman had met the man too. He had been present at the meeting at his client's sprawling estate overlooking Long Island Sound. He wasn't formally introduced to Joe. But Feldman knew Joe was his client's go-to guy in the city for "whacks." He knew because his client had told him so a few years earlier. Nothing was ever written down. The conversation wasn't recorded. It was a passing remark, as if his client wanted Feldman to know how he operated. But he gathered, as well, that it was a way to unnerve Feldman. Maybe a way for his client to let Feldman know that he could be disappeared. Maybe it was simply a way to frighten Feldman. If that was the purpose, it had succeeded.

"Under RICO, Mort, if we nab Joe in the future, we could also technically go after your client."

"Our agreement is quite specific. My client is out of bounds now that the agreement has been signed."

Avery smiled. "Point taken. I know that, as a lawyer."

"Make no mistake, I will not countenance any backtracking on this agreement. I don't like playing hardball if I can help it. But my client has immunity, in effect. The Attorney General has signed off on this. My client is a high-level confidential informant. He has protection. He is permitted latitude for a reason. I'm going to spell it out, Gordon. He is allowed to engage in activities that would otherwise constitute crimes under state or federal law. You know it, so make sure there are no fuckups on this. The first hint of backsliding, and he will walk. That's also in the agreement."

"Relax, I get it. I'm just bringing you and your client up to speed."

"Listen to me, Gordon. This is my final point. You know as well as I do that such criminal conduct, if it was undertaken by my client, is also termed *otherwise illegal activity* or *OIA*. So, we have a double-lock in place so his freedom will not be jeopardized. Be under no illusions; he has cover. He can't be touched by anyone. Not me. Not you. No one. And once he disappears to an unknown location, those agreements will stay in place until his dying day."

"Mort, you're killing me!" Avery smiled.

Feldman stared long and hard at Avery. "I hope my client can trust the FBI to deliver on their promises. He can give you whatever you want. But there are strict parameters."

Avery smiled again. "I get the message. Besides, this deal is too big to jeopardize."

"How far are you prepared to go to ensure this deal stays in place?"

"Don't worry about a thing. The Bureau has been around for a long, long time. We've got it under control."

Twenty

The wide blue Texas sky opened up as Reznick headed west. He rode down a sun-bleached stretch of road. A big, vast emptiness in all directions. Deeper and deeper into the heart of an arid desert. In many ways untamed. Droughts that lasted years. It was easy to see why it would be a tough place to live. To survive. Little towns. Small communities. The endless roads. Oil rigs and fracking operations in the middle of nowhere. Chain-link fences, broken-down homes. A forgotten land. A frontier where only the hardiest made it.

Reznick saw lights up ahead and realized he was riding past the city of Odessa. The heart of West Texas. It was surreal.

He rode on for a few miles, back out on the lonely road. Eventually he pulled off at a gas station in Monahans, a small dusty town. He filled up his bike. He enjoyed an ice-cold Coke as he soaked up the cool air-conditioning in the shop. He checked his cell phone for messages. Then he checked Google Maps. It seemed like he had been traveling for days. But he figured he still had about forty-five miles until he reached Notrees.

He verified his route. He would head north to Kermit and then east back to Notrees. The sun dipped over the far horizon. A bloodred sky hung low as if ready to catch fire.

Reznick rode on toward Kermit, visor down. A hot desert wind whipped in from the south. He turned onto a bone-dry road. Headlight picking out the dusty asphalt. No cars or trucks for miles. Past dilapidated old oil drilling rigs. Long-forgotten gas plants. In the distance, windmills slowly turned, creaking and groaning. Past rundown trailer homes and godforsaken roads.

When was the last time this part of Texas received a drop of rain? Was it months? Maybe even years?

He turned east and headed past parched desert grasses and scrub, as the road encroached on the periphery of the West Texas desert.

The sky was darkening as he arrived in Notrees. A handful of sun-blasted houses spread out before him. It was like a scene out of a long-forgotten America. Barren. Inhospitable. Tough. Unrelenting. Decaying. A ruined testament to the tough pioneers who had made this place a home.

He turned down a near-desolate Third Street and saw the wooden shack. Dark-blue paint flaking off. Overgrown yard. Dusty screened windows.

Reznick pulled up. He had no idea who was in the house. Maybe no one. He could be confronted with one of the fucks at the front door. They might even be watching him now as he dismounted from the bike.

He took off his helmet and left it on the handlebars. He glanced in the bike's mirror. A truck headed past on the only road into town.

Reznick checked that his gun was tucked into his waistband. He walked up to the front door and knocked four times, hard. A deathly silence. He knocked again even harder. Inside, the sound of footsteps.

"Alright, alright, keep your goddamn hair on."

The handle turned, and the door cracked open. Standing before him was a sad-eyed, scrawny woman with leathery brown skin. She ogled him for what seemed like an eternity. "What do you want?"

"I'm looking for Dwayne or Draxler."

"You a friend of theirs? You don't look like a friend of theirs."

"I just got out," Reznick lied.

The woman lit a cigarette and inhaled deeply. "Well, they ain't here." Smoke billowed from the side of her mouth. "They come and go. But they don't hang around here."

"That's a pity. I have something for Dwayne."

"You owe him some money?"

Reznick welcomed the opening. "Yeah, I owe him. Bigtime. Do you mind me asking who you are, ma'am?"

"I'm Mrs. Adams. Mrs. Connie Adams. I'm Jimmy's mother. Did you know Jimmy?"

Reznick felt his insides churn. He realized he was talking to the mother of the triggerman he had killed back in Maine. "Yes, I did, ma'am."

The tears spilled down her face. "Got shot up way up north, they say. He was always a stupid bastard. Just like his no-good father. I told him it would end up like that."

Reznick could have curled up and died. He had brought misery to her door. "I'm sorry."

"He was a mean son of a bitch. But I'm gonna miss him." Reznick stood in silence. "Where you from? You're not from around here."

"Not far from New York," he lied again.

"Is that right? Well, Dwayne and Drax ain't here. Haven't seen them since last night."

"They gone drinking?"

"That's exactly where they've gone." She pointed farther down the street. "Monroe's Bar. Half a mile down Third Street. There's where you'll find them. Good-for-nothing fools. They come and go as if they owned the town. I'm sick of it. And you can tell them that from me."

"Thank you, ma'am." He turned to go.

"Listen, if you find them, tell Dwayne he owes me a hundred bucks still. That's a lot of money to me. Maybe not to him. But I have to pay the bills."

Reznick fished two fifty-dollar bills out of his pocket. "Is that OK?"

"That's nice of you, son." She dragged heavily on her cigarette and squinted against the harsh remnants of the evening sun. "You don't seem like the usual crowd Jimmy hangs around with."

"I'm not."

"A word to the wise, son."

Reznick looked back.

"Don't go looking for Dwayne and Drax. You hang around with them, and you'll wind up like my Jimmy. You hear me?"

"I hear you, ma'am."

The woman pointed a finger at Reznick. "Be careful. They'll kill you as soon as look at you."

Twenty-One

The bar was at the end of a rutted dirt road, just off Third Street. A beaten-up old Chevy outside.

Reznick surveyed the windowless brick building, a hand-painted wooden sign saying "Monroe's Bar." He drove the bike around to the rear of the bar, scanned the scene. Reznick anticipated what delights awaited him. He took a few moments to collect his thoughts and get in the zone. He had no idea what he was walking into. But he guessed this was the kind of back-of-beyond desert hideout where an Aryan Brotherhood crew might gather.

He turned off his engine, put his keys in his front pocket, slung his bag over his shoulder. He took off his helmet and hung it from a handlebar. He walked back around to the front of the bar and pushed open a dusty screen door. His senses were on alert. The sound of an old ZZ Top song playing on the jukebox. He spotted two tattooed, muscle-bound, dead-eyed crazies staring at him, guzzling beer from large glasses.

Reznick walked up to the bar.

The bartender had short hair, eyes like ice. "How you doing, stranger?"

"I'm doing OK." Reznick turned and looked around. "This looks like my kind of place." He faced the bartender. "Serious drinkers, huh?"

"What you having?"

"Cold Corona and a double Scotch."

"Coming up."

Reznick took off his backpack and laid it on the floor as he stood at the bar, his back to the two men in in the corner. He sensed they were watching him. He caught sight of them in a mirror behind the bar.

The bartender served up the drinks.

Reznick handed over a fifty-dollar bill. He knew that money was a good entry point to keep on people's good side. Usually loosened up their tongues. "Keep the change."

"You sure, man?"

"Absolutely."

"You got it, thank you."

Reznick took a couple of gulps of cold beer. It felt good, cleansing his bone-dry throat.

"So, how the heck you find this bar? No one knows we're here."

"My brother lives nearby. He's a roughneck. And he mentioned this place."

"You visiting your brother, huh?"

"That's right."

Reznick glanced at the reflection and saw the two guys whispering. He had no idea if these were the guys he was looking for. But he had a feeling he would be finding out soon enough.

The bartender poured himself a beer and raised his glass. "Well, nice to have you in Texas. Your first time down here?"

"No, I've been down here a few times. Galveston way, Gulfport, a friend of mind had a condo in Corpus Christi. Nice place to hang out."

"Well, a word of warning, man. Things are slightly different in West Texas. There's not much to do here apart from drinking and fighting."

"Could do a lot worse than that, let me tell you."

A murmur from the two guys in the corner.

Reznick sensed it was going to go down.

"Hey," one of them shouted, "you a long way from home, mister. Never seen you around here."

Reznick saw fear in the barman's eyes as if he knew it was about to get nasty. He smiled and turned around. He looked over at the two guys and scrutinized them. He recognized Dwayne McLellan and Bernard Draxler from the mug shots Williams had sent. It was them, alright. He observed their sneering, red, weather-beaten faces. Necks inked. AB and swastika tattoos on their forearms and knuckles. He stared long and hard at both of them, knowing it would rub them the wrong way.

"What the fuck you looking at, Yankee boy?"

Reznick stayed silent as he eyeballed Dwayne. He had seen the type before. He was physically imposing.

Dwayne got to his feet and shook his head. "So, what do we have here?" he said. "You deaf, Yankee boy? You think this is your town? You think this is your part of the world?"

Reznick kept smiling, hoping his silence would trigger the man.

Draxler also got to his feet. Dwayne kept sauntering forward. "I'm going to enjoy beating the shit out of you. Something about you I don't like. Now why do you think that is?"

Reznick put down his drink and stood still. He wanted them to make the first move.

Dwayne pulled out a knife and took a couple more steps forward. "I think we're going to have to teach this Yankee boy some manners."

Reznick was ready. Still in the zone. He stood and held their eyes, waiting for Dwayne to make the next move.

Dwayne lunged forward.

Reznick turned slightly and blocked the attack, grabbing Dwayne's wrist and locking it tight. Then he kicked him hard in the groin. And again.

Dwayne moaned and crumpled to the dusty concrete floor.

Reznick twisted his wrist farther until the knife fell from it. He smashed him hard in the side of the head. The fucker was laid out cold.

Draxler got into a martial arts fighting stance. He pulled back his right arm. But Reznick drop-kicked him in the balls before a punch was landed. The fucker screamed and lunged at Reznick.

Reznick punched him in the throat before he elbowed him in the side of the head. Draxler was now out cold on the floor.

He kicked the knife away and turned and looked at the terrified bartender.

"I don't want any trouble, man," he said, hands in the air.

"Leave by the front door. And don't look back. Do not call for help. I know your face."

The guy sprinted out of the bar, leaving Reznick alone with the two unconscious felons.

The jukebox switched over to the Stones.

Reznick rifled the men's pockets and took out their cell phones, then put them in his back pockets. He took off their leather belts and hauled the unconscious men onto chairs. He tied them tight around their chests.

He went outside and found a five-gallon container of kerosene, picked it up, and headed back inside.

Reznick poured it over the two men and took the container to the rear of the bar. He stepped back a couple yards and fired a shot at the jukebox. The music stopped, glass shards on the floor. The gunshot woke up the two maniacs.

Dwayne screamed threats and obscenities and struggled like a madman for a few moments as he realized what had happened. He tried to move from the seat. But the belt didn't budge. "You better hope that I don't find you and your family. I'm going to hunt you down, you motherfucker."

Draxler's face was red, blood trickling from his nose and mouth. He began to blink as if he had splashes of kerosene in his eyes. "What the fuck you want? Who are you?"

"Why did you kill Bill and Elspeth Eastland in Maine?"

Dwayne struggled hard, teeth clenched. "What the fuck you want?"

"I just told you."

"Fuck you! Who sent you?"

"I'm asking the questions, you stupid fuck. And I want answers. And if I don't get them, I will burn you and this bar to the fucking ground."

Draxler shook his head, eyes shut tight.

Reznick took out a box of matches. He lit one and held it at arm's length. "So, am I going to get answers?"

Draxler clenched his teeth. "Man, I don't know who you are or why you're here, but I swear, it wasn't personal. We got paid."

Reznick blew out the match and placed it in an ashtray on a table behind him. "Now we're making progress. The next match will burn you fuckers to a crisp. Have you ever seen a man get burned alive before? I've seen burn victims. It's not pretty, let me tell you."

Draxler blurted out, "It was supposed to be a hit. A simple hit."

"Who paid you?"

"A guy from a strip club."

Reznick kneeled down and picked up the box of matches again.

"Don't do that, man. Listen, I just told you, it was a hit job."

"Tell me what went down."

"We were paid to kill this guy up north in Maine."

"Why?"

"I don't know."

Reznick turned his attention to Dwayne. "Mr. McLellan, do you know?"

"How the fuck do you know my name?"

"I make it my business to know people's names. Especially when they killed a good friend of mine."

Dwayne clenched his teeth and struggled hard. "I swear I'm going to rip your fucking throat out!"

"I'm running out of patience, boys."

Dwayne snapped, "He owed some big shot a ton of money—couldn't pay it back, alright? Satisfied?"

Reznick's blood was boiling. He struggled not to shoot them both dead. But he needed to know who was responsible. "A name. Who hired you?"

Draxler stammered, "The guy runs a strip club in West Odessa. I know him as Lucky. He's a piece of shit."

Reznick stepped over the puddle of kerosene and circled them, standing in front of them. He lit a second match.

Dwayne braced himself away from Reznick. "What the fuck are you doing?"

"Are you telling me the truth?"

"Yes! Fucking yes, I'm telling you the truth!"

"I hope so. For your sakes."

Reznick smirked at the wretched bastards as he held the match above the kerosene puddle around their feet.

"Man, I'm telling you the goddamn truth!" Draxler screamed.

Reznick blew out the second match and tossed it away from the puddle. He tucked his gun into his waistband and smiled at Dwayne. "How does it feel?"

Dwayne's eyes were filled with hate. "Motherfucker! You gonna pay. Son of a fucking bitch!"

Reznick went over to the pool table and picked up a cue. He turned back and proceeded to beat both men unconscious, leaving them in a pool of blood and kerosene. He checked their pulses. They were still alive. He was sorely tempted to burn the two of them and the bar to the ground. But he didn't.

He dropped the pool cue and picked up his bag. Then he headed out the back of the bar into the near darkness.

Reznick started up the Harley and headed farther down the dirt road, away from the town, the last remnants of the West Texas sun spreading like a cancer in the distance.

Twenty-Two

The mood around the conference room table was grim, everyone glued to the footage on the big wall screens, faces like stone.

Meyerstein watched as an Odessa SWAT team stormed the dive bar in Notrees, West Texas. The shocking scenes of the two bloodied and battered Aryan Brotherhood men tied up, soaked in kerosene. She had already read a report of what had transpired. And none of it looked good from her point of view. She had wanted to defend Reznick. But he'd crossed a line. Bigtime.

Franklin Masson pinched the bridge of his nose, exasperated. He picked up the remote control and paused the action. He looked across at Meyerstein. "This is the work of Jon Reznick, of that I have no doubt. The Director has called me in to give an explanation within the hour. This is not good."

Meyerstein sat calmly as she felt all eyes on her.

"And here's the kicker, Martha. The SWAT team tracked down the bartender. He was found hiding in his mother's attic, terrified. The bartender has given a very detailed statement. The description matches Jon Reznick, no question."

"It might very well be Reznick. But we do not know for sure."

Crabtree fixed her icy gaze on Meyerstein. "Is it just me? You sound more and more like an apologist for an out-of-control rogue operator, who doesn't seem to understand the law."

Meyerstein bristled with fury. She hated being belittled in front of her colleagues. But Crabtree, annoyingly, had a very good point about Reznick's lawbreaking. "Let's look at the facts. Exactly what proof do we have, if any, that Jon Reznick was responsible? The fact of the matter is that there is no footage of Jon Reznick doing this. And obviously these two AB crazies said nothing to the cops. But, while I am not defending Jon Reznick's actions, if indeed this was his handiwork, I think the bigger issue is that I believe we have a case against this Aryan Brotherhood gang. We know the masked man who was shot in Rockland, James Adams, has close links to the two men in the bar, Draxler and McLellan. I'm not going to say that what happened was right. It was clearly illegal, whoever did this. But I think it is best to deal in facts."

Crabtree shook her head. "Point taken. But it's a mess."

"Let's not forget about the execution-style murder of Bill Eastland and his wife. I don't think we should lose sight of that."

"He can't be judge, jury, and executioner, Martha."

"Absolutely right. And he's accountable, like everyone else. But we're also accountable. We need to find out who committed this heinous double killing. This is our investigation. And we need to get on top of it."

Masson interrupted. "Martha's right. But Rachel is also correct. With regard to Reznick, he worries me as much as he worries the Director. My thinking is that we cut him loose. Let him hang in the wind."

"I disagree," Meyerstein said. "Absolutely disagree. We don't cut and run on people who have risked their lives, put their necks on the line throughout several classified operations. And ultimately, we have to establish facts on what happened down in Texas. Reznick will be brought to heel, I give you my word. I just need a bit more time. This Texas crew, as we can see, will stop at nothing. Connell wasn't part of that inner circle. While he might have sported the usual shamrocks and swastikas and AB tattoos on his forearms, he was not a member of the Aryan Brotherhood of Texas."

Mendoza said, "Martha, what concerns me and the rest of us is that Jon Reznick is effectively rogue."

"So, what do you suggest?"

Crabtree interjected, "I say we find him and arrest him. We can't allow these actions to continue without consequences. It's untenable. Can you imagine if this got out? Can you see how that would look?"

"It's not good, I know."

Masson grumbled, "Thing is, Martha, this isn't the first time. The Director was incandescent at his involvement in Mallorca."

Meyerstein felt herself flush. "May I remind you, Franklin, I was the one he came to find and rescue at the behest of my father. That's what happened. He came to find me. And I'm grateful."

Mendoza's gaze dropped to his notes.

Meyerstein's mind flashed back to the moment the luxury yacht she was staying on was blown to pieces. She had somehow survived. The wounds were healing. And the mental scars still lingered, waking her up in a cold sweat most nights. "I've got Jon Reznick to thank for finding the man responsible for my attempted murder."

"And executing him," Franklin added.

"Correct."

"We came within a hair's breadth of an international incident because an American citizen, known to work with the FBI, was starting a one-man war. He's a renegade. He held a gun to a Spanish military intelligence officer's head."

"I know all that. But I want you to put all that aside until this is over. We will find Jon Reznick. And we will take him out of the equation."

Crabtree cleared her throat. "Can we get back on track?"

Masson nodded.

"There is one final thing I want to bring to this meeting as a matter of urgency. It's not on the agenda, I know that. But the information was passed to me literally a few minutes before the meeting began."

"What are you getting at?" Meyerstein said.

"I was talking to the field office in New York earlier as part of my work with the National Security Branch."

Meyerstein was astonished that Crabtree was being allowed to play such a prominent part.

"Special Agent in Charge Andrew Collins is up to speed with regard to conducting investigations into possible Mob links with this hit. And I'm sorry to say, the FBI has a problem. A new problem. A far bigger problem than the one you're facing at the moment."

Masson frowned. "What kind of problem?"

"Andrew has been passed information just in the last hour. We believe the guy who ultimately ordered the killing of Bill Eastland and his wife is one of the FBI's most prized high-value confidential informants."

Twenty-Three

The strip club was located on the dustiest stretch of road by the railroad tracks on the outskirts of West Odessa.

Reznick knew he would be a wanted man. He needed to keep moving. He sensed the Feds and the cops would soon be on his trail after his little stunt in Notrees. But in the meantime, he had business to attend to.

He sat astride the Harley as he kept watch on the rear entrance to the strip club. It would open in an hour's time. No security in place. At least not on the outside. But he saw two surveillance cameras covering the parking lot.

He took out his cell phone and ordered a pizza and a Coke. Fifteen minutes later it was delivered to him by a skinny Black kid on a mountain bike.

"What you doing, man?" the kid asked.

"Just waiting for a buddy of mine."

"He inside the strip club?"

"Maybe, I don't know."

Reznick handed him a fifty-dollar tip.

The kid looked at the bill for a few moments as if doubting his own eyesight. "This is too much, man. You must've made a mistake."

"Keep it."

"That's crazy, man."

The kid got back on his bike, grinning like a jackal. "Take care, man," he said. "And thanks."

Reznick wolfed down a slice of pizza and wiped his mouth with a napkin as he watched the kid cycle off down the road. He shut the pizza box, got off the Harley, and put his helmet back on. He took the hunting rifle out of his bag, quickly assembled it, and carried it up to the entrance, the pizza box in his other hand. He tried the handle. Locked.

Fuck.

Reznick leaned the rifle against a wall. He buzzed the video entry three times before it was answered.

"We're closed! Come back in an hour."

"Pizza delivery."

"No one ordered a pizza in here, pal."

"Special delivery order for Lucky."

A beat. "Lucky? You sure?"

"That's what I said. Do you want to open up so his pizza isn't cold?"

The door opened and a bull-necked bouncer with a shaved head stood in his way. "Nobody ordered pizza."

The rifle hidden behind his back, Reznick thrust the pizza box into the bouncer's huge hands.

"We didn't order this."

Reznick slammed the butt of the rifle into the bouncer's bloated face. Blood spurted from his nose as he crumpled in a heap. He pointed the rifle at the poor bastard's head. "Where's Lucky?"

"He's in his back office!"

"Get the fuck out of here!"

The bouncer scrambled to his feet and sprinted out the door.

Reznick headed down the corridor with the rifle, breathing hard inside the helmet. He saw a girl in skimpy panties, no bra, sauntering around.

She screamed.

Reznick pointed at her. "Get out of here now!"

The girl ran for her life.

Reznick crossed the main room, past tables, as he headed to the rear of the club. He walked down a dimly lit corridor. Black-and-white photos of strippers naked and seminaked lined the walls. He saw a door ajar. He kicked it all the way open.

A stocky balding man was rifling through his desk as if looking for a weapon.

Reznick pointed the rifle at the guy's head. "Freeze, motherfucker!"

The man complied.

"Are you Lucky?"

"Who the fuck wants to know?"

Reznick took a step forward and smashed the rifle butt into the man's face. A muffled moan as the man slumped in his seat, blood spurting onto the desk and papers.

"Who are you?"

"You Lucky?"

"Of course I'm fucking Lucky."

"Not tonight, pal."

Reznick leveled the rifle at the man's bleeding head. "You answer truthfully, you live. You lie, I kill you. Got it?"

"What do you want to know?"

"Why did you give the order to kill Bill Eastland?"

"Who the fuck is that?"

"The retired cop in Maine, you dumb fuck!"

"I swear to God, whoever you are, I didn't step out of line. I got the go-ahead from New York."

"I need a name. A name in New York."

The man shook his head. "They'll kill me. I can't."

Reznick hit him again with the rifle. "You've got a choice. Either you give me a name and you live, or I will put a bullet in your fucking fat head. You tell me, you can get the hell out of here and disappear. That way, you have a chance. Your call."

The man scrunched up his face in pain and fear.

"Don't be shy, I won't tell."

"It was Crazy Joe."

"Who?"

"Crazy Joe told me to hire some people."

"Who's he?"

"Joseph Torrio. He's a crazy fuck. Runs a crew up in New York. He was the one who called. He gave me the name Bill Eastland."

"Why?"

"Money. Eastland owed a lot of money. So, I got the call."

"Why did he call you?"

"I sometimes do favors for them. That's what I like to call them."

"Favors?"

"He passes work my way, money my way, girls my way, and I give them something in return."

"So, you were instructed to hire people to kill Bill Eastland?"

"I was told, specifically by Joe, the triggermen couldn't be from New York. Out of state. So there would be no trace. He wanted to use people from my neck of the woods."

"Are you lying to me?"

"I swear on my mother's life. Please don't kill me."

"Slowly, very slowly, hands on head."

Lucky complied, blinking away tears. His mouth was twisted, his jaw hanging loose. "Goddamn, I think you broke my fucking jaw!"

"Where's your cell phone?"

"Top drawer."

Reznick walked around the desk, rifle still pressed to Lucky's head. He opened the top drawer and saw an iPhone. "This it?"

Lucky nodded, eyes closed tight.

Reznick pushed the screen in the man's face. The cell phone unlocked. He changed the passcode to the easy-to-remember 0909. He put the phone in his back pocket. "So, Lucky, a few more questions, and I'll be out of your face. Where does Joe Torrio live in New York?"

"I got no idea. I know he's in and around Manhattan a lot."

Reznick gazed at the man long and hard. "That's a big, big place. I know you can do better than that."

"That's all I know. Do you want money? I got money in the safe."

Reznick smashed the butt of the rifle into Lucky's forehead, splitting open his head. Blood spilled out of a gaping wound.

Lucky groaned and collapsed to the ground, struggling to breathe.

Reznick smashed the rifle butt hard onto his head again. It split open like a watermelon. Blood poured out.

Lucky's eyes rolled back in his head before he lost consciousness.

Reznick knew he had to move. He headed back through the now-deserted strip club, down a hallway, and out a fire exit into the broiling darkness of West Odessa. He got on the Harley, bag strapped to his back, and rode away from the club.

He accelerated down a side road, across the railway tracks, as he rode hard in the direction of Midland. It was twenty miles away. He accelerated.

In about fifteen minutes, Reznick was in Midland. He needed to move. Get out of Texas. He pulled up outside a diner. He got off the bike, leaving the keys in the ignition.

Reznick headed inside the diner. He sat down at a window seat with line of sight to the bike.

A waitress walked up to his table. He ordered a steak sandwich, fries, and a cold beer.

Reznick ate his food and drank his beer as he kept watch on the bike. A few minutes later, he saw a young guy slink up to the Harley, hanging around for a few moments. It looked as if the kid was admiring the bike. Maybe the guy couldn't believe his luck.

Reznick smiled as the kid put on the helmet, started up the engine, and rode away. He checked his watch. It took eight minutes for the bike to be stolen. Not bad. He knew the bike was hot. Someone would have gotten the license plate.

He finished his meal, left a fifty-dollar bill, and headed to the Greyhound bus station.

Twenty-Four

It was nearly dark as the helicopter carrying Mort Feldman swooped low over Long Island Sound. He felt nervous at the best of times when he was visiting his reclusive client. But the lurching feeling of terror seemed to hike up a notch during the bumpy journey. He caught sight of the floodlit estate of his client in the distance.

Feldman closed his eyes as they came in to land. Despite not being a religious man, he said a silent prayer the moment he was back on the ground. A bodyguard with a Doberman escorted Feldman across the manicured lawn.

"You're late," the bodyguard snarled.

Feldman said, "Ten-minute delay taking off."

His client wasn't a man known for his patience. Feldman was shown into the library.

The client looked up and smiled, glass of red wine in hand. He wore a pale blue button-down shirt, jeans, sneakers, and tortoise-shell glasses. He waved his hand at his bodyguard. "That'll be all."

The bodyguard nodded and left Feldman and his client alone.

"You're late."

"Apologies. Delay getting takeoff clearance, apparently."

"So, what are we meeting about? I thought we had discussed everything there was to discuss."

Feldman cleared his throat. "First, nice to see you again."

"Cut the bullshit. We got a problem? You know I don't like problems."

"Not really a problem, thank God. I was talking to the FBI's counsel, and he was very accommodating. I just wanted to give you an update. He's looking out for you on this."

"I like to hear that. You told me he was a stand-up guy. He doesn't want any more gifts."

Feldman smiled. "He is being paid handsomely to help us out. His connections to my firm are paying dividends."

"As long as it fucking continues. I can't abide people I can't fucking trust."

"You can trust Avery. He did ask me to pass on some sensitive information to you."

The client knocked back the rest of his red wine and shrugged. "What've you got?"

"Remember I told you about that guy who went after the crew that killed the ex-cop in Maine?"

"Sure."

"So, last we heard he's down south looking for them. But he's a very, very dangerous individual, like I said."

"You got a name?"

"No name, but Avery is concerned."

"I thought our deal was carved in stone?"

"It is. That's not what he's concerned about. He's concerned that this renegade will go after you."

The client laughed out loud. "Bullshit. Are you kidding me?"

Feldman shook his head. "The Feds are hugely committed to our deal with them. So much so that they're letting you know they don't want you to be harmed."

"Me? Are you kidding me? Harm me? Who the fuck is this guy?"

"I believe he was Special Forces. Worked as a consultant for the FBI before."

"Listen to me, Feldman. Number one, I ain't afraid of no fuck. Second, I ain't going to get whacked by him or anyone. It's me that does that sort of stuff. Three, tell Avery, from me, I look after my business. Stay the fuck out of my way. And don't think he can tell me what I should be afraid of. This Special Forces nutcase, whatever the hell he is—he will never get to me. I sleep safe and sound at night. No one but you and my boys gets within ten miles of me."

"I just want you to not only be aware of this development, but perhaps add some security precautions."

The client grinned. "Mort, I have all the security in the world. No one makes a move on me. But if that guy tries something, he's going to wish he was never born."

Twenty-Five

The night journey was long. Hours dragged in the Texas darkness.

Reznick sat alone in the back of a near-empty Greyhound bus, unable to fall asleep. He smelled of sweat and dirt and dust. But thankfully the nearest passenger was a kid down front, headphones on, singing out loud to the hip-hop music Reznick could hear despite the headset.

He seriously needed to freshen up. Bad. But more importantly, he needed to get the hell out of the Lone Star State.

Reznick dug out Lucky's cell phone. He keyed in the passcode. Then he called up Trevelle.

"Yeah, who's calling?"

"It's me."

"Man, where the fuck did you get to?"

"You don't want to know. Listen, the cell phone I'm making this call on, can you help me out?"

"What do you need?"

"It belongs to a sleazeball named Lucky. I'm assuming you can remotely access it and all the data?"

"I'd be pissed if I couldn't."

"Good. Download everything on this cell phone for future reference. But also, I'm looking for specific information which might be on this phone. I want to know about any calls to or from a guy called Torrio. Joseph Torrio. Lives in New York, that's all I know. Connected with the Mob in some way."

"Torrio . . . Got it."

"How long will it take you to download everything?"

"Give me a sec . . . I am, as we speak, downloading bespoke software to the cell phone you're using."

"That's crazy. As simple as that?"

"I told you, I'm the best. Stay on the line. I'm downloading the texts and raw data right now. Nearly done . . ."

"Get me an address for Torrio—that's important. But more important, I'm looking for the real-time GPS fix on his where-abouts, assuming the number is on Lucky's cell phone."

"You want to know exactly where Torrio is at a particular moment? In real time?"

"Precisely."

"A ton of stuff on the cell phone. Mostly nasty."

"I can imagine."

"Where you headed?"

"I've had my fill of Texas. I'm headed north."

"You want me to contact you, or do you want to contact me?"

"Give me a call in twenty-four hours. Then we can get caught up."

"You do know you're crazy, right, Jon?"

Reznick stared out the window as the Greyhound headed fur-ther into the darkness of the West Texas desert. He asked himself what had possessed him to get so heavily involved. It wasn't rational behavior. It was pure emotion.

Just looking for answers, that's all, he told himself.

Twenty-Six

The FBI's New York field office was located on the twenty-third floor of the Javits Federal Building in Lower Manhattan.

Meyerstein sat at the conference room table across from Special Agent in Charge Andrew Collins. Sitting beside him was FBI Counsel Gordon Avery. She was surprised to see Avery. She had met him numerous times. He had an unsettlingly unctuous manner, always wanting to praise or flatter those around him. His background was in corporate law, and he had represented major US and Middle Eastern banks on takeovers. "I didn't expect you to be joining us, Gordon. To what do I owe the honor?"

"You don't mind, do you?"

Meyerstein shrugged. "Not at all. I'm assuming your interest has to do with the high-level confidential informant."

Avery perused his notes for a few moments before he looked up and smiled. "Precisely. I've been informed that New York was running this high-level informant. And the Director instructed me to make sure everything is aboveboard."

Meyerstein sensed there was way more to this than met the eye. She had worked on hundreds of investigations over the years. It was strange that Crabtree, a CIA officer, was allowed unrestricted access at the highest echelons of the FBI. And she couldn't remember a single instance wherein the FBI's chief counsel took such a hands-on role. Avery seldom left the Hoover Building. "I just would have appreciated a heads-up that you would be here."

"It's not a problem, is it, Martha?"

Meyerstein sensed Avery was the Director's eyes and ears on this. She decided to let it go. "Let's get down to business," she said. "Are you up to speed, Gordon?"

Avery scribbled some notes on a legal pad. "*I don't know* is the honest answer. Tell me what you know, Martha, and we'll take it from there. How this started. And let's stick to facts and not suppositions."

"So, a brief recap," Meyerstein said. "We have Bill Eastland, ex-police chief, and his wife, Elspeth, killed in cold blood in Rockland, Maine. We have audio surveillance of one Thomas Egan in Texas, linked to the Irish Mob and the Aryan Brotherhood, receiving instructions to take out Eastland. We have Jon Reznick responsible for tracking and shooting one of the gang in Maine. We're still trying to fit all the pieces of the jigsaw. But it appears the orders for the murder originated from a New York crime family. The Gambinos. You want to pick it up there, Andrew?"

"Martha, first of all, nice to see you again," Collins said.

"Likewise."

Collins turned to Avery. "Appreciate any guidance you can offer on the legal pitfalls."

Avery gave a tight smile. "Of course."

"Listen, this is complicated," Collins said. "It isn't helped by having a guy like Reznick in the middle of everything. I personally admire him, but he's making our life very, very difficult. He's getting in the way."

"Forget about Reznick for now," Meyerstein interjected. "We'll find him. Let's talk about exactly why we're here. Namely, that the hit was ordered by a confidential FBI informant. And this is being handled by the New York field office. That's all I know. I want to get to the bottom of that. But I also want to know why Rachel Crabtree, a CIA officer, took such an interest."

Collins was quiet for a few moments as he leafed through his briefing papers.

"You do know that's not how the confidential informant is supposed to act," Meyerstein said. "Criminality is illegal, right? We can't turn a blind eye."

Avery interjected. "If I can jump in here. The informant is the highest-level FBI informant we have ever had."

Collins nodded.

"Reznick's actions," Avery said, "are going to blow everything out of the water."

Meyerstein shook her head. "Sorry, did I miss something?"

Collins said, "Martha, I've spoken to Gordon already."

Martha sat in stunned silence for a few moments. "I'm sorry, you two have already had a chat about this?"

"We have."

Meyerstein leaned back in her seat. "Interesting."

Collins cleared his throat. "Martha, it's clear we can't make a move against this informant. At least for now."

"Why the hell not?"

"Can we just back up for a few moments?" Avery said.

"Sure," Meyerstein said.

Avery took off his glasses and rubbed his eyes. "Let's get this conversation back to facts. The audio conversation we have is of Joseph Torrio, certified Mafia psychopath and Gambino captain. He is very, very powerful. And he put out the word to this strip joint manager down in Texas, Alfredo 'Lucky' Drago. Eastland had apparently issued death threats against Torrio at a gambling joint in New York. And from there it snowballed. Torrio got in touch with

Tommy Egan in Texas. And from there, the crazies at the Aryan Brotherhood of Texas."

"Cute."

"We got a break, as the conversation Torrio had was picked up by a surveillance bug in Lucky's car."

"But this doesn't stop at Torrio, does it? That's what I'm getting at."

Collins said, "We don't know for sure."

"Andrew, listen to me," Meyerstein said. "I have investigated numerous crimes committed by Mafia crime families. And for a hit of this nature to go down, you need the head of the family to give the ultimate go-ahead."

Collins nodded. "Makes sense."

"So, why is the Mob fixated on Eastland?"

"My sources have indicated, anecdotally, that Eastland threatened, very publicly, in a gambling joint, to kill Torrio. And he said that he knew people in the NYPD who would shut the place down. So, there's your link."

"Getting back to this high-level informant."

Collins nodded. "This is an incredibly sensitive area. But this particular person . . . We can't make a move."

"Says who?"

Avery put up his hand. "Says me."

Meyerstein noted the conversation on her legal pad. She turned to look at Avery. "Says me . . . Interesting. I've just taken a little verbatim note of that."

Avery sat in silence.

"Who knows this guy's identity? Do you know, Gordon?"

"I'm here solely to advise and guide on legal matters."

Collins said, "Martha, his identity is known only to the confidential informants coordinator and an undercover FBI agent, both here in New York City."

"And no one else?"

"I believe that is correct."

"You believe . . . Interesting. So, do you believe this high-level confidential informant greenlit this murder?"

"We're looking into this. We can't say for sure. While I welcome any input you have that could be of assistance, I've got to be frank: I very much object to you turning up like this and pulling rank."

"No one's pulling rank."

"I run the New York side of things. So, I don't welcome putting my hardworking agents in the spotlight."

"Don't be so sensitive, Andrew. I'm just asking questions. Is that OK?"

"You don't need to be so sarcastic."

Meyerstein smiled. "Let's get back on point. Can I just recap so I'm not misunderstanding? You are not aware of the man's identity?"

"That is correct."

Meyerstein fixed her gaze on Avery. "Are you, Gordon?"

Avery took a few moments. "I've answered that already."

"Could you recap so I'm sure what the position is?"

"My department is aware of this case, of course," Avery said, "but I have no personal knowledge of this person's identity."

"No personal knowledge. Andrew, did you ask who this informant was at any time?"

"I did, but both the coordinator and the agent said from the outset the informant wouldn't work for us if more than two people knew their identity. Under any circumstances. Take it or leave it."

Meyerstein made a note of that. It wasn't unheard of for a special agent in charge not to know the identity of a high-level informant. But it was unusual. "Two people, huh? Does the Director or anyone else in DC, outside of Gordon's office, know? And this leads me to ask again about Rachel Crabtree's obsessive interest in this case."

"I'm not sure I feel comfortable divulging any more than I already have."

Martha noted his comments once again. "Why is that?"

"I'm going to spell it out for you. Right now, to remove all doubt."

Meyerstein scribbled down some more notes.

"This high-level informant will be invaluable in assisting us with known arms dealers and terrorists in Eastern Europe who could potentially target America. We can't jeopardize that intel. Now do you understand?"

Meyerstein noted down what he said. "I appreciate your candor, Gordon. That explains why the CIA is involved. Do you know if this high-level Mafia informant is known to someone in DC?"

"I'd rather not say any more. Suffice it to say, this is the most extraordinary breakthrough in disrupting and dismantling international terrorist plots and operations."

"You're not telling me that these two agents are the only ones who control this whole thing with this high-level informant? Where's the oversight?"

"DC."

Meyerstein scribbled that down as well. "Fine. I'm assuming you're fully up to speed with the Justice Department's rules on FBI confidential informants?" Collins and Avery both observed her, stony faced. She seemed to have struck a nerve. "Namely, the informant is expressly forbidden to carry out serious illegal activity. No matter how supposedly important this informer, he is not above the law. No one is."

"This is a gray area, Martha. You know what sort of people these are."

"A gray area? Is that what you said?"

Avery closed his eyes, clearly wishing for the conversation to end.

Meyerstein pivoted. "Have we established who gave the orders to Torrio? He's a made man. But he's not the top dog, is he?"

"That's right."

"So, who was it? Was it the consigliere, the underboss, or the boss himself?"

"I can't say."

Meyerstein noted his remark. "I can take this up with Gordon's department in a more direct way."

Collins shifted in his seat. "Just hang on a minute, Martha. Take what up?"

"An investigation into your procedures here."

"That's outrageous."

"Is it? Is it as outrageous as you asking me to believe that only two special agents are in the loop about something so important to national security? Listen to me: someone in DC has the identity. I want to know who it is."

Avery held up his hand. "If I can jump in here again. Can you leave that to me, Martha? I'll make a few discreet inquiries of my own."

"I'd appreciate that, thank you."

Collins's face was flushed. "I'd like to be more upfront. But I'm playing catch-up here too. The cultivation of this source was underway before I took over the field office eighteen months ago. I was told about it after the fact. But I was also told not to divulge anything."

"Who told you this?"

"Rachel Crabtree," he blurted out. Meyerstein sat in stunned silence. "She's running this informant. She's the one. That's all I know."

Twenty-Seven

It was nearly dawn as the Greyhound bus pulled up in downtown Oklahoma City.

After the long overnight bus ride from Midland, Reznick was glad to stretch his legs and check in to a cash-only motel by Will Rogers World Airport. There he showered and shaved. He felt like a human being again.

He headed out to a nearby diner. He ate a full breakfast and drank three strong black coffees.

Reznick felt waves of tiredness washing over him. He discreetly popped a couple of Dexedrine. He was getting pulled into a quagmire of his own making. A twilight world of hardened thugs, shady businessmen, and New York's criminal underworld. He knew that someone in the Mob had given the go-ahead for the hit. He began to feel the same killer instincts honed in Delta Force coming to the surface once again.

He felt that everything that had happened so far was only the beginning of a fraught investigation. He wasn't stupid. He knew that if you fucked with people like that, you might end up at the bottom of the East River. The Mafia didn't play by the rules. But the problem for them was that neither did he.

Reznick wasn't constrained by working for the FBI or Delta or even the CIA. The first rule in his world was that there were no rules. It made life more straightforward. His cell phone rang, snapping him out of his thoughts. "Yeah?"

"You OK to talk?" asked Trevelle Williams. "I know I'm calling earlier than expected, but this seemed like stuff you needed to know right away."

Reznick sipped his fourth coffee. "I'm still here. What've you got on Lucky's phone?"

"It's like a devil's résumé, what he's involved in. Human trafficking, child prostitution, drug smuggling, pimping, pornography, calls to Aryan Brotherhood shot callers in and out of Leavenworth, blackmail and bribes with local cops using his strip clubs, you name it."

"Send all that stuff to Meyerstein. I want that slimeball where he belongs. In jail."

"Be my pleasure. Right, down to business. The calls between Lucky and Joseph Torrio. They're extensive. So, it'll take a ton of time to analyze them all."

"Give me some fundamentals on Torrio. Where does he live?"

"He moves around a lot. His wife lives in a nice house in Staten Island with the kids."

"Not interested in them."

"Torrio doesn't stay in one place for longer than a couple of nights. It might be a friend's house. Might be a swanky Midtown hotel, from the GPS location. The St. Regis, occasionally the Peninsula. Sometimes he's up in the Bronx, then he's out in Queens. He gets around."

"Where is he at this moment in time?"

"I don't have a fix on his location. Not just yet. I might in an hour. Maybe he's got a second, third, or fourth cell phone. That would make sense."

"If you had to make a guess, where would you say he was right now?"

"Rockaway Beach."

"I thought you didn't have a fix on his location."

"I don't. But I do have a fix on the cell phone of his personal bodyguard, his brother, Sammy Torrio."

Reznick smiled. "Now, that is interesting. Good work."

"I wouldn't stake my life on it. But if I had to guess, I'm figuring the brother is beside him nearly 24-7, for protection but also for when he's meeting his crew."

"Would make sense. So, what's the exact location?"

"He's at an auto repair shop in Rockaway Beach. I've done a quick check on the NYPD database. The business is a front used by the Mob. They've been reported to take people there—people who owe them money—and torture them. Electric cables, drills to the head. They're fucking nuts. You really need to think twice about fucking with these guys."

Reznick's mind flashed back to the darkest day of his time in Iraq. He had lost count of the blackened bodies of torture victims found in dusty alleys in Baghdad. Fallujah. Holes drilled through bone by death squads. Shia and Sunni. The more he saw, the more he wanted to get out of the hell America had unleashed. He remembered the images, seared into his brain.

"Jon, are you still there?"

"Yup. So, I'm guessing that makes it impossible to pin down where he'll be at any moment. Interesting."

"What's the plan?"

"OK, first, get that data on Lucky to Meyerstein. Make sure it's encrypted. That's a priority. She can deal with him and let the Feds investigate. He's clearly an important link with the New York Mafia. He might be Mafia himself. But he's also got links to this Aryan Brotherhood crew in and around Texas."

"The FBI should be able to nail them on RICO, right?"

"I would hope so. Tell me more about this Joseph Torrio. Anything that might be of interest."

A sigh. "Let me see. Well, he has a major stake in high-end poker clubs, in and around New York."

Reznick shook his head at how Eastland had gotten mixed up with such crazies. "I don't understand why Eastland would need to go to New York to gamble. You can gamble online, if that's your thing. If anything happens to me, I want you to get every piece of data you accumulate to Martha."

"Don't you want me to just send it to her now?"

"No. Only if something happens to me."

"You headed to New York?"

Reznick finished his coffee. "That's the plan. I think I'll have to go the scenic route to avoid easy detection at major transport hubs."

"I've done some checking on important US infrastructure surveillance, with regard to terrorism. Definitely want to avoid flying. If you catch a flight, they'll be waiting for you. Same with trains. You step off at Grand Central, they'll be waiting for you. And if you use your credit card, it'll be flagged by the system. But I'm guessing you know all that."

Reznick smiled sadly. "Pretty much. But I appreciate the heads-up."

"So, how are you going to get there? It's a long, long way from Oklahoma."

Reznick turned his head to the windows and saw a trucker pull in outside. The chunky Black guy who jumped out wore a camouflage baseball cap with the words *US Army* emblazoned on it in black lettering. "Don't worry about that. I'll get there, one way or the other."

The trucker walked into the diner and sat three booths away from Reznick.

Reznick waited until the guy had finished his meal and was enjoying a Coke, texting on his cell phone. He sat down at the same booth. "Hope you don't mind me interrupting. I'm wondering where you're headed."

The trucker put down his cell phone and took off his hat. "I'm headed east."

"You going as far as New York?"

"That's the end stop for me. Why? You hitching a lift?"

"If you don't mind."

"What's wrong with catching a flight?"

Reznick grimaced. "It's a little complicated."

"Complicated. What the fuck does that mean?"

"I saw your hat, and I was hoping, from one veteran to another, that you could help me out."

"You in the Army?"

"Used to be in the Marines. Then Delta."

"Fuck, seriously?"

"Yeah."

"So, what's the story? You on the run? You killed someone?"

"Listen, if you're able to offer me a lift, great. If not, no hard feelings."

The guy looked at Reznick long and hard. "You're not going to go crazy on me, are you?"

Reznick shook his head.

"I'll be on the road in twenty minutes. Don't be late."

Twenty-Eight

Meyerstein felt a migraine coming on as she walked down the seventh-floor corridor and into the FBI conference room.

"Apologies for my tardiness." She took her seat.

Masson smiled across the table. "How was New York?"

Meyerstein arranged her briefing papers. "It was illuminating, to say the least. Very worthwhile. I'll give you the lowdown in a minute."

Crabtree cleared her throat. "Well, firstly, I want to talk about Jon Reznick."

"I thought you would."

Crabtree held up a grainy black-and-white photo of Reznick. "He's resurfaced at a sleazy Mob strip club in West Odessa, Texas."

Meyerstein scribbled down the details. It was the first she had heard of Reznick's whereabouts for forty-eight hours. "How did we hear about this?"

"The El Paso field office."

"When?"

"Three hours ago. They have a dozen agents chasing down leads."

"So, what did Jon Reznick do there? I'm assuming he didn't go for a lap dance."

Crabtree smiled. "Not quite. He beat the owner of the strip club, a guy known as Lucky. He's believed to have links between the Aryan Brotherhood of Texas in and out of jail, including shot callers. And this attack comes hot on the heels of the savage beatings Reznick dished out to the two Aryan Brotherhood psychos in Notrees, West Texas. So, we've got a pattern emerging, Martha."

Masson shook his head as he rubbed his eyes. "Martha, this is not acceptable."

Meyerstein could have done without the extra grief. Her migraine was drilling into her head, her vision momentarily blurring. She took a few moments, sipped from the glass of water in front of her. "I agree with you, Franklin, this is not acceptable."

"We can't turn a blind eye to this."

"No one said we should."

Crabtree said nothing as she took notes.

"However, what I will say in his defense is that he's shaking things up."

Franklin said, "What the hell do you mean?"

"Despite all our resources, he was the one who found these two guys. Draxler and McLellan. I think it's important that we don't lose sight of the crime that began all this. Reznick never started this war."

"The problem is," Crabtree said, "it looks like he's going to finish it. That is, if we can't find him. He's dropped off the grid."

"We'll find him."

"When?"

Meyerstein leafed through her notes. "You're absolutely right to bring this to my attention. Our attention. But there's something I want to bring to your attention. Something I found out in New York."

Crabtree's face flushed pink. "What are you talking about?"

"What I'm talking about is the interim report from the special agent in charge, Andrew Collins. Have you read it?"

Crabtree smiled in a vaguely patronizing way. "Yes, Martha, I have read the report."

"It appears they're doing a fine job. They have audio indicating that the Aryan Brotherhood crazies were contracted for this hit. It came via electronic surveillance of organized crime figures in and around Texas. And it includes this Lucky character and Thomas Egan, who's linked with the Irish Mob, among others. But, and here's the interesting thing, it leads to a guy called Joseph Torrio."

Crabtree folded her hands on the table.

Masson looked thoughtful. "I've worked on investigations into the five families, and his name comes up a lot. We talking the same guy?"

"Absolutely. And I did some of my own research on this in New York."

Crabtree flushed again. "What do you mean?"

"I mean this doesn't stop at Joseph Torrio and his crew in New York."

"Where the hell are you going with this, Martha?"

"Torrio didn't give the go-ahead to kill a former police chief in Maine. He was the conduit, in my opinion. It would take the green light from the boss, am I right?"

"I have no idea."

"Rachel, how long have you been assigned with us?"

"Two years and three months."

"Do you understand the importance of sharing information with us here at a senior level in the FBI? Especially information pertaining to ongoing investigations."

"What are you driving at?"

"Why didn't you share with us what you know?"

"What are you talking about?"

"What I'm talking about is that you know the man at the very highest level in the Gambino crime family, who is a high-level confidential informant. A person who has been known to have given contracts to Torrio. I'm talking hits."

Crabtree cleared her throat as she took a few moments as if to gather her thoughts. "I'll be honest; until I read the report from the New York field office, I was unaware of the involvement of Torrio."

"Well, now we *do* know Torrio was the cutout. The intermediary. But I'd like to know now, right now, the identity of the confidential informant. I suspect a person at the top of the tree gave the go-ahead. Because it sure as hell didn't come from Torrio."

"Martha, I might only be CIA in your eyes, but I know that FBI confidential informants are highly prized. And I'm sure you're aware that the identity of confidential informants is strictly need-to-know. A handful of people at most."

"A-plus for stating the obvious, Rachel."

Masson held up his hand. "Enough!" He turned to Crabtree. "Let's back up for a moment. Rachel, are you aware of the identity of this very high-level informant?"

"I'll have to check on that."

"What? You don't know?"

Crabtree shifted uncomfortably in her chair.

"I'm compelling you to share that information."

"This is something I can't get to you."

Meyerstein cleared her throat. "We want answers, Rachel. This is not the goddamn CIA."

"As you know, I work alongside the National Security Branch. And in that capacity I was speaking to the confidential informants coordinator, looking for an update on the situation you are alluding to. Things are in flux. But I can tell you that the informant is someone I've been overseeing. This is a highly sensitive and classified operation."

Meyerstein noted the information. "Are you running a shadow CIA operation here within the FBI?"

Crabtree shook her head.

"You're aware of his true identity."

"I know his name."

"Forgive me for belaboring this point, but why aren't you giving us the information, Rachel?"

"It is paramount that we keep his identity confidential. It's a legal requirement."

"Legal requirement? Are you denying us access to this information?"

"I'm not denying you anything. I'm just stating that, because of legal considerations, I can't disclose this to you here, around this table. At least at this time."

Meyerstein scoffed. "I can't believe what I'm hearing. You're being deliberately obstructive. What are you hiding?"

"I'm just outlining the complicated legal situation. A legal contract is in place."

"A legal contract? This is outrageous. Beyond the norms of what the FBI usually does for confidential informants?"

"That's exactly right. Otherwise, the informant would never have become an informant in the first place."

"That's extraordinary. So, the end justifies the means?"

"Perhaps in this case it does."

"What if this high-level confidential informant ordered the hit on Bill Eastland?"

Crabtree sat in silence.

"We need to know the name of this informant to determine if he was the one who ordered the killings."

"I will share this information . . . in due course."

"In due course! What the hell are you talking about? Do it now, Rachel. Otherwise I'll be taking this up with the Director."

Crabtree sighed long and hard. "How do I know that you won't share this information with Jon Reznick?"

"Seriously? Did you just ask that question?"

"I did."

"Who the hell do you think you're talking to, Rachel? My relationship with Jon Reznick is strictly professional."

"Are you sure about that? I've talked to a few people who said you and Reznick are pretty tight."

"Rachel, this information is required. You either tell me and Franklin, or I will be going straight to the Director. Your choice."

Crabtree shrugged. "I guess you'd better take it up with the Director, then."

Twenty-Nine

It was dawn when Reznick saw the Manhattan skyline. Sun peeking through the skyscrapers in the distance. It had been a grueling journey of more than twenty-four hours in the truck with the Army veteran, with three stops along the way. The guy never stopped talking. Mostly about Iraq. Reznick didn't want to talk about Iraq. No one he knew wanted to talk about Iraq. But this guy—this guy could not stop talking about bombs, bodies, and the bloody carnage on his tour of duty.

Reznick zoned out, occasionally nodding his head. He was relieved to be dropped off in the Meatpacking District.

"Take care, man," the trucker said.

Reznick shook his hand. "You too, bro."

He had asked to be dropped off outside a sleazy two-star hotel. Cash only. That was the appeal. No trace of credit cards. Its interior was a funky primary-color vibe trying to appear fashionable. But it was just a flophouse for those who needed to hire a room by the hour. Judging by the clientele he encountered in the lobby, elevator, and corridor, it was mostly out-of-town businessmen with prostitutes or escorts.

It was a sad place.

Reznick got to his room, went inside, and locked the door. He showered and shaved and put the radio on low. A talk station discussion on rocketing crime levels in New York. He switched it off and heard instead the sound of police sirens outside.

He lay down on the bed. Gathering his thoughts. He felt as if he could sleep for a thousand years. But he was wired.

His mind began to race as he reflected on the events of the last several days. The cold-blooded killing was a rarity in Rockland. It would echo down the years, in and around his hometown. Bar fights happened, for sure. Opiate overdose, yes, even in a tight-knit community in mid-coast Maine.

The more he thought about the killings, the blacker his mood got. While he had been driving home from his cabin in the woods, his friends were being killed like dogs.

Reznick missed Eastland. He missed his gruff humor. The laughter. The dark moods. Eastland wasn't a perfect person. He was flawed. Reznick knew that. But there wasn't a false bone in his body.

He began to reflect again on his own helter-skelter trip down south. Reznick decided he had let the Aryan Brotherhood crazies off lightly. Part of him had so badly wanted to shoot them dead, in cold blood. An eye for an eye. He figured he might even have gotten away with it in Texas. He felt his finger on the cold steel of the Beretta trigger. But if he had gone down that route, there would be no way back. He would be facing homicide charges. No question. He had felt an overpowering urge to kill the psychos in the West Texas bar. But he had managed to rein in his rage, more or less.

He relished whatever awaited Draxler and McLellan. He could only put his faith in the good sense of the jury to put them away for the rest of their natural lives.

That was the best he could hope for. It would have to do.

He knew the Feds would be on his tail before long. Maybe they already were. New York had tens of thousands of surveillance cameras, especially in Manhattan. It was just a matter of time before face recognition picked him out of the crowds.

He had to think. Try and keep one step ahead. He closed his eyes, wishing for sleep. His crazy thoughts ricocheted around his head.

On the other side of the wall, the sound of a couple going hard at it.

"Goddamn!"

Reznick realized he wouldn't get any sleep. He got up and headed into the bathroom, splashing cold water on his face. He downed a couple of Dexedrine with a bottle of Coke.

His cell phone rang. Trevelle.

"Jon?"

"Nice to hear from you."

Reznick pressed his cell phone tight to his ear as the banging next door got louder.

"Is there somebody there with you?"

"Not quite. Tell me about it. What's happening?"

"I've been trying to get a fix on Torrio or his brother. Nothing. Seem to have dropped off the grid."

"Tell me about the poker club that Torrio is in charge of. That might provide a way into his world for me."

"I've got the address. I've checked cell phone messages over the last year from Torrio to his associates, and they mention this joint, Jimmy's."

"Jimmy's? What's the full name?"

"Jimmy's Gentlemen's Club."

"Sounds charming."

"It's down in the Financial District, two blocks from Wall Street. Get a lot of hedge fund stiffs and out-of-town big shots throwing their cash around and swigging the Krug."

"What about the poker game?"

"It's in the back. They're not looking for guys wanting to get a lap dance and ogle naked women. They want guys who splash the cash. Always cash. Bigtime. The sort of cash that buys five-hundred-dollar bottles of champagne."

"How do I get in?"

"Ask anyone behind the bar, and say, *I'm looking for Ramo*. That will get you in automatically. The name is given to concierges in select five-star hotels in Manhattan, so the guests might make it down there for some action."

"Got it."

"The back room is very popular. Opens at ten every night. But it doesn't heat up till after midnight."

"Anything else?"

"Do not go armed. It was busted two years ago by the cops. This is the joint Bill Eastland visited. But it's up and running again."

"And I ask for Ramo?"

"That's it. And Jon . . ."

"What?"

"Be careful. This is the New York Mob. They don't take prisoners."

Thirty

The Uber picked Reznick up at ten o'clock.

"You like the gentlemen club?" the wide-eyed driver asked, looking into the rearview mirror.

"Somewhere to pass the time, I guess."

The driver shook his head. "I'm from Bangladesh. In my village, you would be whipped for going to such an establishment."

Reznick stared out at the crowds on the Manhattan sidewalks. Americans going about their business. He remembered his late wife taking him around the Museum of Modern Art. He couldn't figure any of it out. Cubism. Abstract. Picasso. Whatever. But he still enjoyed it. She took him to see a classical concert at Lincoln Center. A bit of a revelation to him.

She introduced the small-town boy to the sophisticated elements of the city. He felt out of place. But not for long. He loved it. The ups and downs. The highs and lows. The extremes. The anonymity.

His father had told him all about New York in the early 1970s. When he came back from Vietnam, his father and Bill Eastland had stopped off for a day or two in some bars in and around Times Square. It was a time of peep shows and prostitution, everything on show.

By contrast, these days, the city had become Disneyfied. It was cleaner, more welcoming. The floor-to-ceiling glass condos had sprung up. The skyscrapers got supertall. The city looked more cosmopolitan. But it was still rough around the edges in some neighborhoods. Very rough.

Reznick read about the spike in the crime rate. It seemed to be spinning out of control. Killings up. In and around the city. The cops weren't being backed by the city like they once used to be. It was all in flux again. Who the hell knew where the city would be in another ten years?

The cab pulled up at the neon-lit club in the Financial District.

"Enjoy your evening, man," the driver said, grinning.

"I wouldn't count on it."

The driver laughed as Reznick gave him a fifty-dollar bill. "This is too much, man."

"This is America. Enjoy it while you can."

Reznick stepped out of the cab and walked up to the shaven-headed security guy on the door.

"Pay inside. Have a good one."

He brushed past the doorman and headed inside.

A girl sat in a glass booth painting her nails, chewing gum. She looked up and smiled. "Fifty dollars, honey, gets you into our beautiful club."

Reznick handed over the cash.

"Have a great time, sir," she said, blowing on her red nails.

Reznick smiled and walked down a corridor past more rough-looking security, through a metal door, and into the main bar lounge. Huge TV screens on the wall showed ESPN. A few booths of tattooed men splashing cash and guzzling champagne as topless girls in thongs danced and gyrated in front of them.

He sat on a stool at the bar and ordered a beer.

"Cold Heineken OK, sir?"

"Perfect."

"You had a tough day."

"You could say that."

Reznick took a sip of his beer. "I'm looking for Ramo."

The bartender smiled. "Who sent you?"

"Guy uptown. Concierge."

The bartender cocked his head to the far end of the bar. "Press 9-2-5-7 on the keypad at the door. That'll get you in. Enjoy your evening, sir."

Reznick handed him a fifty-dollar bill. "Much appreciated."

"You're welcome. Anytime."

Reznick finished his beer and walked up to the thick metal doors. He pressed the four-digit code and pushed open the heavy doors. A corridor garishly bathed in crimson red light stretched out before him. A security guy walked him the last few yards into what looked like a casino, chandeliers on the ceiling.

A girl wearing a bikini and spike heels walked up to him. "What can I get you, sir?"

"Scotch on the rocks."

The girl winked at him. "Coming up."

Reznick saw a few guys sitting around the poker table. He headed over, pulled up a chair, and sat down. He handed twenty thousand dollars in cash to the twentysomething female dealer. "Deal me in," he said.

"Right away, sir."

The young dealer took the money off the green velvet table and slid across twenty one-thousand-dollar chips. "Welcome to the game, sir," she said. Her eyes were glazed as if she was under the influence.

The three other guys around the table nodded toward him. They looked like regular joes. Middle-aged. Paunches. Hooded eyes. Maybe just trying to forget their humdrum lives for a few hours.

The dealer sniffed hard as she dealt. "OK, gentlemen, very best of luck to you all."

Reznick checked his hand. Three sevens, the two of clubs, and the five of spades.

"Two-thousand-dollar minimum per hand, gentlemen."

Reznick tossed in two chips. He played the hand and lost to the guy opposite him, who had three kings. He drank his Scotch as his gaze wandered around the room. Surveillance cameras covering everything in sight. Mirror on one wall, perhaps a one-way mirror. Was someone on the other side observing the players? He tossed in another couple of chips.

The young dealer curled her hair behind her ears. "First time here, sir?"

"Yeah. It was recommended to me. Close personal friend."

"Good choice. Nice to have you."

"Don't know if you ever met my friend. Bear of a man. From up in Maine."

The dealer went quiet for a few moments as she frowned, opening a new deck of cards.

"You remember him?"

The girl flushed as she shook her head. "I can't say I do, sir. But we have a lot of clients through at the club. Very discerning customers, usually."

"I'm sure."

"Your first time in the city, sir?"

"No, I know New York very well."

The girl smiled as she dealt another hand. "It's a busy city, a lot going on, that's for sure."

Reznick sipped his Scotch. He sensed she was nervous. He sat quietly and played the game. He lost a few thousand more in the blink of an eye. It was that easy. He could imagine Bill Eastland getting loaded on expensive Scotch as he tried to cover his losses.

The young dealer smiled a killer smile. "When the cards aren't falling for you, they just aren't falling for you, sir."

"Yeah, no kidding," Reznick said. "Deal me in anyway."

Reznick pretended to play badly. He lost another two grand.

The guys at his table looked like pros. One had shades on to conceal any emotion. The rotund guy at the far end of the table had headphones on. It was all pretty bizarre.

Reznick surveyed the rest of the room. Tables for blackjack, roulette, craps, and baccarat. The girls were supplying booze as the guys bet and bet.

"How long you worked here?" Reznick asked.

"I'm sorry sir, but I'm here to deal poker."

"Of course. The friend I was telling you about. His name was Eastland. Bill Eastland."

The girl's eyes fixed briefly on the security guy in the corner.

"Name ring a bell?"

"I don't think so."

Reznick leaned closer. "He always came here when he was in New York."

"Sorry, what was that name?"

"Bill Eastland."

"I'm sorry, that name doesn't ring a bell. There are hundreds of customers in here every week."

Reznick finished his drink and ordered another. "Not to worry. Nice place you have here."

"Not my place, sir, but thanks anyway. Are you in town on business, or is it pleasure?"

"A bit of both."

"What line of business, if you don't mind me asking, sir?"

Reznick sensed she knew more than she was letting on. "I'm in the same line of work as your boss, Joseph Torrio."

The dealer cleared her throat. "Very good, sir. I'll deal a new hand, if that's OK."

"Got it."

The young dealer dealt the new hand as Reznick surveyed his cards. He had a bullshit hand. He tossed in another couple thousand bucks to stay in the game.

The waitress served him his second Scotch on the rocks. "Here's your drink, sir. It's on the house."

Reznick thanked her and took a long sip of the Scotch. It warmed his belly. He caught the gaze of the dealer. "What time do you get off?"

"I'm sorry, sir. I don't fraternize with customers."

"Never said you do. I'm just curious, that's all."

The girl rolled her eyes. "I finish at midnight. I've got classes in the morning."

"Classes? You at college here?"

"Columbia."

"Good for you."

Reznick played a couple more hands of poker, had another Scotch, and finished his game.

"Better luck next time," she said.

"I'll need it."

Reznick thanked her and left a thousand-dollar chip as a gratuity.

"That's a lot of money, sir."

"Might help with those tuition fees of yours, right?"

The dealer smiled. "I appreciate that. Thank you."

Reznick got off his stool. "You're welcome."

Then he turned and walked out of the room, down the corridor, and out onto the streets of Lower Manhattan, glad to get the fresh air.

Reznick checked his watch. Not long till the dealer finished her shift.

Thirty-One

Feldman sat on the outdoor terrace of the ultra-exclusive CORE Club in Midtown Manhattan, waiting for his guest to arrive. He sipped a glass of wine as he checked his messages. The private members' club was a beautiful refuge for him. He would occasionally pop in for a drink or meal before he headed back to his apartment on Fifth Avenue, two blocks away.

He enjoyed the casual, hip vibe. It was all so different from other New York private clubs, which were either too stuffy or too full of coked-up twentysomethings. His club was for people in business, politicians, billionaire philanthropists, a confidant to the President who worked out in the private gym, hedge fund guys who talked incessantly on their cell phones. He didn't mind. It was actually part of a theater of the absurd. Feldman found it intoxicating as well as alluring. The money, the power, the exchange of ideas and business cards, and the networking—second to none. Whereas many clubs frowned on using cell phones in and around the club, the CORE Club was very relaxed about that.

Feldman was always amazed at who was hanging around. The place was always buzzing. Especially in the late afternoon and early evening. The excited chatter of deals clinched, new friendships made, corporate firings, and even gossip about executives in therapy. Nothing was too personal or important for them not to discuss. The alcohol was a great loosener of the tongue.

Feldman's gaze wandered to the far end of the terrace. He spotted Avery, walking toward him.

Avery pulled up a seat opposite. "Hope you weren't waiting too long. I just got a heads-up. Real eager to discuss this with you."

"First, you fancy a little drink?"

"Don't mind if I do. Scotch on the rocks."

Feldman caught a waiter's eye and ordered two Chivas Regals. They made small talk for a few minutes. The suffocating humidity of DC in the summer, the midterms, and of course, the Yankees. "What the hell is wrong with them?"

"I swear to God, Mort, they're going to be the death of me. I've got a couple of tickets for tonight's game against the Red Sox. Care to join me?"

"Would love to, but got to meet a new client of mine. Thanks all the same."

The waiter returned with the two drinks.

Feldman raised his glass, as did Avery. "To your good health, Gordon."

They sipped their drinks, swirling the ice around in their glasses.

Avery leaned forward, drink in hand. "We got a problem."

"What kind of problem?"

"The guy I was telling you about, the ex-Delta guy, he's in town. Right now."

"Are you serious?"

He nodded. "I'm hearing he was down in Texas, connecting a few dots. But I have seen one APB Manhattan-wide. He's in town. They're looking for him as we speak."

Feldman was fully alert. "Why's he here?"

"Retribution. He's decided to take the law into his own hands."

Feldman took a sip of his Scotch. "I don't like the sound of that. Don't get me wrong: I very much appreciate you being candid on this issue. But it's a concern."

Avery's gaze wandered around the near-empty terrace. "It should be."

"Has he done this sort of thing before? Gone rogue."

"A few times."

"Interesting." Feldman shifted in his seat. "Do you believe he's a real and credible threat to my client?"

"I do. This guy is like a shape-shifter. He goes into a building. Then he disappears. He reappears at the other end of the country."

"Does the FBI have any proof that my client was involved in some way?"

"Tenuous links at best."

Feldman took a gulp of his Scotch. "Consider this: If I contact my client and say, 'A certain individual is going to kill you,' how do you think he will react?"

Avery cleared his throat. "I'd assume he won't run and hide. He would fight, right?"

"You're correct. One billion percent correct."

Avery leaned in close. "My advice to your client? This is the time to leave his home. Get a jump start. That's my point."

"Gordon, you know as well as I do his home is the best-protected in America next to maybe the White House. You're surely not saying this guy could breach it. That's not feasible. One man?"

"I know. But it's purely precautionary. From our side of the fence, we want your client to remain safe but also focused on his work with us as he moves on to another stage of his life."

"That won't be an easy conversation with my client. I know his temperament."

"He must not get embroiled or dragged into this. It would be prudent and in your client's interests to get to his new home now."

"And if he doesn't?"

"Then his life will be at risk. He will never be safe as long as Jon Reznick is around."

Thirty-Two

It was just after midnight.

Reznick watched and waited across the road from the club. He had been cooling his heels for the last fifteen minutes. He was about to call it a night when he caught sight of the young dealer. She was leaving the club, accompanied by two friends.

The girl hugged her friends tight before the three went their separate ways.

Reznick crossed the street and approached her, smiling.

She turned around. "What the hell?" she said. "Are you stalking me? You better get the hell away from me or I'll get security."

Reznick showed his hands. "Relax. I just want to say I'm sorry for bugging you in there."

"Are you kidding me? This is making me real uneasy."

"I just want to talk. About my friend who visited the club. I think you might know more than you're letting on."

The girl pushed the hair away from her glazed eyes. "Are you still going on about that? Jeez, give it a rest, man."

"I will, I promise. I've just got a few questions. I swear."

The girl shook her head. "You shouldn't hang around outside here. If my supervisor finds out, he'll kill me."

"A couple minutes. Then I'll get out of your face. I'm just trying to piece together what happened to my friend. I believe he was in the club a lot. He spent a lot of money in there."

The girl looked sheepish. "Thanks for the tip. It was real nice of you."

"I don't mean to bug you, honestly."

"Listen, you just scared me. I don't usually get guys hitting on me outside."

"I'm not hitting on you."

"You're not?"

Reznick shook his head.

"I'm flattered by your interest, but you need to talk with the waitresses inside serving the drinks. They might be more accommodating."

"I'm not interested in them. I just wanted to talk. You're the one who deals the cards."

The girl took out her cell phone. "Do you want me to call the cops? Do you?"

"Go ahead if you want. You might want to try and explain what you know about Bill Eastland. I can tell you've seen him before."

The girl put the cell phone away. "Listen, buddy, I'm tired. I've got classes. There's eight million other people to bug in this city. Go and bug them."

"My friend is dead. I just want to ask a few questions."

The girl looked blankly at him. "I'm sorry. But I told you already: I don't know anything about that."

"My friend, I believe, was in the club a lot. He lost a ton of money."

"It happens if you gamble."

"True, very true. He was a good man. But he was flawed, like we all are."

The woman folded her arms. "I don't know who you are."

"My name is Jon."

"This is really unnerving me, Jon."

Reznick put up his hands. "For that, I'm sorry. And if you could just give me five minutes of your time, maybe over a cup of coffee at the diner around the corner. That's all."

The woman bit her lower lip, looking around anxiously. "One cup of coffee? You're not going to drug me, are you?"

Reznick shook his head. "I'm only looking for answers."

"Are you a cop?"

"No, I'm not. But the guy that was killed, my friend, he used to be a cop. A real cop. A police chief in a small town in Maine. That's who was killed."

"Really?" The girl closed her eyes and shook her head. "I should never have gotten mixed up with them in there. It's crazy. They creep me out."

"Do you want to talk about it? You must be starving."

The girl forced a smile. "I am starving. Haven't eaten since breakfast."

"Let's fix that. I swear, five minutes and I'll be out of your life."

They headed to the all-night diner.

Reznick followed the young woman in and walked to a booth, away from the window. He sat down opposite her and ordered coffees and pancakes for two.

"How did you know?"

"Everyone likes pancake and maple syrup, right?"

The woman smiled and laughed. "This is all a bit strange."

"Trust me, I don't usually hang out in places like that. I'm more a dive bar aficionado."

"Sounds like my dad."

The waitress returned with their food. "There you go, folks. Enjoy."

The girl began to wolf down her pancakes, quickly washed down by a mug of coffee.

"Someone was hungry," Reznick said.

"Thank you. I miss too many meals. My dad's always getting on my case about that."

"Where you from originally?"

"A small town in Nebraska. You wouldn't have heard of it."

"Long way from home. You getting a bit homesick?"

"A lot."

"Why did you move to New York?"

"To escape my life. I was pregnant."

Reznick nodded. "That's tough."

"You have no idea. My family are church folk."

"Your kid?"

The girl nodded. "With a friend. Not a great situation. But it's better than being on the streets."

Reznick ate his pancakes as he allowed a silence to stretch between them. He sensed she would be ready to talk when she was ready. She just needed space.

"You need to be on the level with me. You're a cop, aren't you? Undercover, maybe?"

"I'm not a cop. I'm not a private investigator. I'm just a guy trying to find out if anyone knows anything about what my friend got up to before he was killed. I must not have known him as well as I thought I did. Truth is, as I know now, he was a degenerate gambler. I believe he got in over his head."

The girl sipped her coffee.

Reznick took a photo out of his pocket of him and Eastland on a fishing expedition. "Do you recognize that guy?"

The girl gazed at the photo. "Yeah, I recognize him."

"So, he was a regular at the club?"

"I saw him a bunch of times, usually Friday and Saturday nights. He would get loaded in the bar with one of the waitresses. They also turn tricks on the side, adjacent to the room you were in."

"When you say *tricks*, you mean sex?"

"Exactly. So, Bill liked to fuck before he gambled away his money. Big tipper too."

Reznick looked down. He felt ashamed learning for the first time about his friend's sordid private life. He thought back to the man he thought he knew. The burly, ruddy-faced, tough, heavy-drinking ex–police chief and Vietnam vet. But his friend clearly had a far darker side to his personality, hidden from Reznick and everyone he knew. The deception gnawed deep into Reznick. He had thought he knew this man.

It was not only thinking of his friend having sex with tragic, vulnerable young women who were forced to work for the Mob. But also of his poor, devoted, long-suffering wife at home in Rockland. A man she had known since elementary school. Truth was, Eastland was a deviant, a drunk, and a philanderer. And his big mouth had gotten both himself and his wife killed. A sadness washed over Reznick. But as much as he would have liked to hate Bill Eastland and disavow him over his moral failings, and he had every right to, he couldn't quite bring himself to do it. He knew Eastland wasn't all bad. He knew about the man's generosity of spirit. He had a big heart. He knew that over the years Eastland had helped out many veterans who were down on their luck. He wasn't a cold-blooded monster. But he was, most certainly, flawed. Badly flawed.

"Cat caught your tongue?"

"No, just processing. And you saw him losing big?"

"Losing huge."

"The guy that owns the club, Joseph Torrio . . . what do you know about him?"

"I thought he was nice when I started working there, a couple years back. I began as a waitress. A hostess, he likes to call them."

Reznick averted his gaze.

The girl had tears in her eyes. "I did what I had to. Joe Torrio said he would slice my face open with a razor. I was desperate for money. My daughter was hungry. I was going days without food. I was too ashamed to call my parents."

"So, what happened?"

"Mr. Torrio turned up at my apartment up in the Bronx. Well, it was just a room, to be frank. And he said he'd heard I was down on my luck. He gave me a thousand bucks, and I allowed him to fuck me."

"Christ, I'm sorry."

"This went on. And then I developed a habit. To deal with all this shit, I started chasing the dragon, whatever. Drinking. I was still broke. He would turn up, give me money. Then one day he turned up, said I was no longer a hostess, and I was getting a big raise and working the tables. Croupier. My pay doubled. But it wasn't enough to keep me in my habit. So, he supplied that. And he fucked me. Now you know . . . not exactly a golden girl from the prairies of Nebraska."

"I take it that might be in the past?"

"I got clean. I don't fuck him anymore. And at least I can live with myself, thanks to Xanax and Librium."

"You said you've got classes in the morning. What are you studying?"

"Modern history."

Reznick smiled. "Impressive."

"It would be better if I didn't have to work in that sleazehole to make my rent."

"Why don't you head back to Nebraska? Good university there."

"I was offered a scholarship there too."

"Can't you move back in with your folks while you're studying in Nebraska?"

"I don't know if they'd have me back."

"Listen to me. If they're true Christian people with good hearts, they will most certainly have you back. And they would welcome you and their granddaughter with open arms."

The tears spilled out of her eyes. "What would you do if you were in my shoes?"

Reznick opened his wallet and showed her a picture of Lauren. "This is my daughter. She's in her twenties, same as you. If she had been in your shoes, I would sure as hell hope she found it in her heart to come back home."

The girl nodded. "Sorry, I'm getting upset, and you're trying to find out what happened to your friend."

"I guess it was a long shot, but it was good to have confirmation that that's where he lost a lot of money."

"He lost tens of thousands every time. On credit. Just building debt. He was a terrible gambler."

Reznick wondered if an outstanding debt like that was enough to get Eastland and his wife murdered. It seemed like a bit of a stretch. "Is there anything else that sticks out about Bill Eastland? You said he was a big tipper. Is there anything that happened that you saw or heard about involving Eastland at the club?"

"There was one thing."

"What?"

"I remember one night your friend was told to cool it by the pit boss. You know, the guy that looks after the tables. Your friend started shouting and screaming until Joseph Torrio approached him. Then Eastland threatened to kill him. Called him a greaseball."

"What happened?"

"Your friend was thrown out by security. Think it might've been the last time I saw him."

"Eastland threatened to kill Torrio?"

"I saw it with my own eyes."

"Listen to me: I need to ask you one more thing. This guy, Joseph Torrio, I have an idea where he lives. But he's never home."

"That figures."

"He's always moving around, right?"

"I know where he is every day."

"You do?"

The girl nodded. "He has a new girl in his life."

"Who?"

"She's very pretty. Joseph is fucking one of the new hostesses. A Puerto Rican girl. I showed her the ropes the first week."

"What's her name?"

"Carla Santos."

"Where does she live?"

"She lives in a room in the Queensbridge housing project, a dump out in Long Island City. I helped her move into the place when she started working. It's not good."

"So, Joseph goes there. Where exactly?"

The girl gave the address. "She's not in trouble, is she?"

"No, she's not. Have you got a number for her?"

The girl shook her head.

"So, he turns up there every night?"

"Like clockwork. She's on the midnight-to-dawn shift. But he likes to pop in around nine for a quick one. He's very particular about his times. He throws her plenty of cash. But she's shooting up bad."

Reznick leaned in close. "You've been very helpful. Can I say one final thing?"

"Yeah, sure."

"Get yourself back home. Get yourself back to your mother and father. And get yourself free of this bullshit."

The girl had tears in her eyes.

Reznick took out a pen and scribbled an email address on a napkin. "If you need to speak to me about this, don't hesitate to contact me."

"You think Nebraska's a good bet for me?"

"Get yourself home. You need to be surrounded by people who care about you. People who love you."

Thirty-Three

The desk of FBI Director Bill O'Donoghue was typically clutter free.

Meyerstein had been sitting patiently as her boss read the briefing paper she had sent him. It focused on the Eastlands, as well as Reznick's role in tracking down the people responsible for their deaths. She expressed her outrage that a high-level confidential FBI informant had almost certainly ordered the double hit. But she also revealed how the CIA's Rachel Crabtree was privy to the identity, while senior FBI people, like her, were out of the loop.

It was a mess.

Meyerstein shifted in her seat as the Director leaned forward, eyes fixed on her.

"Confidential informants are an incredibly sensitive area, as well you know, Martha. But let's set that aside for a few moments. Let's talk about Jon Reznick."

"What about him?"

"Let me get this straight. Reznick hunted two Aryan Brotherhood members all the way down to goddamn Texas?"

"Correct."

"Without being apprehended?"

"Also correct."

O'Donoghue pinched the bridge of his nose, a mannerism that came out when he grew stressed. "And that's after gunning another one of them down in the road? Seriously? I can't believe what I'm reading. The Aryan Brotherhood guys are in the hospital as we speak. Serious injuries. Broken bones. Smashed jaws. Blood loss. One might be blind in one eye."

Meyerstein sat in silence.

"He's not the goddamn law, Martha."

"I'm well aware of that."

O'Donoghue lifted up a surveillance photograph of Jon Reznick in New York. "Downtown Manhattan, a strip club, chatting up one of the croupiers."

"Where did you get that?"

"Andrew Collins."

"He could've done me the courtesy of keeping me in the loop. It's quite irregular that I'm not informed on matters pertaining to Reznick. That was the deal."

"That *was* the deal, Martha. That deal is history. Do you know who has an interest in the strip club?"

"Joseph Torrio?"

"Indeed. And his associates. Do you know what that means?"

"It means that Jon Reznick is piecing together how this whole thing went down. I'd like to explain or at least try to explain."

"I'm done hearing explanations or excuses from you defending Reznick. Enough is enough. He's working from the ground up. Starting with the Aryan Brotherhood crew in Texas. Then he visits the strip bar owned by Alfredo 'Lucky' Drago, who in turn is associated with the Gambinos in New York. Then he turns up at a Manhattan strip club. Reznick is getting to them, one by one, and dealing with this as if he's a fucking virus. Enough!"

"It's difficult, I know."

"It's not difficult. He's breaking the fucking law, Martha! Don't you get it?"

"I get it, alright. But you know as well as I do what he is. He's a trained killer. And it's personal."

"Gimme a break." O'Donoghue leaned back in his seat and shook his head. "He's a wanted man. A man who you deployed on behalf of the FBI has gone rogue. Again. But he's not going to run amok forever. What happens then?"

"He will face justice like everyone else."

"No one is above the goddamn law."

Meyerstein studied the shadows under his eyes. The older he got from slowly working himself to death, the testier he became. "Is that really true, Bill?"

"What the hell do you mean by that?"

"I want to talk about the role of a high-level informant who I knew nothing about."

"I'm listening."

"First, I would like to know who the confidential informant is, whose identity Crabtree is withholding."

O'Donoghue went quiet before he steepled his fingers on his lap. "I'm going to let you know who it is, Martha. Crabtree is working on a special project within the National Security Branch. And New York reports to her on the high-level informant, everything about him. However, I'm the Director. And I believe you have the right to know more."

"I appreciate that, thank you. Can you tell me when this began, first of all?"

"The general counsel of the FBI, Gordon Avery, was approached by a legal firm in London."

"London?"

"Their client has interests in Europe. The Far East. Russia. Businesses. All legal business interests. The high-level informant felt that news of his involvement with us had less chance of leaking if the approach came from outside the United States. Gordon flew to London and had a discussion."

"Why only Gordon?"

"He was the first one who knew. That was the strict stipulation to test the waters, so to speak. We were investigating the tax affairs of this individual. That's how it all started."

"So, the law firm in London reached out to Gordon before you?"

"Exactly. He then flew back and met with me. And that's how the process began. So, it was then that I was privy to the identity of this high-level source. I believe that New York was then informed, and this brought the Agency into the equation. Rachel Crabtree was assigned here because of the international nature of the high-level informant. National security, international terrorism links."

"Why was I kept out of the loop until now?"

"A lot of senior FBI people were kept out of the loop. This was on a need-to-know basis."

Meyerstein held her emotions in check. It was difficult to hear.

"There's a big picture here, Martha. The head of one of the five families in New York is on the verge of becoming a fully activated FBI asset. He was the one whose international tax affairs we were investigating. And he cut a deal. A landmark deal."

"The head? Not senior, but the boss?"

O'Donoghue nodded.

"That's extraordinary. Is Paul Moretti our informant?"

O'Donoghue nodded. "That's correct. Now listen, Martha. This doesn't go any further. I'm trusting you with this. We're trying to keep this tight."

"I understand. And thank you. You're probably going to know what I'm going to say next."

"Gimme a break, Martha."

"The order to kill Bill Eastland and his wife came via Joseph Torrio. So, he's the conduit."

"I've read the report. Torrio is used by all five families as a go-between. So, it's complicated."

"Torrio does a lot of work for Moretti. You see where I'm going with this? Moretti very well might have issued the hit. We can't brush that aside or ignore it."

"We don't know definitively who ordered it. Besides, a decision has been made."

"We're going to turn a blind eye? We've seen this before. And it doesn't end well. Informants who commit the most serious offenses—you once said it yourself: we can't turn a blind eye."

"This is different."

"How is it different?"

"We're working with the full might of the CIA on this. This guy, Moretti, he has his fingers in every pie. International businesses spanning Europe, Asia, the Middle East, and Russia."

"So, we stop investigating his tax evasions for what, exactly?"

"There are former KGB officers who are running legitimate businesses around the world. And they have tentacles and contacts in many terrorist networks. Bottom line? Moretti's associates and contacts in the former Soviet bloc can serve a purpose for us. Which is bigger than any of this. We can get suitcase nukes out of the hands of terrorists. Interrupt their sources of funding, stop arms deals before they lead to future attacks on the West."

"So, that's the deal? We turn a blind eye to Moretti's serious criminality, including ordering the killing of a former cop to save his own ass? Didn't you host a conference call talking about this not one year ago? And you talked about the FBI's Office of Professional Responsibility where you spelled this out time after time. 'No one is above the law.' That was your mantra."

O'Donoghue's face flushed pink as he loosened the top button of his shirt. "Don't lecture me, Martha. You're in no position to lecture anyone. Your relationship with Reznick has jeopardized investigations in the past."

"The relationship is strictly professional. And what Jon has done for this country and the Bureau has been recognized by the President, no less."

O'Donoghue sat in silence.

"We cannot allow Moretti to go free if he authorized the killing of Bill Eastland. Imagine if the attorney general at the Justice Department got wind of this?"

"He already has. And so has Avery."

Meyerstein took a beat to absorb the information. "Hang on, are you saying the attorney general and our counsel are also OK with us turning a blind eye? To Moretti?"

O'Donoghue stood up to see Meyerstein out of his office. "That's exactly what I'm saying."

Thirty-Four

It was late afternoon when Reznick checked out of the sleazy hotel, caught a yellow cab, and headed uptown.

He sat in the back seat. He wore shades and a baseball hat. He had slept well. He began to strategize. He needed to make sure he kept one step ahead of the FBI and the NYPD. But his thoughts had already turned to Joseph Torrio.

He weighed whether he should head across to the Queensbridge projects tonight to take him out there and then.

The more he thought about neutralizing Torrio there, the more appealing the idea became. The intel from the female croupier was great. He already knew Torrio had given the order to Lucky, who in turn had recruited the Aryan Brotherhood crazies to carry out the hit. But the problem with gunning Torrio down in cold blood was that Jon wanted to know what Torrio knew. He needed to find a way to get Torrio alone, if possible. And, crucially, to be in a position to extract the information as and how he wanted.

He knew a good place to start. He remembered the business from a previous visit to his daughter.

The cab pulled up on West Fifty-Fifth Street, just off Fifth Avenue, outside Malone's Motorcycle Rentals.

Reznick walked into the showroom and looked at the bikes. A collection of gleaming chrome. Yamahas, Suzukis, Kawasakis, BMWs, Ducatis, all top-of-the-line motorcycles. But Reznick had his eyes on a classic American motorcycle brand. He had a penchant for Harleys.

"Morning, sir. Anything particular you got in mind?"

Reznick pointed at the Harley 1200 Sportster. "Beautiful bike."

"Isn't she? You've got to love it."

"How much to rent for a week?"

"A week? I could do you a deal."

Reznick smiled as he admired the bike. He most certainly had an idea in mind. A motorcycle would keep him mobile. A helmet would mean he could go around virtually undetected on the streets of New York. It wasn't a fail-safe system. But it could work to his advantage. At least for a while.

"You can't go wrong with a Harley."

"Very nice. Got a problem, though."

The salesman shrugged. "I'm a problem solver."

"I'm in town for a couple weeks."

"Taking in some shows?"

"That's right. But unfortunately, last night I had my credit cards stolen."

"That's terrible."

"I know, bad luck, right?"

"It's New York—what can I say?"

"Here's the thing. I have cash to rent the bike. And I have my ID."

"Are you kidding me? I love cash! Who doesn't love cash!"

Reznick smiled. "This is America, right?"

"Give me cash any day."

"Good stuff. Thanks."

The salesman lowered his voice as if afraid he would be over-heard. "I can do you a special one-off deal. It's usually for my regulars, but I can do this for you. How does that sound?"

"What are we talking about?"

"Usually, the bike would go for at least forty-five hundred for the week. If you're paying cash, I can do it for four thousand dollars even. You want to shake on it?"

"You got a deal." Reznick shook the man's hand, which gripped his like a vise. He showed him the ID, and the details were quickly scribbled down by the guy. Then he handed over the cash. "And I can take it out now?"

The salesman got the keys and handed them to Reznick with a helmet. "Wheel it out. Phenomenal bike. And the helmet—you can answer and make calls with that baby. It's all integrated for the twenty-first century."

Reznick almost laughed at his stroke of luck. "Thank you."

"You going to be handing it back in exactly one week's time, right?"

"One week from today."

"I love you out-of-town guys. Straight down to business, no angles, no bullshit."

"You got it."

"Enjoy the bike! And watch out for those Uber drivers. Maniacs."

"I'll keep that in mind." Reznick put on his helmet and wheeled the bike onto West Fifty-Fifth Street. He started it up and checked it had a full tank of gas. He pulled away and voice-activated a call.

"I need a home address."

"You on the move?"

"Have we got a fix on a location for Torrio either through his cell phone or his brother's?"

"Gimme a minute. Hold on . . ."

Reznick edged through the near gridlocked Midtown traffic as he got used to handling the powerful motorcycle.

"Jon, I have another client on the other line at the moment. A pressing issue. You'll need to wait."

"Not a problem. Let me know when you get a good fix on his position."

Thirty-Five

A couple of yachts could be seen in the sparkling waters of Long Island Sound, just off the huge Connecticut property of Paul Moretti.

Feldman felt uneasy as he sipped a mojito. He sat in a chair in the middle of the sprawling gardens as his client brooded and paced. Moretti hadn't taken the advice from the FBI's legal counsel well. "I just thought it was important that you know what the FBI thinks is best. Their assessment is that you should make the move now. That's what they said."

Moretti wore a crisp Ralph Lauren polo shirt, chinos, and expensive dark brown loafers and smoked a Cuban cigar as he worked himself into a fury. "I swear to God, I feel like heading across to New York and grabbing Avery by the fucking neck and telling him, face-to-face, what I think of him. I thought we had a deal."

Feldman sat quietly. "It's still in place."

"Is it? Who do they think they're dealing with? Tell them to go fuck themselves."

Feldman cleared his throat. "Not a good idea, with all due respect. The reality is that, in my view, it would be mutually beneficial for you to make an early move. It's the best outcome for you *and* the FBI. You and your family will be safe, no one able to know where you've settled. New identities, the whole nine yards. And the Feds? They make sure their highest-level informant is in a secure, safe place, ready to start his new life. And all you have to do is make the move a little bit sooner than you expected. You were going to make it anyway in a couple of weeks, so what's the difference?"

"What's the difference? The difference is *I* decide when the time is right."

"I'm begging you to take this advice from the FBI. It's the smart move."

His client puffed on the cigar. "I can't believe what I'm hearing. Are you telling me the Feds' lawyer actually told you that? Seriously?"

"That's what he said. He spoke to me face-to-face. In New York. This guy doesn't do favors. But trust me, this is a favor."

"A favor? I don't want no fucking favors. Especially from some lawyer fuck, no disrespect."

"None taken. Listen, he wasn't telling you. It was just advice. Guidance, if you like. That's what I am passing on. Lawyers offer their best advice to their clients. It's about weighing the situation and making the right call."

"And what do you think?"

"You sleep on it. Gives you time to think about it. But the choice is entirely yours. What does it matter if you leave tomorrow or in a few weeks' time?"

"I'll tell you why it matters. I do things how I want to do things. I don't like being ordered around. And not by some FBI smart-ass lawyer. Who the fuck do they think they're dealing with here? I leave when I decide it's the right time to leave, and not a minute before."

Feldman gazed out over the water while his client went red in the face. "I know it's not easy. Change is never easy."

His client sat down at the table and crushed the cigar out in a glass ashtray. "Very true. I think I'm going to miss staring at the water. The calm. The sense of . . ."

"Well-being?"

His client snapped his fingers. "That's it: well-being. I can look out here and see fucking yachts. I won't be able to see yachts or the water in Arizona."

"I don't disagree with you. I love it here too. And I get it. It's a sanctuary for you."

"Thank you."

"I was in Manhattan this morning, and I swear, I was stressed the moment I walked out of my apartment. My blood pressure, it's not good."

"You need to move out of the city."

"I'm thinking about it."

"Mort Feldman, leaving New York?"

"Maybe."

"It ain't gonna happen."

"Who knows?"

"Where you got in mind?"

"I saw a little place in Montauk."

"Montauk? That's nice, very nice. East end of Long Island is beautiful. I have cousins out there."

Feldman rubbed the corners of his eyes. "How long have I been your lawyer?"

"Ten years?"

"Twelve years."

"It that so?"

"In all that time, have I ever given you bad advice?"

"Never."

Feldman smiled. "I represent you to the absolute very best of my abilities. I do everything I can to further your interests. Personal and business. Now, this decision to become a confidential informant for the FBI is both profound and life-changing for you and your family. I get it. But you've weighed up the pros and cons, as have I, and you're making the right call. No doubt about it. But here's the thing: curveballs come at us. This advice is a curveball. It's unexpected. But we deal with it, right?" His client stared off into the distance, distracted. "If push comes to shove, and I had to give my honest legal opinion as to what is in your best interests, after my discussion with the FBI legal counsel, I would say this: head down to Arizona tomorrow night. I'll get a flight lined up, and it's done."

His client looked out over Long Island Sound. "Who the hell can get to me when I'm here? I'll tell you who: no one. I've got this covered. I use the best security system in the world."

"I have no doubt you are a very resourceful and intelligent man. But this Special Forces guy is out of control. He's a wild card. And he's crazy."

"I can deal with him. I've dealt with crazy people my whole life. Besides, I have twenty trained men living here on my estate. Day and night. They work in shifts. I'll feed the fucker to my Dobermans, huh?"

Feldman felt queasy at the very thought. He hated dogs. And the idea of someone being savaged to death by one brought on palpitations.

"Mort, listen to me. Nothing will happen to me."

"Is that your final word?"

"Final word. I don't want to hear any more. I move on the agreed date. I keep to my agreements."

"So, you want me to go back to the FBI and relate that message?"

The client shook his head. "Tell them nothing. We move when I say so."

Thirty-Six

The hours dragged for Reznick. He had been waiting for the call from his hacker friend. He checked his watch. It was now nearly midnight. He shifted in his seat as he hung out in a Midtown diner. A handful of others sitting around. Reading papers. A trucker eating a burger and fries. He watched the guy's gargantuan stomach under the tight-fitting T-shirt moving in time with his mouth. He felt a bit sick. He popped a Dexedrine. He had nursed a succession of cups of strong black coffee as he waited for Trevelle to get in touch. The waiting went on. And on.

Fox News was playing on the TV. The footage showed a reporter talking from the deck of an American aircraft carrier somewhere in the South China Sea. He wondered if Uncle Sam was lining up another foreign war. He twitched a bit when the amphetamines kicked in. He felt wired. Alert. Switched on.

Then his cell phone rang.

Reznick picked it up. "You got any news?"

"The guy is on the move. I have a fix on him."

Reznick finished his coffee and put on the motorcycle helmet. He pulled on the backpack. He dropped a twenty-dollar tip on the table and headed out a side door to the nearby parking garage where he had parked the Harley.

"Are you still there?"

It was weird to have the conversation with his helmet on. "Yeah, I'm still here. So, where is he?"

"I got a visual. He's just leaving the Lincoln Tunnel and is now in Manhattan."

Reznick put his cell phone in his pocket and started up the motorcycle, revving it hard. "Copy that."

A few moments later. "He's twenty blocks south of you."

Reznick checked his mirror and pulled away into the late-night traffic. Dazzling headlights all around. A yellow cab beeping its horn. "Keep the line open."

"Copy that."

Reznick turned the bike around and headed down Fifth Avenue.

"Where, exactly? I'm going at this blind."

"I'm with you. Port Authority Bus Terminal."

"I know where that is. But it's a big fucking place. Can you try and get a fix on exactly where he is? Is he in the terminal? Is he outside the terminal? Is he in the elevator? Give me some triangulation!"

"It's a huge place. I'm working on a precise location."

"I can't imagine him taking a bus, can you?"

Reznick was getting closer. He took another turn and headed south on Ninth Avenue. He sped past an Irish pub he had spent blackout days in when he first returned broken from Iraq. Sitting slumped at the bar, not talking to anybody. A shell of a man. His wife a victim of 9/11. And the horrors of war scarring his mind forever.

"You're ten blocks away."

Reznick saw a panhandler up ahead, crawling on all fours in the middle of the road. He braked hard to avoid running him over.

"I'm into the bus terminal computer systems, surveillance cameras. And . . ."

The panhandler was helped across the road. The lights changed, and Reznick pulled away.

He looked up and saw the monstrous concrete edifice of New York's main bus station. "Are you still there?"

"He's in the parking garage."

"Where, exactly?"

"Hang on. There are hundreds of cameras in and around the terminal. I'm trying to . . . OK, I'm in."

"Where is he?"

"He's on the roof!"

"What?"

"The parking garage of the Port Authority."

"Seriously?"

"It's a black Mercedes SUV."

"And he's parked up on the roof? Right this moment?"

"Affirmative. Real-time. He is sitting behind the wheel."

"Where's his brother? I thought his brother was always with him."

"No sign. Just him."

"What about any of his goons?"

"Nothing. I repeat: he is on his own."

Reznick wondered if Torrio was meeting an escort for some action. He saw the parking garage looming in the next block.

"Yeah, you got it. Entrance coming up."

Reznick felt his heartbeat quicken as he rode up the ramp into the parking garage. "Heading up. You still there?"

"I've got you. Signal is strong."

Reznick edged higher up the garage. He braced himself for what he was about to encounter. A part of him began to wonder if this was a well-laid trap. Maybe it was. But he would find out soon enough.

He rode the bike up the last ramp.

A few moments later, he was on the roof, amid scores of cars.

Reznick slowed down as he looked around.

"Northeast part of the roof. He's parked two from the end."

"Copy that." Reznick turned his bike around and rode twenty yards to the north side of the roof. He edged past the gleaming black Mercedes SUV and spotted a silhouetted figure inside.

"I got eyes on target vehicle. I repeat: got eyes on the vehicle."

"I've got eyes on you too, Jon. That means so will security. But I'm watching the whole roof."

"Copy that."

"Helmet is a nice touch, by the way."

Reznick craned his neck to look up at the surveillance camera.

"Your face is not visible on the camera. I repeat: not visible. Another thing—that corner of the garage, three cars down from where the SUV is—that's a blind spot. Do you copy that?"

Reznick knew what Williams was saying. "Appreciate the heads-up. Do you have his cell phone number?"

"Affirmative. He has his cell phone with him. Be careful."

Reznick parked in the blind spot beside the concrete wall.

"I'm not seeing you."

"Good. Radio silence until this is done."

"Got it."

Reznick got off the bike.

Out of the shadows emerged a man with a gun. "Who the fuck are you?" the man said.

Reznick shrugged. "What the hell is this? I'm a delivery guy."

"What are you delivering up here?"

Reznick feigned ignorance. "I'm on my break."

The guy stepped forward and pressed the gun to Reznick's chest. "My boss doesn't like surprises. I want to see your ID. Who do you work for?"

Reznick nodded, helmet on.

"I said I want to see some ID!"

Reznick leaned forward an inch as if he hadn't heard the man properly. He grabbed the wrist holding the gun and twisted it hard, pointing the muzzle away from him. He twisted the hand as he held the gunman's arm. The man headbutted Reznick's helmet and groaned. "Motherfucker!"

Reznick snatched the gun and smashed his fist hard into the man's neck, right on the carotid artery. The man collapsed, gasping, holding his throat as Reznick stomped on his jaw until it broke. The man passed out, lying prostrate between the cars.

Reznick gathered himself as he put the man's gun in his bag.

Reznick let his gaze wander around the rest of the rooftop parking garage. He walked toward Torrio's car and tapped on the driver's side window.

The window rolled down. Torrio was staring up at him. "What the fuck you want?"

"You got a flat, buddy."

"What the fuck are you saying?"

Reznick raised his voice, not wishing to remove the helmet or lift the visor. "I said you've got a flat."

"Are you kidding me?"

Reznick shook his head. "Rear right, check for yourself."

"Motherfucker. Never a fucking break!"

Torrio got out and walked around to the rear of the car. "What the fuck are you talking about? I can't see no flat."

Reznick pulled out the 9mm Beretta from his waistband and pressed it tight to the back of Torrio's head. "Walk to the motorcycle by the wall."

Torrio instinctively put his hands up. "Who are you?"

"Walk or you die."

Torrio walked toward the bike until he was at the corner. He turned around, his back to the low wall. "You are making a big fucking mistake, pal. Do you know who I am? Do you want money?" He showed a chunky Rolex. "Take this, you dumb fuck!"

Reznick stepped forward and kicked the man hard between the legs.

Torrio crumpled to his knees, face red and contorted in pain. "You're a dead man!"

Reznick smashed the grip of the Beretta into Torrio's temple. He pistol-whipped the cowering mafioso until the blood flowed. Then Reznick grabbed him by the neck and lifted him to his feet. He bent down and got a grip on Torrio's ankle. It seemed like he was going to throw him over the edge. But he didn't. He tipped Torrio headfirst and dangled him over the edge.

"What the fuck are you doing, you maniac? Let me up!"

"I want a name."

"Don't drop me! Please! Mary, mother of Jesus!"

"Why did you order the killing of Bill Eastland?"

Torrio's eyes were black. Terrified. "What the fuck are you talking about?"

"The guy up in Maine. Why did you have him and his wife killed?"

"Please! Please! I just gave the order!"

"Who told you to have him killed?"

"I don't know."

Reznick took away one hand, holding Torrio tight by the right ankle. "I'm losing patience!"

"Moretti! It was nothing to do with me!"

"Who's Moretti?"

"The boss. Paul Moretti got the message to me."

"How did he get the message to you?"

"I was handed an envelope by his lawyer. Little snake."

"Name?"

"Feldman. Mort Feldman."

"Where did he give you the note?"

"A church in the Bronx."

"Tell me once more: Who gave the order from the top?"

"Moretti! I told you! It was him! I swear on my son's life!"

"Did you keep the letter?"

"I burned it. Let me up!"

Reznick held Torrio for a few more lingering moments. He was sorely tempted to let the fucker fall to his death. "You better not be lying to me. Are you lying to me? You're getting heavier!"

"I swear on my mother's life, my son's life, my wife's life. I swear to God, it was Moretti who gave the go-ahead!"

Reznick hauled up Torrio, who collapsed in a crumpled heap, cowering, crying, and bloodied. He smelled of piss.

"Happy now?"

Reznick stared down at him. "You motherfuckin' piece of shit!" He stomped down on Torrio's head until the man slipped into unconsciousness. He rifled Torrio's jacket and pulled out a cell phone. He put it in his pocket.

Then he walked over to the Harley and climbed on. He knew he needed to get out of there. Fast. He turned the key and rode across the rooftop parking lot and down the ramp. Down and down.

Then he was out on the dark streets of Midtown Manhattan.

Thirty-Seven

Meyerstein watched the drama unfold in real-time on the big screens in the FBI's fifth-floor Strategic Information and Operations Center in DC. Her heart was in her mouth as Reznick sped through the streets on a motorcycle, weaving at high speed in and out of traffic as he rode onto I-95.

She adjusted the Bluetooth headphones, allowing her to communicate with her staff watching on laptops.

"Do we have any idea where he's headed?"

"Ma'am," Josh Abrahams, a rookie agent and IT specialist, said, "we believe he might be directed via a third party at this moment. Cell phone signals are changing channels. And this indicates an encrypted conversation is going on as we speak."

"Do you have a positive fix on Reznick's cell phone?"

"We do. But the signal is flipping wildly between GPS locations. There's also some sort of white noise on the line. We're trying to strip it out, but no luck so far."

"How is this possible?"

"The signals show a level of advanced encryption. Military grade."

Meyerstein shook her head. She knew it had to be Trevelle Williams.

Letitia Banks, who was on loan to them from the NSA, said, "I'm running a program. And I've detected advanced jamming technologies being deployed to a program on Reznick's cell phone."

Meyerstein watched the figure on the bike doing ninety on the freeway, chopper overhead. Suddenly, the chopper veered sharply off, losing sight of Reznick. "What the hell happened? Talk to me."

Josh Abrahams said, "Ma'am, the pilot is reporting a drone within fifty feet. He took evasive action."

"A drone? What kind of drone?"

"A quadcopter, he thinks. A civilian drone. You can buy them off the internet for a thousand bucks."

"Well, that's just great. I can't believe what I'm hearing. Get that chopper back onto Reznick!"

"Working on it," he said.

Meyerstein surveyed the footage of traffic on the Union City Turnpike as the helicopter swooped low. The minutes crawled by as the chopper tried to locate the bike. "Come on, people—he's getting away! I want a visual!"

A few moments later, on the big screens, a fast-moving motorcycle headed north.

"Forty-Third Street in North Bergen," Letitia Banks said. "We got a fix!"

"Copy that," Meyerstein said. "Let's not lose him this time. Can we apprehend?"

"Not at this time, ma'am. We have two vehicles en route. Five hundred yards from target."

The chopper kept the motorcycle in its sights.

"Talk to me, people!" Meyerstein said, raising her voice.

The voice of FBI Special Agent Harry Schultz: "He's right up ahead of me. Just say the word."

"Intercept with immediate effect! I repeat: intercept!"

A minute later on the big screens, two black SUVs sped into view as they overtook Reznick and expertly boxed him in.

He screeched to a halt, narrowly avoiding smashing into one of the vehicles.

The agents emerged from the SUVs, guns drawn, as traffic thundered past.

Reznick got off his bike and kneeled down, hands on his head.

An agent stepped forward and yanked off the helmet.

Reznick faced the chopper camera, no emotion visible on his face.

Thirty-Eight

Meyerstein hadn't slept in twenty-four hours and was struggling to stay focused. She freshened her makeup in the bathroom. Then she picked up her papers from her office and headed into the conference room. She felt all eyes on her. She was responsible for Reznick. She was going to have to take the flak.

Crabtree glanced at her briefing paper before she fixed her gaze on Meyerstein. "Hard to know where to start, Martha. Your guy, Jon Reznick, has jeopardized one of the Agency's most sensitive operations against international crime gangs."

"That's correct," Meyerstein said. She looked at Franklin. "I take full responsibility for what happened."

Franklin Masson looked benevolently at her. "He was not under your direction for this, so I don't think it's appropriate for you take responsibility in this case."

Crabtree shook her head. "Sorry, but I strongly disagree. Jon Reznick is only hanging around because Martha has allowed this whole messed-up situation to develop. I mean, it's ridiculous. He was photographed holding Joseph Torrio by his ankles."

"He wasn't identified. But I agree, it's not good."

"Not good? Seriously, Martha, it is beyond the pale. I've never heard of such violations of protocol and ethics."

"That surprises me, since you work for the CIA."

Crabtree glared at Meyerstein. "It'll be all over the *Post* today. And it will be picked up by all the channels under the sun. It will be on YouTube. But perhaps most worryingly, our informant might get cold feet on our deal. That's how serious this is."

Meyerstein didn't flinch. "I don't think I need any lectures from a CIA employee on ethics or protocol."

Franklin flung up his hands. "Enough! Both of you! Now listen, I don't entertain feuds of any sort. I don't want any interagency rivalry bullshit. I'm not having it. Rachel, your tone was uncalled-for. I'd like you to apologize."

Crabtree nodded and forced a smile. "Martha, I'm sorry. I did cross the line there. I hope you accept this apology in good faith."

Meyerstein sat impassively. She felt like walking over to Crabtree and grabbing her by the throat. "I accept, of course, and I'd like to apologize for snapping back."

Franklin went on. "The big picture comes first. I'm talking Paul Moretti. That's the call that was made. And we will abide by this. We can't allow anything to get in the way of obtaining the names and associates of Moretti in Europe and Asia."

Martha realized that Franklin's use of Moretti's name meant everyone in the room had become privy to the knowledge.

"Our priority as of now is to get Moretti to a safe house, so he can start his new life as one of our most prized informants with a new identity."

Martha said, "Without trying to get too bogged down, I would like to put it on the record, Franklin, that Torrio categorically did not greenlight the killings of Bill Eastland and his wife."

Franklin scribbled down the details. "It's a fair point. Rachel, what else have we got?"

"I disagree with Martha. As I pointed out at our last meeting, we have confirmation through the cell phone conversation that Joseph Torrio gave the go-ahead. There is nothing linking Moretti."

Franklin frowned. "Do we have Moretti's personal cell phone or his wife's or any of his closest circle to confirm any connection to this?"

Crabtree shook her head. "Absolutely nothing."

"So, we have Torrio in the frame. Torrio most likely would not have acted without the go-ahead from those above him. Besides, there is no electronic surveillance or anything else to otherwise indicate anyone else's involvement. Torrio, as of now, will take the fall. And he might decide to throw his boss under the bus to save his skin."

Cesar Mendoza looked up from his laptop and cleared his throat. "That is absolutely true. This had to have come from Moretti. And when the Aryan Brotherhood wackos go on trial, it'll lead to Torrio, and when it comes to Torrio, his defense will point out that he was carrying out orders. And the orders would point to the boss. Moretti. It's problematic, alright."

Crabtree said, "It's a hypothetical scenario. It may or may not be the case. He may have known about it. But without proof, we have nothing."

Meyerstein said, "Then, if Moretti knew about it or knew it was in the works, he should have alerted us."

"I guess that's correct. But we're still tying up the loose ends to have him as a bona fide confidential informant. I think this is big-picture stuff. The specter of international terrorist groups potentially getting their hands on suitcase nukes . . . that's the priority. Far more important than domestic killings."

"I disagree," Martha said. "We can't turn a blind eye to a double murder, no matter the possibility of receiving some kind of intel further down the line. We could nail Moretti and disrupt any potential terrorist network at the same time."

"Answer me this, Martha," Crabtree said. "Why would Moretti take such a risk, ordering the killing of Eastland and his wife, when he's so close to dropping off the grid?"

"He's crazy," Meyerstein said. "Wasn't he once diagnosed as a psychopath? So, he would have no qualms. Besides, maybe that's how he gets his kicks? He kills for fun."

Franklin said, "It's a possibility, I accept that."

"Then, as it stands, he would be an accessory to murder, would he not?"

Crabtree looked around the table. "The fact remains, there is no evidence that Paul Moretti was aware of this double hit. No evidence at all. Any lawyer would have the case thrown out."

Franklin took more notes, as did Mendoza, tapping away on the laptop. "We are confident that once we get our teams of forensic accountants to pore over the business interests of Moretti in the Caymans, Bermuda, Switzerland, Panama, and Russia, it will take down the terrorist network. It will also rake in potentially tens of billions in assets for the US Treasury. It's that big a deal. Also, the names of all those who are hiding behind seemingly respectable businesses will be laid bare for us. If Moretti can give us that . . ."

Crabtree said, "We need to stop being so queasy. My overriding concern is the same as the FBI's. We need this deal to happen, no matter what. But the actions of this renegade might spook Paul Moretti. He is not a man to be messed with. If he suspects that this is bringing heat on him from the other families or unwanted publicity before he disappears off the radar, he could pull out."

Meyerstein sat in silence.

"We're so close, we cannot—dare not—jeopardize this further. Which is why I propose that Jon Reznick be charged with these offenses and detained until this is over. House arrest. And maybe even have him moved to a black site, out of sight, somewhere overseas."

Meyerstein shook her head. "This is not the CIA, in case you hadn't noticed." She sensed she was losing the argument. "OK, listen: I get the importance of this deal with Moretti." She turned to Franklin. "So, the legal agreement which we're going to put in place for Moretti—how far are we from having that finalized?"

Franklin shrugged. "A matter of days. It should be signed and sealed by his legal team and ours. And then, we can get to work. Perhaps we can get Reznick released from custody once that's all over with."

Meyerstein couldn't countenance that. "I'm sure if Reznick gets a great lawyer, which he will because he's smart, he'll be out in seventy-two hours, max."

Crabtree nodded. "I understand. And I agree with you: a great lawyer would get him out. So, what do you propose? Can we come up with a solution for Reznick that would satisfy everyone?"

"Here's what I propose. I would like us to draw up a legally binding agreement with Jon Reznick."

"To do what?" Crabtree said.

"The contract would be that Reznick agrees that he and anyone he knows—his associates, Delta buddies—can't go anywhere near Paul Moretti. And we would put a six-mile exclusion order in place around Moretti's main property in Connecticut. So, if Reznick breaches that order, he will open himself up to a host of charges, including the attempted murder of Joseph Torrio, torturing Lucky down in Texas, and so on. You get the picture. Quid pro quo."

Crabtree rubbed her face and leaned back in her seat. "I might be able to live with that. He would have to sign it and understand that under no circumstances may he or his associates go anywhere near Moretti's home. He's too important. And I would widen the scope. I would insist on a clause that states that Reznick cannot enter New York State or Connecticut until this is over. I don't want him bumping into Moretti if he's in Manhattan or out in the Hamptons or at his place in coastal Connecticut."

"Good point," Meyerstein said. "Franklin?"

"I can live with that too. I like that idea, Martha. Very creative."

Mendoza grinned. "I'm in. I say we get the Director to agree, and if he's fine with it, we get this buttoned up. I don't want Reznick anywhere near Paul Moretti."

Thirty-Nine

Reznick sat in a basement cell in the cockroach-infested Manhattan Detention Complex, also known as the Tombs. It was as if the room had been designed to crush the human spirit. The concrete. The bleakness.

He had already done hundreds of push-ups and sit-ups to stay sharp and focused. His training kicked in as soon as the cell door shut. It was important not to feel like a prisoner. It was important to stay mentally and physically strong. It was no sweat to him. But looking at the other poor saps who moped around, weeping and staring at the walls, he could see the despair. He didn't blame them. He felt sorry for each of them. Druggies, wannabe gangsters, street thugs, alcoholics, and a smattering of the homeless.

A guard walked over to his cell and pointed at him. "You Reznick?"

"Yeah."

The burly guard opened up the steel door, then cuffed Reznick. "A lady wants to see you," he said. "You going to behave?"

"I'm always on my best behavior for the ladies."

The guard laughed. "You're fucking crazy. What's with all that fitness stuff?"

"Keeps my mind occupied. You should try it sometime."

The guard gave a rueful smile. "The last time I did exercise like that, I was in boot camp."

"Never too late, man."

The guard shook his head as he led Reznick down a series of dirty and dingy corridors until they entered a windowless room.

Meyerstein was standing, hands clasped in front of her. She stood beside a small wooden table, a briefcase on top, a chair on either side. "Uncuff him, please."

The guard grimaced. "Ma'am, that's not our protocols."

"I'll take full responsibility. Your boss has my details. I trust that will suffice."

The guard shrugged as he unlocked the cuffs. "I'll be outside if you need me, ma'am."

"Appreciate that. Thank you."

The guard locked the door behind him, leaving them in the concrete room together.

"Take a seat, Jon."

Reznick pulled up a chair and slumped down. "How you doing?"

"Not great."

"Why's that?"

"Why's that? Well, let me think. You gun down one of the Aryan Brotherhood guys who you believe killed Bill and Elspeth Eastland, then you head down to West Texas to find the rest of them, after which you stop off at a strip club where you proceed to beat up a business owner with Mob ties. And then, you track down a Mob enforcer named Joseph Torrio. To cap it all off—and the reason why you're here in jail in Manhattan—you dangle him off a parking garage roof in Midtown. Do you want me to go on? Are you out of your mind?"

"Maybe I am."

"Don't be so goddamn flippant. This is outrageous!"

"Not half as outrageous as that fucker ordering a hit on Bill."

"My colleagues say you've gone rogue. Again. Do you ever think for one moment about the impact your actions will have on my job? A job I love. What about me? What about us?"

"What about us?"

"Have you considered how this behavior impacts our relationship?"

"Not a whole lot."

Meyerstein stared at him, hurt in her eyes. "That's it, then? There is no us?"

"Of course there is. But I can't in good conscience walk on by after my friend and his wife were killed in cold blood. Don't forget, I didn't start this."

"That doesn't excuse your actions. You're acting as if you just don't care what you do or who you hurt."

"Martha, listen to me. You have your job to do. And I respect that."

"Do you? It looks like you're hanging me out to dry. From where I'm standing it sure as hell doesn't look like you respect the job I do, my responsibilities, or me for that matter."

"What the hell does that mean? I most certainly do respect you and care about you. I care about you more than I have about anyone for a long, long time."

Meyerstein jabbed her thumb into her chest. "Do you know I'm doing everything in my power to keep you free? Do you know how much slack I'm cutting you?"

Reznick bowed his head. He had no doubt Meyerstein was doing everything she could to get him out of jail.

"Who was the one who ensured your hearing in Maine was private so not a soul would know about it?"

"Point taken."

"Yes, it was good for the FBI too, protecting national security and all that. I accept that. But it was also good for you."

"Quid pro quo and all that."

"That's the way it works. It helped us both."

"I appreciate that."

Meyerstein's gaze wandered around the concrete walls. "Well, you've got a funny way of showing it. Who the hell do you think you are?"

"I'll tell you. I'm a guy who caught that bastard escaping from Rockland, masked up, then firing on my vehicle. I confronted him. And he got what he deserved."

"I believe that was self-defense. But you're on shakier ground with what went down in Texas. That wasn't self-defense, was it? You are not acting in a rational manner."

"I'm not facing rational men. The type of men who did this have no scruples. They don't give a shit for rationality. The end justifies the means in their world."

"Here's what's going to happen: you are going to go home. The funeral is the day after tomorrow."

Reznick bowed his head again. He felt guilty that he had clean forgotten about the funeral. He hadn't been back in touch with Tom Cain.

"I have spoken to the district attorney's office in Rockland, and we have come to an arrangement. I'm vouching for you, and they are happy with that. Get back to your old life."

"That's easier said than done."

"You need to move on."

"What if I don't want to?"

Meyerstein shook her head. "I'm going to give you an opportunity to make the call. It will be your decision. You can either take the deal I'm offering and go back to Rockland, or you can dismiss the deal. If you take the deal, you are free, with some conditions."

"Which are?"

"You must never go anywhere near Paul Moretti, nor send any-one else after him. You must leave New York State and not enter it again, or Connecticut for that matter, until we say so."

"What the hell for?"

"We have our reasons."

"And if I don't take the deal?"

"You will be refused bail. I'll make sure of that. You'll be held until your trial for threatening the life of Joseph Torrio and others."

"Are you serious?"

"What do you think?"

"I have to leave New York State and not enter Connecticut, until you say so?"

"Correct."

"You're protecting someone, aren't you?"

Meyerstein opened her briefcase and pulled out an envelope. She handed it to him. "Open it up; it's a legal contract. All you have to do is sign."

"Can I discuss this with a lawyer?"

"Of course. I suspect they will advise you to sign. But by all means, speak to a lawyer."

Reznick opened the envelope and scanned the contract. It was dense legal prose. "So, let me get this straight: I'm a free man, apart from not being allowed anywhere in New York State or Connecticut or anywhere near Moretti, right?"

"Correct."

"And if I don't sign, I can't go back for the funeral?"

"Your choice."

Reznick smiled at Meyerstein. "You're playing hardball."

"Take it or leave it."

He signed and dated the document, before handing it back to her.

"Collect your things. You'll be flown back to Maine under escort by two of my best."

Forty

Feldman leaned back in his chair. Outside his office window, the sky darkened by the minute, rain clouds rolling in. They were in for a thunderstorm.

He wanted to escape the treadmill of work. Being at the mercy of a certified maniac, his number one client. He had begun to contemplate retirement. He just wanted to close his eyes and not have to worry. He imagined what a world without work would look like. A world without deadlines. A world without billable hours. A world without cell phones. A world without psychotic clients screaming over the phone.

He imagined a house down in the Lower Keys, Florida. Azure sky. Turquoise waters. Maybe a boat. Stopping by a laid-back bar for a beer. Maybe a Bloody Mary at sunset. He had visited Sugarloaf Key. He knew people who lived down in the Keys throughout the winter. He could do with that.

He was sick of working night and day for Moretti. The money was great. Actually, the money was sensational. But it wasn't even about money anymore. He had $23 million in three bank accounts. He had blue chip stock in Apple, Tesla, and biotech companies, among others. He even had some Bitcoin.

Feldman had no ties. He had been divorced for ten long years. His kids were all grown up. Two lived in Europe, one in California. His ex-wife had headed back to North Carolina.

He preferred to live in Manhattan. It was where his clients expected him to be. But empty beaches and endless blue skies and long days ahead of him had begun to appeal to him like never before.

Maybe once he got his main client, Moretti, to his safe house in Arizona, he could give it all up.

Feldman's desk phone rang, snapping him out of his reverie. He picked it up. "Yes?"

"She's arrived, sir," his secretary said.

"Send her in."

Feldman opened his door to greet her.

Gillian Rossi flashed her trademark smile. She wore a perfectly cut honey-brown suit and killer heels and carried an elegant brief-case. "I haven't got long, Mort," she said.

Feldman shook her hand. "I understand." He had dated her for a few months five years earlier. The two realized they didn't have much in common. He liked watching ball games on TV. He enjoyed a drink. She, by contrast, was a Pilates nut. Working out night and day. It was exhausting. Now she was the US Attorney for the Southern District of New York.

He pointed to the sofa in the far corner of his office. "Please."

Rossi sat down demurely, briefcase at her feet. She looked around the office. "This is nice. Good aspect."

"Yeah, moved in a couple years back. Anyway, lovely to see you again." Feldman pulled up a seat and smiled. "Very much appreciate seeing you in person. I know you have a tight schedule today."

Rossi shook her head. "You have no idea."

"Problems?"

"You could say that."

"What's wrong?"

"Fox News are bastards."

Feldman wanted to laugh. He really did want to laugh. He had been watching the interview a couple of hours earlier. "What happened?" he asked.

"Reporter bitch kept on bugging me about my son being busted for pot in his dorm at Duke."

Feldman shrugged. "Are you kidding me?"

"I swear to God, Mort. They're already making memes on Twitter."

"To hell with them. Pot? Jesus Christ, I thought it was compulsory to smoke pot in college."

Rossi closed her eyes for a moment. "It's tough."

"I get it. When it gets personal, it hurts, I know. Listen, can I get you a cup of coffee? Glass of water? Fruit juice?"

Rossi smiled. "No, I'm good. I just wanted to say I have now formally authorized and signed the necessary legal documents in connection with your client's high-level confidential informant status. I know you've worked hard to get this over the line."

"Hey, that's what we're here for, right? To help our clients. But it's also in the government's interest too, don't forget."

Rossi smiled. "Our last meeting, you mentioned you had a little something for me."

Feldman snapped his fingers. "Nearly forgot, of course." He walked over to a painting on the wall, lifted it up, and punched in the code for his personal office safe. He reached in and pulled out a briefcase. The same kind of briefcase Rossi had at her feet. He locked the safe and put the painting back in place. He set the briefcase at her feet as she handed over hers. "Are you sure this is how you want it?"

"Secret bank accounts aren't as secret as they used to be. Bitcoin is trackable. Gold is heavy. No, this works for me."

Feldman slid the briefcase under his desk. He turned to face Rossi, who was already on her feet, holding the new briefcase, arm outstretched.

"Sorry this is a brief meeting," she said, shaking his hand, "but my car's waiting."

"Do you want to check it before you go?"

"I trust you. We're lawyers, after all."

Feldman grinned. "It's just a small gift for your future political ambitions. But also a thank-you from my client for ensuring his arrangement gets the green light."

Rossi winked at him as he opened his door for her. "Let's set up something next week. Lunch?"

"With pleasure."

Rossi brushed past him as her cell phone began to ring. She pressed the phone tight to her ear. "Tell them I'm on my way."

She strode through his outer office to the elevators before he shut the door again. The US Attorney for the Southern District of New York had walked out with a briefcase stuffed with nonsequential hundred-dollar bills totaling one million dollars. A little thank-you present from Paul Moretti.

Forty-One

Night had fallen as Reznick stared out over Penobscot Bay.

A place and space to think. His mind flashed on fleeting images of the last few sweltering days chasing the Aryan Brotherhood crew down south. Then the showdown at a crummy bar in the middle of West Texas. The back of beyond. He was glad to have made it home in one piece.

It had always been his sanctuary. But Eastland's killing had shattered the peace and calm of the town.

He closed his eyes for a few moments. The sound of the waves crashing onto the rocks below. It was good to have made it home. But a lingering sadness remained.

Reznick could never again look forward to seeing the beaming face of Bill Eastland in a bar. No more growly voice over the phone. No more meandering conversations long into the night over beers and whiskey. But more than anything, no more animated conversations about Eastland's old pal, Reznick's father. They were cut from the same cloth. Old-school toughs. No compromise. No bullshit. What you saw was what you got. If you didn't like it, so fucking what. They were as hard as nails. They had to be, to be the sort of men you would want by your side as you fought in the jungles of Vietnam, hunkered down and ready to attack.

Reznick's cell phone rang.

"Dad?" The beautiful voice of his daughter, Lauren.

Reznick sat up and smiled. He hadn't heard from her for a few days. It was so nice and comforting to hear her soft voice. "Hey, honey, how are you?"

"I'm OK, thanks."

"How's work?"

"Crazy busy."

"Glad to hear it. You in New York?"

"Yeah, just finished for the day. Just winding down now."

Reznick sighed. "I'm sorry I haven't gotten in touch. You know the service for Bill and Elspeth is coming up, right?"

"I'm so sorry, Dad. I can't believe he's gone."

"It's a big shock."

"I know how much you liked him." She sighed. "Martha told me what happened down in Texas and in New York."

Reznick closed his eyes. He wished Meyerstein hadn't talked to his daughter about his vengeful actions. But he was most concerned his behavior would jeopardize her job at the FBI.

"She also told me about how you shot one of the guys."

"I don't want to talk about that, Lauren."

"I'm glad you took one of them down."

Reznick felt his throat tighten.

"Martha said you went down south after the rest of that crew."

"I really don't want to talk about it."

"You also dangled some New York Mafia guy off a Midtown roof? Dad, seriously? That's crazy."

Reznick shook his head. "These are crazy people. Sometimes violence is the only language they understand."

"Dad, this leaves me in a difficult position. I felt awkward when Martha told me."

"I know that."

"I work for the FBI. I love you; you're my dad. But, come on, Dad, what about me? My career?"

"It is what it is, honey."

A silence stretched between them for a few moments. "Your actions reflect on me."

"I don't want this to reflect on you. It's on me."

"That's not how I felt after I spoke to Martha a few hours ago. Like I said, it puts me in a really difficult position. I don't want to take sides."

"You don't have to explain. You work for the FBI, I get it. Don't sweat it."

"Yeah, but I do. You're my dad."

"What did I always say, honey?"

"'Do your job. And do it well.'"

"That's right. And I'm very proud of you."

"Martha was seriously pissed. I've never heard her like that before."

"She's got a lot on her mind. And I probably don't help matters."

Lauren let out a small laugh. "You're right there."

"Listen, I'm back home. I cleared the air with Martha. And we're good. So, hopefully we can all move on. What do you say?"

"You're not going to do anything like that again?"

"All you need to know is I love you, and I'm looking forward to seeing you soon. What happened happened, OK? I don't want to talk about that. Time to move on."

"I will, if you promise to consider your actions in the future. Dad, I'm begging you: think of my career."

Reznick closed his eyes. She was right. He hadn't considered for one moment the impact his actions would have on his daughter's nascent career in the FBI. The fact that she was based in New

York, where her father was acting like a crazy man, wasn't a good look for her.

"It can't go on."

"Like I said, I don't want to talk about that. Listen, it's the funeral the day after tomorrow. Will you be able to get home for that? I was hoping you would."

"I'd like to, Dad, but that's not an option just now. I have back-to-back twelve-hour days."

"Of course, I understand. I'm very proud of you. You get your work ethic from your mother for sure."

"Why don't you come down to New York after the funeral?"

Reznick groaned before he could stop himself. "That's just not possible at this time."

"Why not?"

"I don't want to get into it. I would love to see you. You know that, right?"

"How about I head up in a couple months? I'm sure things will have quieted down on my end."

"That sounds terrific."

"Listen, I've got to go. Got a Pilates class in half an hour."

"Take care of yourself. And remember one thing. I love you. I always will."

Forty-Two

Reznick stood at the graveside in an overcoat, collar turned up. The slate-gray skies hung low as a soft rain fell. He watched as the polished coffins of Bill and Elspeth Eastland, peppered by raindrops, were lowered into their final resting place.

The minister, who knew Bill, said a few well-chosen, heartfelt words. "Bill Eastland was born in a one-bedroom house less than half a mile from where we stand today. He was brought up in this town, he fought overseas, he served Rockland and Knox County with distinction as a highly respected police officer. He cared about his town. And he cared for the lives of countless veterans who had reason to thank him for his charity. He might have been a tough, gruff man to some of you. But the Bill we knew, so beloved by his wife, had a heart of gold. He will be sorely missed by us all."

The sound of a woman crying filtered through the assembled mourners.

Helen Eastland sheltered under an umbrella with her husband. She was an only child and had moved down to Washington, DC, to become a corporate lobbyist. She was two years younger than Reznick. They had gone to the same school. But he hardly knew her.

His gaze wandered around the mourners. A sprinkling of dead-eyed Vietnam veterans from the Rockland area. He saw the same stoicism his father had shown. The same demeanor as Eastland. Impassive. The hurt was inside, so deep inside. Invisible. But none of them let the mask slip.

It was the way they were made. The way that war and fighting and death had scarred them. To show feelings was to show weakness. It was only those who developed such steeliness, such coldness, who survived.

Reznick felt all the same old feelings tugging at him as the rain fell. The shame. The rage in his soul. The terrible darkness and anger which could not be doused.

"Ashes to ashes, dust to dust," the minister said, clasping the Bible tight to his chest.

Reznick stood for what seemed like a lifetime. He thought of Eastland. The memories of the tough-guy cop and veteran. The man who had lived with honor.

A few moments later, the assembled mourners drifted away, out of the cemetery, back to their cars.

Reznick hung around until there was only Helen and her husband. He stepped forward.

"I just wanted to say I'm so sorry for your loss, Helen," he said. "I knew your mother and father very well."

"Jon?"

Reznick nodded. "That's right. Long time no see."

"Oh my God." Helen hugged him tight. "Thanks for coming. The police told me what happened. And how you got one of them."

"I'm just sorry I wasn't there to prevent it."

Helen dabbed her eyes. "My dad talked about you a lot."

"Your father was someone I looked up to. He was a great friend to my father, as you know. The whole town will miss him."

"What exactly happened? The police said you went after them. And you seriously injured one."

Reznick was reluctant to go into details. "It's a long story."

"I'm glad. I'm not a vengeful person. But my parents didn't deserve to die like that."

"No, they did not."

Helen clasped her husband's hand. "We're having a drink afterward at the Haven Hotel, if you'd like to join us."

"That's very kind of you. And once again, sincere condolences."

Reznick turned away as Helen and her husband thanked the minister. He watched them slowly walk back to a waiting limo.

Reznick stood alone in the rain as the mourners drifted away. He was the last to leave. He stood at the graveside for a few minutes in silent contemplation. He thought of the last time he had seen Eastland, propped up at the Rockland Tavern, watching a Red Sox game. He had sat there with his friend, knowing nothing about Eastland's descent into the abyss with his degenerate gambling. The man had always been larger than life. But not once had Eastland confided in Reznick the extent of his gambling addiction and his colossal debts.

The more he thought about how his friend had been killed for a debt, the angrier Reznick got. A burning fury deep down inside. Raw. He felt angry at his friend. Not only for jeopardizing his own life and that of his churchgoing wife. But for the pointlessness of it. All for the sake of gambling. What a waste. What a wretched waste of life.

Reznick felt an ache in his heart. An emptiness. He turned and headed back to his car. A couple of guys wearing suits stood beside a black SUV. Reznick thought they looked like Feds. A generic look.

The back door of the SUV opened.

Martha Meyerstein got out and walked toward him. "Hi, Jon."

"Hey."

"We need to talk," she said.

"What about?"

"About you. We believe your life is in danger."

"From who?"

"That's what I want to talk to you about."

Forty-Three

The rain abated as the FBI tailed Reznick all the way home. The Feds stayed inside the SUV. Meyerstein followed him inside.

Reznick made them both some strong black coffee and headed out onto the back deck, overlooking the choppy waters of Penobscot Bay. He got a blanket for Meyerstein and wrapped it around her.

Meyerstein flushed. "Thanks."

Reznick sat down next to her. "So, what's on your mind?"

"A lot, as you can imagine."

"I'm guessing this might have something to do with my trip down to Texas."

"And other incidents."

He grinned. "Like dangling the Mafia sleazeball off a parking garage roof?"

Meyerstein's eyes grew cold. "Jon, we're talking life and death. Your life."

Reznick nodded as he sipped his coffee. "So, you're saying I'm being targeted by them."

"You catch on quick."

Reznick sat in silence.

"We have credible information from a couple of sources within a prominent crime family. They are actively trying to track down who was responsible for that stunt you pulled in New York."

"It figures."

"The fact you were wearing a motorcycle helmet works in your favor, but there is a $500,000 bounty on your head."

"So, what do you want me to do about it?"

"That's why I'm here, in person. I think the wise move would be to move you to protective custody, at least until this is all over."

Reznick gulped some of the coffee. "I've already agreed not to go back into New York or Connecticut until this blows over. Isn't that enough?"

"Our best guess is that we're better safe than sorry, and that for your own good, a move into secure FBI protective custody is the best course of action. Maybe somewhere on the West Coast."

Reznick groaned. "The West Coast? I don't think so."

"Jon, listen to me. I care about you. But you've crossed so many lines over the last week. You've broken laws. You've killed a man. You've tortured multiple others. I'm being put under enormous pressure from within the FBI to make sure you are kept on a tight leash."

Reznick bowed his head.

"I'm still here for you. I want to help. But you have to help me help you."

"Let's get something straight. I don't hide from anyone. I'm not that kind of man."

"No one said you were. But we are talking a sophisticated crime family. People who play for keeps. People who kill as and when required."

"I know that, Martha."

"They strike at their choosing. It might be a few weeks, months, maybe years. But you are in danger until this situation is resolved to our satisfaction."

Reznick mused on that point.

"We need to get you to someplace safe."

"Not interested."

"What do you mean, you're not interested? This is a serious and credible threat."

"I'll take my chances. Besides, I figure I have a better chance of survival outside of FBI protective custody."

"That is nonsense! We will take care of you."

"Any guarantees with that?"

"You're a stubborn man, Jon. You're not making the right move or the smart move."

"I'll decide what's right for me."

Meyerstein got up from her seat and took off the blanket. "I'm sorry I couldn't persuade you."

"I've agreed to the deal where I stay put. I'll honor that."

Meyerstein turned and headed for the door. "Just make sure you do."

Forty-Four

Feldman's head swam from the Xanax. He had been picked up by a limousine outside his Fifth Avenue apartment and driven all the way up to East Harlem. He walked into a classic old-school Italian eatery, Freddy's. The place was empty apart from one diner. The jukebox was playing Frank, of course. "Come Fly with Me."

He saw Paul Moretti sitting at the best table, talking to the owner of the restaurant.

Feldman sat down. "I didn't expect to be meeting in such a public place, Paul," he said.

"Relax. This is private dining. Just me and you. Let's eat. Then we can talk."

Feldman could not believe Moretti had left his Connecticut compound. He knocked back a glass of red wine to calm his nerves even more. He had mixed booze with Xanax before, during a flight out to the West Coast a couple years back, and slept all the way there. Then when he arrived at his Beverly Hills hotel, he slept for an additional twelve hours straight.

His anxiety had risen to new levels now, though. Maybe it was something to do with overwork. Maybe the stakes involved in Moretti becoming a full-fledged FBI informant. Maybe it was because he was concerned that his client was out and about with a Special Forces guy after him. Maybe it was the months and months of work in setting up Moretti with his new life in Arizona. Maybe he was worried that Moretti was going to have him killed. It had all taken its toll on Feldman, recently waking him up in the night in a cold sweat.

The more he thought about that, the more depressed he got. It would make sense if Feldman got whacked. Killing the one man who knew what Moretti was about to do—become the highest-level FBI informant in the Italian-American Mafia. Christ, if Moretti didn't have him killed, maybe the other crime families would.

Feldman concealed his fears and smiled as they exchanged small talk, eating a beautiful meal of lobster, spinach, and mushroom ravioli. He finished his red wine, head swimming. Booze and chemicals. Christ, this was so fucked up. Why wasn't he in Florida enjoying an early retirement? No stress. Days by the pool. Walking in the fresh air. Blue skies. A bit of shopping in Bal Harbour. Lunch in South Beach.

The waiter brought a fresh glass and filled it with fine red wine.

Feldman dabbed his mouth with the napkin and took another sip. "Very nice, thank you." He waited until the table was cleared before he started up a conversation. "Paul, really nice to see you again. But I'm surprised, if I'm being honest. I thought your plans were in place. You were to stay in Connecticut until the move."

"I understand your feelings. And you're probably correct about me getting out and about. But the family who runs this restaurant—I've known them all my life. Besides, I've read the contract. The conditions are quite clear. The old life I had will be gone. Forever."

Feldman had never felt so much tension throughout his body. It was as if his heart was going to explode at that very moment. "That's correct, Paul. It's just that at this delicate point, what with this special forces crazy on the loose, I'm not sure this is a prudent move."

"Who gives a fuck about prudent? I know I don't. I live my life as I wish. And I've got to be honest: I don't give a fuck what the

FBI or the government says. Might never get this chance again. It's like a last supper, right?"

Feldman could see there was no point in arguing. His gaze wandered around the intimate restaurant. "What, am I one of your disciples?"

Moretti laughed, pointing a fork uncomfortably close to Feldman's nose. "You're a funny guy." He lowered his voice. "I made sure there were no other customers tonight. Called in a little favor."

"How you feeling?"

"About what?"

"The move."

"Mixed feelings. I'm going to miss my apartment in New York and my house in Connecticut. But the weather will be a hell of a lot nicer, so that's a plus."

"Arizona is favorable to income and business taxes. So, once we restructure your new companies, it'll be quite a bit more in your pocket. And no high taxes ever again!"

"Thank fuck. I can't stand taxes." Feldman didn't say a word. "But I'll miss New York. Meeting old friends, family, this and that." Moretti sipped his wine. "What a situation."

"It is what it is, Paul. I, for one, am going to miss you."

Moretti, perhaps for the first time in his life, appeared vulnerable. He shifted in his seat. His eyes filled with tears. "I deal with a lot of people, Mort. People I thought were my friends. My family. But none of them has acted with the same dignity, calmness, and straightforwardness as you. You never let me down. And for that, I want to say thank you so much."

"It's been a pleasure, Paul. Can I ask one favor from you?"

Moretti shrugged and leaned back in his seat. "A favor? Anything. How can I help you?"

"Make sure this is the last time you're seen in public in New York."

Moretti stared into his glass of wine. "I know . . . Rest assured, it's over. You won't see me around New York ever again."

"Fair enough."

"Mort, I want to get to the reason why I really asked you here. Two birds with one stone, so to speak."

Feldman felt his insides move. "I see. Why's that?"

"A final request. Actually, it's not a request. I've got an instruction for you."

"I'm a lawyer. That's what we do for our clients."

"Mort, I'm going to ask you this one last time."

"Sure."

"I want to know the identity of the fuck that's supposedly after me. The fuck who held my friend Joseph Torrio from a roof. I want a name."

Feldman leaned in close and whispered, "Paul, listen to me. This is something the Feds are not going to divulge. I've asked about this, in a super low-key way, but they're not saying a thing, even someone like Avery, who knows who it is."

Moretti pointed the fork at him again. "I want to fucking know, Mort! I don't want to have to hire private investigators or people like that. I expect my lawyer to get things straightened out."

"Paul, I am dedicated to making sure your interests are aligned with the law. As much as they can be. But I'm telling you this, as a friend and as your lawyer: this is something you can't get from anyone in the FBI. I know, I've tried."

"You need to try again. And try harder. I want a name. I'm not interested in how you get that name. But I want you to get it."

"Doing this goes against a lot of legal ethics as well as imping-ing on my ability to advise you as your lawyer."

"Get me the name. I don't care about legal ethics. Whatever it takes, just get it."

Forty-Five

Reznick stood on the Rockland breakwater, his mind troubled. It was a place he returned to often. A place to contemplate. A special place for him. He often stood alone on the granite wall beside the lighthouse. A shelter from the storm.

He had lost count of the number of times he had walked along the breakwater. It provided a safe haven for the fishing boats in winter storms. But for Reznick, it was where he'd spent sacred hours and days with his father. A man he revered.

Reznick was at a crossroads. He had broken the law. He thought of his father. How would his father have reacted to the murder of Eastland and his wife in cold blood? Would his father have grieved? Perhaps. Probably. His father would certainly have wanted vengeance. His father believed in an eye for an eye. Biblical justice.

His father had taught him to fish from the breakwater. He remembered his huge, calloused hands baiting the line. He remembered the ominous tone when he spoke, demanding attention. He remembered the times they had sat in beautiful silence, fishing together, father and son. But there were also dark times. He remembered the times his father had broken down and cried as he sat with his back to his son. Maybe crying for comrades who had fallen in Vietnam.

Reznick never did ask his father why he was crying. He knew it would be no use. His father was a man of few words. He knew in a way that his father was broken. Broken by the war. Broken by years of working to keep his head above water, working in the sardine-packing factory, night and day. Bleeding hands, red and raw from the cold and the cuts from handling fish scales. No money to spare. The quiet, blue-collar American. A man who served and worked until the day he died.

It ate away at Reznick that money was so tight for his father. He wished he'd had money when his father needed it. Now he was gone. His father had borrowed cash from Eastland. He remembered Eastland stopping by when his dad was sick with a collapsed lung, no money coming in. He had thrust hard cash into Reznick's father's fist. Jon didn't know if his father had ever paid Eastland back. He remembered his father once raising his voice, saying, *I can provide for my family.* But Eastland just turned and walked away. *I never said you couldn't. This will tide you over.*

He knew Eastland couldn't have been earning that much money at the time. Maybe he was better at looking after his money. Then again, maybe it was money Eastland had won at the track. Maybe in Vegas. Maybe at illegal poker clubs in New York.

Reznick questioned what more he could do. He had gone after those who had carried out the killing. The gang responsible for murdering Eastland and his wife. He had dealt with Torrio, probably put the fear of God into him. But the head of the snake was still in place.

Paul Moretti. Moretti's home would be a fortress. Wherever his home was. He assumed Moretti had a house in Connecticut, too, if the Feds were stopping him from entering the state. That would make sense.

Reznick noted to check if the FBI was spying on him. Electronic surveillance, perhaps. That would also make sense. He needed to be careful. As a rule, he only used military-grade encrypted devices. The occasional call on a public pay phone.

He ran scenarios through his head. Even if he did find out where Moretti lived, the chances were that Reznick would be shot on sight and his body dumped in the East River. Maybe he would be tortured.

Reznick knew he was facing a man who had the means to protect himself and his property. He began to pace the breakwater. The name *Feldman* skidded across his brain. The man who had passed along the information from Moretti to Torrio. That's what Torrio had told him in New York.

He considered if Feldman might be a weak link. Could Reznick kidnap Feldman from his office, take his cell phone, and send a text message to lure Moretti out of his fortress? It was a possibility. It might just work. But he also thought of the binding contract he had signed with the FBI.

The contract was clear. The Feds could apprehend him en route. Maybe he would face a second-degree murder charge for the killing of Jimmy Adams. But that's not all. His daughter would lose her father *and* her career. Maybe worse, the Mob might kill her too.

The smart move was to forget it all. But according to Meyerstein, Reznick had a price on his head.

It was then he realized there were no good options.

The middle of the night, and Reznick couldn't sleep. Scenarios raging around in his head. He got up, dressed, opened a bottle of beer from the fridge, and headed down to the sandy cove. He lit a fire. He sipped the beer and listened to the sound of waves crashing against the rocks as he contemplated his situation.

The smart move would be to just do nothing. He could do as Meyerstein and the FBI wanted. He called Williams.

It rang three times before he answered. "Do you ever sleep?"

"I was going to ask you the same thing."

"I see you're back home."

Reznick smiled. "I thought my cell phone had the best technology to mask my whereabouts."

"It does. I'm the only one who's able to pinpoint stuff like that."

"Listen, you've been a huge help so far. But I need more information."

"What do you need?"

"I believe a guy named Mort Feldman is the lawyer for Paul Moretti, boss of the Gambino family in New York."

The sound of tapping in the background. "Feldman . . . Gimme a few minutes, and I'll pull up his stuff."

"Mort Feldman," Reznick repeated.

"It's going to take a few minutes . . . Hang on."

Reznick put the bottle down in the sand.

"I'm in. I'm accessing his emails and messages."

"That was quick."

"Yeah, OK, I see there's business with Swiss banks and financial companies in the British Virgin Islands being conducted on Moretti's behalf. But I don't see any number for Moretti, not surprisingly."

"My next question. The other four crime families at this moment in time: Who are the lawyers who represent them?"

"That is going to take a lot longer than a few minutes. I'm going to need a little time to gather that information. Is that a problem?"

"I'd like to know within the next twenty-four hours."

"A bit of advice, man. Let it go. I think you've done enough. What do you think?"

"Maybe."

Williams sighed. "It would be for the best."

"It would be the smart thing to do, I get it."

"I can get you this information. How much do you want it?"

"Get it."

"You sure?"

"Positive."

"OK, I'll get on it. But I'm telling you, as a friend, these guys don't like people interfering in their business. You go after them, it never ends well."

Forty-Six

The cab pulled up outside Feldman's favorite restaurant, Umberto's, in the West Village. He headed inside and shook hands with the maître d', Angelo.

"How are you this evening, sir?" Angelo asked.

"Happy but hungry."

"You've come to the right place. Follow me."

Angelo escorted Feldman past the other diners. The restaurant had been a favorite with movers and shakers in the city since it opened. A few lawyers he recognized, a baseball star he had once represented, and a cocaine-addicted harpist with the New York Philharmonic he had once dated. He gave a polite nod to them all as he passed.

Gillian Rossi was already seated, cell phone pressed to her ear. A glass of sparkling water with a slice of lemon sat on the table. She motioned with her free hand for Feldman to take a seat.

Feldman sat down and ordered a bottle of their finest red wine. He perused the menu as Rossi barked orders to some poor sucker in her office. She always seemed hyperstressed, usually over the trivial, like vacations by senior staff she didn't know about.

A waiter appeared and uncorked the bottle of wine. He poured a small glass for Feldman to sample.

Feldman took a sip and savored the gorgeous, deep, full-bodied wine. "Excellent."

The waiter filled his glass as Rossi ended her call. "Are you ready to order, sir?"

"Give us ten minutes while we check out the menu, thank you."

The waiter nodded and left them alone.

"What an asshole," she said.

"The waiter?"

"No, my call."

"Another happy customer?" Feldman joked.

"If only. The bullshit I have to put up with, Mort, you wouldn't believe."

"Tell me about it."

Rossi took a deep breath and let it out.

"Everything OK?"

"It is." She looked around. "Nice restaurant you've chosen. First time I've been in here."

Feldman picked up his wineglass and took another sip. "That's delicious."

Rossi raised her glass of sparkling water. "I need to watch my weight."

"You kidding me? You look fantastic."

Rossi blushed.

"How about we eat and then we talk business."

"Sounds like a plan."

Rossi motioned the waiter over. She ordered warm spinach and kale followed by vegan lasagna. It wasn't Feldman's idea of lunch. He ordered the best filet mignon on the menu and fries and onion rings. He was a man of simple tastes.

The lunch was convivial as they made small talk. The mayor, what an asshole he was, the stifling weather, the broken air-conditioning in Rossi's West Village apartment, a shooting three blocks from her home a couple of nights earlier. But she also talked gloomily about her wayward son, Frankie.

Feldman listened as he ate. A good lawyer had to know when to listen. Her errant son was her weak spot. She'd do anything for him. The kid was smart. But he was lazy. A bad combination. He had seen it before at law school. Very bright students who didn't put in the hard work and hundreds of hours of study required to pass exams. They thought their intelligence was enough to allow them to breeze through. That was rarely the case. Even the brightest needed to work their tails off, reading—devouring the law books, the case law—to stand a chance of passing the bar. Frankie wasn't even there yet. He was an undergraduate. Feldman had made a few discreet inquiries, and that turned up a dark secret.

When the table was cleared, Rossi checked her watch. "I didn't realize the time. I've got an appointment with the mayor in forty minutes!"

"I won't keep you. Just a few more minutes of your time."

Rossi looked surprised. "I thought we were done with your client's case. I thought this was just a little lunch to thank me."

"In a way it is. You're right. My client is grateful that you were able to address any issues that might have been an impediment to him moving on to a new life."

Rossi pursed her lips. "So, why am I here?"

"I think I can help you with a serious problem. It's about your son."

"I'm sorry, what do you mean, Mort?"

Feldman leaned in. "I have a good friend," he said in a quiet voice. "She works down in Durham, North Carolina. In the DA's office."

Rossi went ashen.

"She mentioned your son's name, you know, with regard to the pot found in his room. She made a throwaway remark."

"A throwaway remark. What did she say?"

"Your son, Frankie. She said, *If they only knew the half of it.*"

Rossi's pupils were black pinpricks.

"I didn't tell her that I know you well."

"Appreciate that."

"She mentioned that Frankie had been investigated by cops, and the information passed to her department."

"What the hell are you talking about, Mort?"

Feldman's voice was a whisper. "Your son is alleged to have drugged and raped a student on campus. That's what she said."

A stony silence opened up for a second too long. "There must be some terrible mistake. He's a good kid. My son? No, absolutely not."

"I thought it had to be a mix-up with names. I thought the same as you: great kid. But she clarified, saying despite his mom being a big-shot attorney in New York, her son couldn't abide by the law. She called him a monster. Her word."

"Why are you telling me this, Mort?"

"First, I thought it only right that you know. But second, I think I can help Frankie with this issue."

Rossi blinked away tears. "I don't understand."

"I can sort this out."

"I need to speak to Frankie about this."

"How do you think he'll respond?"

"He'll deny it, and we'll argue like last time, and the time before that. And he'll accuse me of hating him. Which is nonsense. I love him, but I want to protect him. That's all I want to do, Mort."

Feldman was a master at feigning concern and appearing to care. "I tried to put myself in your position, and my first reaction would be to speak to my son. But think about it: How will that work out?"

"We'll fight, he'll get drunk and high, blame me . . ."

"Exactly. And all the time the DA's office in Durham will be investigating. Maybe leaking this information. It happens. I'm amazed the cops haven't leaked something already. It might just be a matter of time, I don't know."

"Mort, this is a lot to take in."

"Listen to me. I can help you. If you leave this with me, I promise I will resolve this issue for you. You're a good friend. I know you're thinking about running for governor, right?"

"A bit down the line. Three, maybe four years, I don't know."

"If this comes out, your ambitions will be dead in the water. But I can make this all go away."

"How?"

"That's for me to worry about. You just say the word, and I can help you. But there is a small favor I'd like to ask in return."

"Quid pro quo?"

"Precisely."

"I'm listening."

"The Special Forces guy. The identity of this guy. I need to know who he is, so I can help my client work on any future lawsuits against him."

"Mort, I can't do that. That's not fair."

"If you get me that name, I'll make this problem go away."

"You just want a name?"

"A name. There's no time to waste. Get the name, and I guarantee your son won't have any more problems with that allegation."

Forty-Seven

It was early afternoon when Reznick's cell phone rang.

"Hey, man, it's me."

"I was starting to think you had gone AWOL on me."

"Not quite, man."

"You got something already?"

"It took a few hours, a lot of cross-checking, and some data analysis to make sure I had the right people, but I think I got something."

Reznick's home phone and cell phones were encrypted. His instincts told him to be extra careful if Trevelle really did have the names and numbers he was looking for.

"You still there?" Trevelle asked.

"Listen, do you know that number I called you from before?"

"Before when?"

"First time I called you this month."

"Yeah."

"Call that number in ten minutes."

"Why?"

"I don't know. Better safe than sorry."

"You got it."

Reznick ended the call, got in his car, and drove down to the harbor. He pulled up beside the pay phone. He hung around for seven minutes, then picked up after the first ring. "Yeah?"

"You paranoid about your cell phone?"

"Maybe."

"It's fine, I've remotely analyzed it. It's got the best encryption. You're good."

"I'm a bit analog and old school about such things."

"Fair enough."

"So, what you got? You got four names of the Mob lawyers?"

"Nope."

"I thought you got something."

"I do. But it's not four lawyers. It's *one* lawyer."

"I guess that's better than nothing."

"You don't understand. There's just one lawyer who represents the other four families."

"Are you sure?"

"Don Lieberman. He works for Lugton, Kronklow, and Melecki on Lexington, Midtown Manhattan. Lieberman is the Mob's guy. He represents the four other families. Has for nearly ten years."

Reznick took a few moments for the information to sink in. "Holy fuck."

"But I got something else. I accessed the records of Mort Feldman, who represents Moretti. Now, that makes for some interesting reading."

"How did you get into his files?"

"The oldest trick in the book. His documents are backed up to the cloud."

"Does that not make it safer?"

"Not really. He uses a company to store his documents. I found a weakness in their coding."

"Could anyone do that?"

"Definitely not. It's a backdoor technique; it would take a week to explain. Anyway, I downloaded hand-coded rogue software on his emails, both personal and work emails. He was completely unaware. No trace. And from there, I found all sorts of stuff."

"Spit it out."

"I have a ton of documents. One in particular got me really excited. Are you listening?"

"I'm still here."

"It's a legal agreement between the United States Department of Justice and Paul Moretti. Paul Moretti lives on a huge estate in Connecticut, right by the ocean. Hence why you were barred from entering Connecticut. But here's the kicker: I have a document which states the preconditions and conditions for him becoming an FBI informant."

Reznick stood beside the pay phone in partial shock. "Bullshit."

"I shit you not. I got it in front of me. Signed, sealed, and delivered. He has been a high-level informant to the FBI for the last six months."

"That's unbelievable. I can't seriously wrap my head around that. He's in charge of one of New York's families? And he's a snitch? You just blew my mind."

"There's something else. I don't know what it means. A bit cryptic. But it's a letter from the Director of the US Marshals Service to Feldman."

"What about?"

"Not sure. 'Delighted we got there in the end, Mort. Hope you get your long-awaited vacation on September fourth.'"

"That's in five days." Reznick theorized what it meant. "I don't understand. Moretti isn't a fugitive. He's an informant." His mind began to race. "I wonder . . ."

"What?"

"You're right, Moretti isn't a fugitive. But you know as well as I do that the US Marshals don't just hunt fugitives."

"So, what else do they do?"

"Think about it."

"I honestly never gave them much thought."

"The US Marshals also run the Witness Protection Program. It's part of the Department of Justice. Is that possible?"

"Fuck."

"What if, and it is a big *what if*, Moretti is being lined up for the Witness Protection Program?"

"I don't know. That's very speculative."

"I don't know for sure, that's true. But think about it. What if Feldman has struck a deal so that Moretti disappears? And this is what the US Marshals director is alluding to when he talks about enjoying a long-awaited vacation. Is September fourth the date when Moretti will be safely ensconced in protective custody?"

"You mean Paul Moretti just disappears? As simple as that?"

"It's brilliant. New identity. New backstory. Who knows? It doesn't say where he's going to be relocated, not surprisingly. But it would give a rationale for all this bullshit going down."

"Christ Almighty. That's fucking nuts!"

Reznick pressed the phone tight to his ear. "Here's what I want. I want you to access the US Marshals Service files, if you can."

"OK, I'm listening."

"The director in particular. If this is the plan, that office must have the documents."

"I can get them for you."

"Are you sure?"

"Piece of cake, man. My record for the Department of Justice is four minutes."

"You can hack them in four minutes?"

"No, it means if this is actually happening, I can get you the documents in four minutes."

"Bullshit."

"You don't believe me? Hang up and call me back in five minutes. If there's something concrete, I will have it."

"Do it." Reznick ended the call. His heart was racing like he had swallowed a handful of Dexedrine. He wondered if this was indeed the endgame for Moretti. He would hand over the keys to his criminal empire to the Department of Justice to save his skin. The minutes dragged. He checked his watch endlessly. Then the five minutes were up. He called Trevelle's number. "What you got?"

"Sweet Jesus. I swear to God, it's happening."

"Witness Protection Program for Moretti?"

"And his entire freaking family."

"Are you sure?"

"I am staring at the documentation right now. Classified top secret."

"Do we know if these are authentic documents?"

"They're authentic. Zero day, as they are calling it, is in five days. September fourth. I could send it to you if you want."

"Absolutely not. If that's intercepted electronically, Moretti will be compromised. I don't want that."

"What do you want me to do with it?"

"Save everything you've accessed on Moretti in the highest-level encrypted file you can, and leave it on your private server until I say so. Don't tell a soul. And don't back it up to the fucking cloud."

"Copy that. So, tell me, how the hell are you going to get to Moretti? And if you figure that out, you are going to be out of time very, very soon."

"That's my problem. Listen, I owe you one."

Reznick ended the call. He got back in his truck and drove around town, trying to get everything straight. A thousand ideas were ricocheting around his mind. He had a big call to make. He pondered if he should put an end to his personal vendetta against Moretti. It would be the smart thing to do. He knew that. But something deep within his guts, within his soul, within his very being, was telling him the opposite.

He thought of Bill Eastland. He thought of Elspeth Eastland. Then he thought of his daughter. Her career might be over if he pursued this to the bitter end. How would he feel about that? It didn't sit well with him. But neither did Moretti getting a sweetheart deal for turning snitch.

Reznick asked himself if he could really live with that thought. He asked if he was reminiscing about Eastland, in a year or two, what he would make of his actions. He could let it go. He could just turn the other cheek, knowing he'd done the best he could. But the reality was Moretti would get away with it.

His instincts told him to go after Moretti. But he needed help. It would be a high-risk strategy. And he needed a foolproof plan. But he wasn't stupid. A conventional assault on Moretti's compound would be in vain. He needed a plan. Was there anyone who could advise him? Assist him? He had less than a week.

He turned around, drove down Main Street, and headed back to the harborside. He got out of his truck and checked his cell phone contacts. He saw the name of a highly intelligent veteran. One he trusted.

Reznick picked up the pay phone and called the number of an old pilot friend of his. "Sam, it's Jon Reznick."

"Jon, what the fuck, man? Great to hear from you."

"You back in Boston?"

"Where the hell else would you find me?"

"You still up for a beer?"

"Me? Are you kidding? I'm always up for a beer."

"Listen, I also need a favor."

"Name it."

"It's a long story. I want to pick your brain."

Ripley laughed. "Yeah, good luck with that, bro. But I'll be glad to help. You want to talk in person?"

"I think it's best. You want me to head down to Boston?"

"No, much prefer to see you in good old Rockland. Haven't been there in years."

"That works for me. Listen, there's a daily flight out of Logan at four. Will get you into Rockland just after five. We can grab a bite of dinner while we shoot the breeze. I want to discuss something with you."

"Sounds like a plan."

"You're OK with this, short notice and all?"

"Jon, relax. It'll do me good to get out of town for a night. I'll see you soon."

Forty-Eight

It was beers and tequila shots at the Rockland Tavern as Reznick reminisced with Sam Ripley. He had been on countless missions with Ripley flying them into and out of war zones or extraction points. He never failed. Ripley seemed not to have changed much.

But the longer Reznick talked with him, the more Ripley opened up about everything that had gone wrong since. Ripley had suffered crippling financial losses after a business deal went bad.

"Why didn't you call me, man?" Reznick said.

"Too proud, I guess. I felt like a fucking failure. It was a hard life lesson."

Reznick patted Ripley on the back. "I might be able to help you out."

"Appreciate that. I've got enough to last me a few months. I sold a lot of my belongings. The bank repossessed the house. But I'm slowly getting my shit together. The NATO consultancy paid well. So, I'm hoping that's something I can build on."

Reznick leaned close. "You working now?"

"The contract ended. But I'm looking."

"I can help you with that. I know a few people that would love to have your skills."

"I really appreciate that, Jon. I feel bad, though, that I'm telling you all this sob-story bullshit."

"Fuck it. Give me your bank account details."

"You don't have to do that."

"I know I don't. But I'm doing it for the guy I knew. The guy sitting in front of me right now."

"I'll pay it back when I'm straightened out."

"No chance. I owe you. We all owe you for getting our asses out of some tight spots. Remember Ramadi?"

"Do I ever. What a fucking nightmare."

"Give me your bank details. We all need a helping hand from time to time."

Ripley reluctantly pulled out his cell phone and gave him the details.

Reznick took out his cell phone, opened his bank app, and transferred $20,000 to Ripley's account. "There, it's done."

Ripley closed his eyes and shook his head. "I don't know what to say."

"Shut the fuck up and let's have a drink. I think you might be able to help me."

"How?"

"First, let's enjoy our drinks." He gulped his beer and ordered another round.

Ripley grinned. "I heard you worked for the Agency."

"A few years back, yeah."

"How was that?"

Reznick leaned in closer and whispered. "You know how it is. Black ops, middle of the night, target neutralized, I fly out."

Ripley stared into his bottle. "It's like a million years ago, all that stuff. I was approached by a guy about doing some consulting in Europe. Bosnia, in particular. But I need to think it over. I'm not that interested in getting back into that game."

"Correct me if I'm wrong, Sam, but besides being an ace pilot, didn't you do some advanced courses at the Army College in Pennsylvania?"

Ripley nodded. "Yeah, I took a year off to do some studying."

"I thought you mentioned that once."

"Advanced courses in asymmetric warfare. Thought that would look good on my résumé."

"Interesting. Listen, I'm looking for some help."

"Shoot."

Reznick smiled. "The money I gave you—consider that an added consulting fee for picking your brain."

"I can live with that."

"Here's the thing, Sam. I have an idea how I might deal with a particular situation. I'm just seeking expertise on how you might approach it."

Ripley motioned the bartender for two more shots. "You want to tell me more?"

"Let's drink up. We'll talk in private back at my house."

Forty-Nine

The pair headed back to Reznick's house on the outskirts of Rockland.

"Sam, what I want to talk about," Reznick said, "you can't divulge in any way, shape, or form."

"That's a given, man."

"It's a hypothetical scenario."

"Let's imagine this is a training exercise."

"Sure."

Ripley shrugged. "I'm all ears."

"OK, let's talk asymmetric, like you studied."

"It was a few years ago. But I had some really interesting insights into irregular warfare and tactics."

"The kind of stuff we faced in Iraq, right?"

Ripley nodded. "Precisely. So, when the insurgents, for example, see that the enemy, America, for example, is far more powerful, then they can't go head-to-head, or they would be pulverized. So, their tactics change. And that causes serious problems."

Reznick fetched two beers from the fridge and handed one over. "I want to talk about a scenario. Like I said before, hypothetical."

Ripley popped the cap. "I'm intrigued."

"There's a guy . . . here on American soil, right?"

"OK."

"He's a Mob boss. The top guy. He lives alone in a huge fuck-off mansion, by the water in, let's say, Connecticut."

"Lucky him."

"Now, bearing in mind what you've just said, assuming he has far more firepower, manpower, the estate is a virtual fortress, cameras everywhere. How can one man get to him?"

Ripley cocked his head to one side as if considering the scenario. "Can you tell me more?"

"The compound will be heavily protected, of course. Infrared security sensors all over the place. I don't know for sure. But I think that's a given."

"Sure. So, if you're thinking traditional asymmetric tactics, you obviously wouldn't go head-to-head with this Mob boss, right? That would be nuts."

"Precisely."

"Does this guy ever leave the compound?"

"I don't know."

Ripley nursed his beer before taking a large gulp. "So, we're talking, perhaps, an element of surprise."

"Perhaps."

"If he leaves the compound, you could do the traffic-cop-stop routine on the Mob boss's car. But that poses a real threat to the assailant. So, there would be collateral damage. It could get messy."

Reznick had already considered that option. "What else?"

"He lives by the water?"

"Yeah."

"The chopper approach. Drop a team in. But again, potentially very messy. And no guarantees he wouldn't be in a secure panic room, which I'd imagine he'd have. Room by room. Could be dozens of rooms."

"Don't have the manpower. What else?"

Ripley gulped some more beer. "You're not asking much."

"I'm thinking stealth. Where the assailant could do the hit and still get away."

"Sniper on a boat, five hundred to a thousand yards away. Slow approach. Maybe even disguised as a fisherman if stopped. But yeah, take the shot."

Reznick smiled.

"What?"

"I already thought of that."

"What's wrong with it?"

"Nothing's wrong with it. It's brilliant. But the variables—the tides, the currents, could be stormy, he might be sitting in his bedroom jerking off for days at a time. Maybe he's playing tennis on the other side of the estate."

"You want a guarantee. You can't get a guarantee that it will work 100 percent. It might be an 80 to 90 percent probability, I guess."

"I want 100 percent certainty it would work. Using stealth."

Ripley shook his head. "I guess you might want to deploy a drone for surveillance. But I'm assuming a dude like that would have a security team to blow it out of the sky."

"Probably. And I'm guessing a dude like that might have a patrol boat or night-vision cameras on small rocky islands if you approach by water."

"Shit, I guess. Ninety percent is my best estimate, man."

Reznick growled. He wanted a slam dunk.

"Thinking off the top of my head," Ripley said, mulling it over, "you could get his cell phone number and send a fake text message, luring him outside. But that has its limitations."

"It's not bad."

"So, how would you do it?"

Reznick smiled at the dark waters of Penobscot Bay. A plan was already forming in his head. "I've run about six different scenarios, including the ones you mentioned, in addition to remotely setting off the fire and smoke alarms, so he evacuates the house, then he gets taken out. But I'm still not sure."

"Maybe spray-paint a car to look like a cop car and gain entry to the compound on the pretext of a prowler having been reported by a member of the staff . . . Perhaps remotely switch off all the surveillance equipment, but I'm guessing he would have a localized back-up generator."

"Interesting. What I'm looking for is something way out of left field. The sort of thing he wouldn't see coming."

"A classic aspect of asymmetric warfare, as you know, would be avoiding an open battle, which he might expect. Maybe get to him through a close member of his family."

Reznick nodded. "I like the direction of travel. But ideally I want to disguise the source of responsibility and pin the blame on his enemies."

"Now you're talking." Ripley knocked back the rest of his beer. "So, we're in the realm of a false flag operation, bro. Nothing more, nothing less."

Reznick felt his stomach tighten. Was this what he needed to do? A false flag on the Mob boss?

Ripley had his *aha* moment. "I've been doing a lot of reading recently. Had a lot of time on my hands. One guy especially, Sun Tzu. You've heard of him. Chinese strategist."

Reznick nodded. He had read his classic, *The Art of War*.

"Know my favorite quote from him? And it most certainly applies in the scenario you outlined."

"What's that?"

"'The quote about the superiority of vanquishing an enemy without fighting.'"

"I think I know how I can do this. Using the same principles you outlined."

Ripley grinned and shook his head. "You seriously contemplating this?"

"Oh yeah."

Ripley laughed. "You're out of your fucking mind, Reznick. And I love it."

Fifty

Late the following morning, after talking well into the night, Reznick drove Ripley to the small airport at Owls Head to get a flight back to Boston.

The dialogue with Ripley about asymmetric warfare had gotten Reznick's juices flowing. He was beginning to think outside the box. He needed to get all the pieces in place. The problem with his plan was that it would require him to physically get to New York. Manhattan. That was a major stumbling block as it would violate his contract with the FBI.

A place smothered in surveillance cameras. Transport hubs, bus stations, office buildings, highways, housing projects—the all-seeing eye seemed to have the city covered. But like all systems, it could be defeated. It would just take a touch of guile and a few strokes of luck.

Reznick picked up his cell phone and called Trevelle. "What's the weather like in Iowa?"

"No longer in Iowa, man."

"What happened?"

"Nothing happened. It was way too quiet. I mean eerily quiet. I like seeing people."

"Where are you?"

"I'm back down in Florida."

"Very nice. Listen, you at your desk?"

"If I have a computer or phone on me, I'm at my desk."

Reznick smiled. "I guess. Don Lieberman, the guy that represents the other four Mob families in New York. Where exactly does he work?"

The sound of Trevelle tapping away at his laptop. "Why are you interested in him? Surely you would be interested in Feldman, if anyone."

"I think I might have a way to get to Moretti in a roundabout route."

"Don Lieberman works at 435 Lexington Avenue, Manhattan. His company has a suite of offices on the thirty-eighth floor."

"I want you to try and access his diary. I'm assuming his appointments are kept up to date on an online calendar."

"Most certainly. Who the hell uses paper today, right?"

"You'd be surprised."

"Let me see. Hang on . . ."

"What is it?"

"OK, I'm in. So, that's interesting . . . Lieberman is in wall-to-wall meetings today, lunch at Cipriani with his wife, and tomorrow very busy again. His first in-person appointment tomorrow is a breakfast meeting at 8:30 a.m. He has a call scheduled with one of his clients, Robert Grasso, at 7:00 a.m. in his office. He's scheduled to leave for his breakfast meeting at 8:15. I guess the only slot would be eight."

"Are you sure?"

"Copy that: it's the only available moment. It's not much of a window of opportunity."

"It'll have to do."

"So, what's the plan?"

"Tomorrow morning at that time, I want you to remotely disable the surveillance cameras in that building. Is that possible?"

"It's a big ask. I'll need to do a remote assessment, as I call it. But I don't foresee any problems."

"It needs to work. Once I'm inside that building, I need to be a ghost. Unseen."

"Copy that. 0755 hours tomorrow, I could deactivate surveillance cameras in that entire building on Lexington. I'm assuming that includes the cameras in the elevators."

"There needs to be no trace of me going in or out."

"The only problem is the streets are covered from every angle. That area has the most cameras per square mile. It's really short notice. I would have preferred a week or so to do a test run of the systems."

"I know. We're against the clock. Zero day is only four days away. That's why I need you to be on your A-game tomorrow. This needs to happen. And it needs to happen tomorrow."

Fifty-One

Reznick scrolled through all the contacts in his cell phone, past and present. He saw the name Tom Hewson, ex-Marine and part-time mercenary. Tom hailed from Ohio. He had been involved in more coups than Reznick could remember. But now he was living in a trailer on the outskirts of Rockland.

The last time Reznick had spoken to Tom, he mentioned in passing that he was trying to sell his old motorcycle. Another beautiful old Harley.

Tom had picked up the bike for cash at a chop shop salvage yard in Ohio three years earlier. But it would fit Reznick's need for a one-off, quick job.

Reznick's idea was coming together in his head. He drove to Tom's trailer. He knocked three times.

The door opened, and a huge bear of a man wearing a torn Led Zeppelin T-shirt and cargo shorts stood there, smoking a joint.

"Hey, man," Tom said. "You're lucky you caught me, Jon. I'm headed overseas in a month's time."

"Where to?"

"Dubai."

"What the fuck are you going to do out there?"

"Bodyguard for some little wealthy Middle Eastern brat in a gated community."

"Sounds like a lot of fun."

"Hell no. You wanna come in? Excuse the mess, by the way."

"No, I was just checking if you still had the old Harley."

Tom dragged hard on the joint. "Around the other side of the trailer, man. You interested?"

"Sure. I'm looking to buy an old bike."

Hewson walked around the trailer. Jon saw a brand-new Kawasaki and a beaten-up old Harley. Hewson pointed at the Harley tank. "It's scratched bad. Had a fall about a month ago. It's a piece of junk. But you know me: soft spot for Harleys."

"Love them. Beautiful bikes."

"Don't get me wrong. It runs strong. And it's powerful, let me tell you. A real handful—a bit like my ex-wife!"

Reznick smiled. "She was nice."

"She was a fucking nutcase, Jon. I got no money. No fucking anything."

"Maybe I can help you out."

"Appreciate that, man. That's why I'm doing that shitty job in Dubai for a month. Need the hard cash."

Reznick kneeled down and began to inspect the machine. "Tell me about this Harley. You said you bought it from a chop shop in Denton, Ohio, right?"

"Yeah, both the Kawasaki and the Harley. See, a crazy old guy and his son had a warehouse. Old stolen cars and motorcycles. Cannibalized them for parts, sometimes bought stuff at salvage auction that had been badly destroyed in accidents. But they wanted them for their VINs."

"Vehicle identification number?"

"That's right. Did the same with motorcycles, including this Harley. Although I think there are Suzuki parts in there somewhere."

"Sounds like they've got quite an operation going."

"You better believe it. Here's how it works. They steal a car of the same make and model. Then they do the classic switch. They change the VIN plates, usually found inside the door and the dash, and they resell, claiming they repaired a totaled car. That's just one of the ways they were able to operate."

"How much do you want for the Harley?"

"It's probably worth a hundred bucks, maximum."

"What if I give you a thousand bucks, cash?"

"You kidding me?"

Reznick took out the wad of bills. He counted out the thousand and handed it over. "And I want the helmet."

"You drive a hard bargain, you motherfucker!" Hewson laughed.

Reznick shook his hand and felt a viselike grip. "One final thing: I'll need you to drop it off at my house."

"When?"

"Right now. And I'll get you a cab ride back home."

Fifty-Two

Reznick spent the hours that followed in his workshop in the garage attached to his house.

He needed to make sure the machine—made of many parts from different makes of motorcycle—was in working order. He checked the electrics and tire pressure, replaced the clutch fluid and the engine oil, checked the brake torque, and on and on, making sure the bike would get him to his destination and back in one piece. He polished up the bike and took it for a spin around town for twenty minutes.

It ran well, just like Tom said. Chop-shop bike or not, it was a fine runner.

Reznick headed back to his house, parked the bike in the garage, and showered. He put on an old leather jacket, faded jeans, and old Nikes. He popped three Dexedrine and washed them down with a can of Coke.

His cell phone rang.

Reznick picked up on the third ring. "Yeah?"

"You OK to talk?" asked Trevelle.

"Sure, what's going on?"

"Turn on the TV, man. Fox News is going big on this."

Reznick picked up the remote control and turned on the TV. He switched channels until he got to Fox. A young reporter was standing in some scrubland in the Hamptons. Police chopper swooping low in the background.

The reporter said, "The jogger reported the body found floating in shallow water near Montauk, at the easternmost tip of Long Island. Joseph Torrio, a New York businessman who is widely believed to have links to Mafia crime families in the city, was found at first light this morning."

Reznick switched off the TV. He knew in his bones Torrio had been killed for dishonoring the family. It was a reprisal.

"Are you still going ahead with whatever the hell you're going to do tomorrow?"

"That's the plan. Everything still in place?"

A deep sigh. "So, I'm going to do a dummy run tonight to make sure my system works. Basically going to probe the law firm's firewall and security protocols."

"I'll be in touch." Reznick ended the call. The conversation gave him pause. His plan could fail if he was intercepted en route and detained by the cops. His name would appear on an NYPD computer. It would be flagged by the FBI. And all hell would break loose. But if he had a slice of luck, he might just be able to pull it off. If it didn't? He could well wind up dead.

It was dark when Reznick did a final check of the bike. He knew the route he was going to take. He had a burner phone charged to 100 percent in his pocket to keep in touch with Trevelle over the next twenty-four hours. He had left his usual encrypted cell phone safely in the house, no GPS signals getting pinged until he got home.

Reznick pulled on the helmet and zipped up his leathers and started up the bike's engine. It growled into life like any classic bike. It sounded to his ears like there was a Triumph engine in there.

He turned the bike around and rode along the old dirt road that led into town. He got on US-1 South.

Reznick would rest twice on his way south to New York. He would stop to fill up with gas and coffee at truck stop diners along the way. He had it all mapped out in his head, how it was going to go. He felt the amphetamines kick in bigtime as he opened up the throttle. He picked up his speed on the open road. He had unfinished business to attend to in Manhattan.

Fifty-Three

The text pinged Meyerstein's cell phone at 0503 hours.

She reached over and switched on the bedside lamp in her Bethesda home. She picked up her phone.

The message read: *Call SIOC regarding Jon Reznick. Urgent.*

"Never a goddamn break," she muttered.

Meyerstein got up and opened the drapes to darkness. She called the direct number for the FBI's twenty-four-hour command center in DC.

"What's the problem?" she said.

"Martha, sorry to wake you." The voice of Franklin. "I just wanted to give you a heads-up."

"Is Reznick OK?"

"Honestly? We don't know."

Meyerstein's heart skipped a beat. A feeling of dread inside her. "So, what's the issue?"

"He's not at home. We had a deal, remember."

Meyerstein racked her brains. "I don't know . . . Maybe he went fishing or shooting or whatever he does up in Maine."

"Maybe."

"So, how did we learn of this disappearance?"

"Tom Cain, sheriff's investigator, rolled by Reznick's home just after one o'clock this morning. He saw a light on, but no one home. He knocked, but no answer."

"Do you think he collapsed or something?"

"I don't know."

Meyerstein rubbed her eyes. "He's an outdoor guy. He might've gone for a walk. He might've been out on the beach. Maybe on the breakwater. I know he likes the solitude there."

"In the middle of the night?"

"I'm playing devil's advocate."

"Sure. Cain has apparently tried all those familiar places in and around Rockland. He went around the back of his house, peering in windows. Checking down on the beach."

"I don't know where he could be. I assumed he was going to be sitting tight after everything that happened."

"Martha, I hope he's not going to do something really dumb. He'll wind up getting killed."

"Doesn't he have a place up in the north Maine woods?"

"I sent a team there. They're on their way."

"Jon always has his cell phone on, wherever he is. He always wants to be available, especially for his daughter."

"That's what worries me."

Meyerstein sensed Reznick was up to something.

"I've heard enough. Get the police involved. Let me know as soon as we hear something."

Fifty-Four

A blood-orange sun peeked through a gap in the bleak housing projects up ahead.

Reznick was filling up the bike at a gas station in the Bronx. He figured he was about ten miles from his destination. It might take him half an hour until he hit Midtown Manhattan, depending on traffic. But he was on schedule. He had time.

He checked his watch. It was 6:50 a.m. The sooner he got there, the sooner he could get in and out.

Reznick headed into the station, helmet on, and paid by cash.

The cashier was yawning his head off, headphones on, flicking through a porn mag.

"You mind if I use your bathroom?"

The cashier pointed to a door at the far end of the gas station shop without looking up. "In there. And don't be jerking off like the last guy."

Reznick felt as if he had entered a parallel universe. He walked into the bathroom, took a leak, flushed the toilet, and washed his hands. He pushed through the bathroom door. He turned to the cashier. "Thank you."

The cashier was busy checking the surveillance cameras behind the glass on his desk. "Yeah, whatever."

Reznick got back on the Harley and eased away, not wanting to attract any attention. He was back on the expressway, the traffic already snarled up. A few minutes later, it was down to a crawl. It wasn't long before he realized there had been an accident up ahead.

Filthy fumes from the exhausts of old cars were all around as the traffic ground to a halt.

Reznick sat astride the bike and looked around. A few drivers leaned out of their vehicles to see what was happening. A truck driver began to pull a U-turn.

A white guy in a shirt and tie got out of his car. "Are you fucking serious, man?" the guy shouted at the trucker. "Don't you see there are people waiting? You're fucking up everything, you dumb fuck."

A huge Hispanic trucker got out and walked slowly toward the driver, monkey wrench in his right hand. "What're you saying?"

"I ain't saying nothing, man! I'm just pissed about why the hell the traffic's not moving."

"Sounded like you were shouting at me, son. You want to shout at me?"

"No, sir. Get back in your truck. I'm serious."

The trucker stared the guy down. "I'm just trying to make my delivery." He turned slowly around and headed back to his truck.

Reznick sat on his bike as he observed the whole scene behind the tinted visor.

The voice of Trevelle in his ear. "Welcome to the Bronx, my friend."

"Tell me about it."

A few minutes later, traffic was moving again.

Reznick rode on as he headed south on the FDR Drive toward Midtown Manhattan. He weaved in and out of the cars and trucks as he got closer to his destination. He saw a sign for the parking garage. He headed up a ramp on East Forty-Third Street and parked on the fourth level. He was only a couple of blocks away from the office. He checked his watch. It was 7:54 a.m. He had made it in time. Just.

Reznick sat on the motorcycle, helmet still on. His burner cell phone rang in his pocket.

A voice in his helmet. "You OK?"

"I'm good. Talk to me."

"Activation in place. I repeat: activation in place."

"Copy that."

"I'll be standing by if needed."

Reznick turned off the ignition and got off the bike. He took a few moments to get his bearings. He walked over to the nearest stairwell and headed down a few flights.

The stairs led Reznick out onto the bustling, noisy East Forty-Third Street. He turned onto Lexington.

It was then he saw a crowd of people had gathered—police lights, cops everywhere, paramedics too.

Reznick tried to get closer. People were holding up their cell phones to take photographs of the scene. He searched around for what the hell had happened.

A cop pushed him back. "Get out of here, sir."

Reznick peered through the crowd of cops and onlookers. A blood-splattered white sheet. And a body underneath.

"What happened, Officer?"

"I don't know the full story. Some poor bastard was gunned down when he arrived for work. Just happened. You need to move!"

Reznick watched the bloodstained white sheet for a few moments. He noticed a finger protruding from the sheet. He turned away and headed back to the parking garage. "I can't deliver the package. Someone has been shot outside. I want to know who it is."

"I'm watching the whole thing in real time. This whole thing is fucked up."

"Can you ID the guy? Do the police have a name?"

"Someone got to him."

"Don Lieberman?"

"It's him, alright. Two bullets to the head, point blank, execution style."

Fifty-Five

Feldman sat at his kitchen table drinking a cup of coffee, reading the front page of the *New York Times*, when the breaking news came on the TV. He turned to the screen.

A reporter was standing in Midtown Manhattan, police tape and a handful of NYPD in the background. "We're just hearing from police sources that a sixty-two-year-old man was shot by masked gunmen outside his office here in the heart of New York City less than an hour ago. Multiple sources have confirmed to us that the man is believed to be Don Lieberman, a prominent New York City attorney. Mr. Lieberman is one of Manhattan's top-earning lawyers, and his clients are believed to include several prominent New York crime families."

Feldman felt as if his world had exploded into a million pieces. He knew how these Mafia guys would read this. Who did this? Who was responsible?

The more he thought about the killing, the more he feared for the future. His future. He pondered who had given the orders. Had Don run afoul of one of the four Mob family bosses? It was a distinct possibility. He remembered Don mentioning that one of the Mob bosses had moaned and questioned the billing for a property transaction in Nevada. In particular, the billable hours.

But when Feldman ran the scenarios through his head, he concluded that it wouldn't make sense for one of the four families to kill Lieberman. He was their guy. Unless Lieberman had been helping himself to some of the money sloshing around in the myriad business accounts he would have set up. That could certainly get him taken out.

Then it hit Feldman like an oncoming truck. What if it wasn't one of the four Mob families? What if Moretti was responsible? Was this his work? But that would make no sense.

Moretti would know better than anyone that it would and could ignite an internecine Mafia war across New York. No one wanted that. No one besides a man who no longer had a stake in the status quo.

Feldman felt sick to the pit of his stomach. The usual way he communicated with Moretti was when one of his goons turned up at his door driving a limousine to whisk Feldman to the helipad before flying off to Moretti's estate in Connecticut. No questions asked.

Feldman paced his living room, hands in pockets, thinking about what the hell he should do. He couldn't do *nothing*. That wasn't an option. But he did need to speak to Moretti. His client would expect nothing less.

He put on his jacket, picked up his car keys, and took the elevator downstairs to the parking garage. He got in his car and began the journey to Connecticut.

The security guy at Moretti's gatehouse smiled.

Feldman wound down his window. "Hey, I'm here to see Paul."

"I'm sorry, but he isn't taking visitors today, Mr. Feldman."

"This is a matter of utmost importance."

"It's not the way we do things, Mr. Feldman. No disrespect."

"Listen to me: I need to speak to Paul! I'm not leaving until I do. This is urgent business!"

The security guy smiled. "Let me see what I can do." He took out his cell phone and tapped in a number. "This is Ricky at the north gate. We got a visitor. Mr. Feldman. He says it's urgent business. And he's not leaving until he speaks to Mr. Moretti." The security guy grimaced. "I'll hold. Sure."

Feldman nodded. "I appreciate you checking on this, Ricky."

"Don't sweat it. We'll see what they say."

"Thank you."

The security guy pressed the cell phone tight to his head and turned away. "Are you sure? OK, you got it." He turned and stooped to speak to Feldman. "You're in luck. Straight through. But I need you to hand over your cell phone and any electronic devices to me. Standard security protocol."

Feldman reluctantly handed over his cell phone.

The security guy pointed farther down the road. "Don't stop until you get to the main house."

"Thanks, Ricky. And look after that cell phone."

"You got it. Nice and slow. Twenty, tops."

Feldman put his window up and pulled away slowly. He drove through the manicured estate fringed by fir trees and oaks. The estate had been the setting of the summer home of a relative of the Sultan of Brunei, who sold it when he got divorced. But Moretti had had the house demolished when he bought the property.

In its place stood a twenty-five-bedroom monster of a property, which Moretti had gotten designed by a prize-winning New York architectural firm, Mondale & Fisher. It boasted two wine cellars and an Olympic-size swimming pool in the basement as well as one on the grounds. But the overriding consideration had been integrating high-end security throughout the property. It had taken a painstaking five years to construct, from the first drawings to the final coat of paint.

He pulled up outside the home as two men in suits, Moretti's private security detail, approached.

"Mort," one of them said, "we weren't expecting you today. Is everything OK?"

"I need to speak to Paul right away. And before you ask, no, it can't wait."

The guy cocked his head. "Follow me, Mort."

Feldman's heart pounded as he was led through the sprawling property, past oil paintings worth millions and photos of Moretti out and about in Manhattan.

He was shown out the back of the house, where Moretti was admiring a flashy car, the latest addition to his collection.

Moretti turned around and smiled. "What do you think? Ain't she a beaut? Limited edition."

Feldman forced a smile.

"Bugatti." Moretti beamed. "I love it. Three million bucks. I think it's a bargain. A great investment too."

Feldman looked over the car. "Yeah, it's a beautiful car, Paul. What do you want me to say?"

"What's wrong? I thought you liked the nice things in life." Moretti motioned for his security guy to make himself scarce. "You hungry? Of course you're hungry. I'll get you a sandwich."

"I'm not hungry. I want to talk."

Moretti tilted his head. "Follow me. It's a bit more private."

Feldman walked alongside Moretti as they ambled around the huge grounds and into the rose garden, shielded by huge twenty-foot hedgerows.

"What's on your mind?"

"I'll tell you what's on my mind, Paul. Don Lieberman. That's what's on my mind."

Moretti shook his head. "Is he causing you a problem?"

"He's fucking dead, Paul. Shot outside his office in Manhattan a few hours ago."

"Are you kidding? They do say crime in New York is on the rise. A lot of crazies running around. You can't be too careful."

"Paul, are you listening to me? We're talking Don fucking Lieberman. He's dead. Do you understand?"

Moretti shrugged. "Are we talking about the same Don Lieberman?"

"Yeah, the same Don Lieberman. Don't bullshit me, Paul. Are you saying you have no knowledge that he died?"

"First I heard of it. That's too bad."

Feldman felt waves of revulsion at the seeming lack of understanding or empathy in the wake of the death. His client seemed oblivious to the ramifications. "Paul, do you know what this will mean?"

"I'm guessing the shit will hit the fan. But who knows? The guy might've been whacked for stepping out of line. You know how it is. Maybe he's been helping himself to a little piece of their money? I heard he had a pretty bad coke habit."

"That's bullshit. I know Don."

"I don't know. Maybe he pissed off one of the families he represented. Maybe their interests didn't align. Maybe one thought Lieberman was giving preferential treatment. Maybe one of the families got sick of all the dipping. I don't know."

"Paul, Don Lieberman was a lawyer of the highest integrity. He was a close personal friend. You're acting as if his death means nothing. Don't you understand what this could mean? The families could go to war."

Moretti laughed. "Go to war? Most of those stiffs couldn't go to the bathroom unaided, let alone go to war. Gimme a break, Mort. This ain't like the old days. These things happen."

Feldman felt his blood run cold. The way Moretti was speaking was as if Lieberman's death didn't matter. As if it didn't change a thing. It was impossible to kill a Mob lawyer without repercussions.

Moretti plucked a stick out of his koi pond and set it on the path for someone else to discard. "I don't get involved these days. I like to focus more on my family and my life moving forward. I'm making plans."

"Paul, this changes everything. I'm deeply worried about what's going to happen."

Moretti shrugged. "Mort, I love you, man, but you need to tell me what's in your heart. Don't try and talk around whatever happened with Lieberman."

"Did you have Don Lieberman killed?"

Moretti's eyes were black as night. A deathly glassy quality. Unfathomable. "What kind of question is that?"

"I'm just looking for a straight answer. Yes or no will suffice, Paul."

"Mort, do you want me to remind you that you are my lawyer? I don't do confession. And if I did, it would be to a priest. Do you understand?"

"You either tell me the truth or I walk."

Moretti eyeballed him. "Don't you ever try and pressure me in any way whatsoever. Do you understand?"

"Did you have Lieberman killed?"

"Mort, why the hell would I bother with that guy?"

"You told me in the past you didn't like him. You didn't like when I met up with him. You didn't trust him."

"I don't trust anybody."

Feldman felt sick. "You did it, didn't you, Paul? I feel it in my bones. But I can't for the life of me understand why you felt the need to do that."

Moretti pointed a stubby finger at him and jabbed him hard in the chest. "Don't fuck with me."

"If you had anything to do with this, you could be signing your own death warrant. And I want no further part in it. I'm out of here."

Moretti grabbed Feldman by the collar. "Where the hell do you think you're going?"

"I'm going back to New York. I quit. I'm no longer your lawyer."

Moretti grinned. "That's not how it works, Mort."

"Get your fucking hands off me! How could you? Don was an honorable man. He was a fine lawyer. And a friend."

"He's a fucking snitch!"

"What?"

"Every fucking conversation you had with him, the Feds knew about. He was wired."

"How do you know that?"

"I make it my business to know everything."

"He was wearing a wire?"

"A guy at the Justice Department passed it on to a friend of mine."

"Do I know them?"

"I don't think so. But that's all you're getting. So, I don't want to hear any more bullshit about Lieberman being honorable and all that shit. He was a fucking rat." Moretti smiled and grabbed the sides of Feldman's head. "I love you, Mort. I trust you. You're like a brother to me. And I don't say that lightly." He kissed him lightly on the cheek. "Are we good?"

Feldman felt like he was losing his mind. His bearings. His grip on reality. He was screaming inside. "Paul, I want out! I've reached the end of my rope."

Moretti dropped his hands from Feldman's head. "I see."

"You're all set to move out on the date agreed with the Feds. So, you don't need me anymore. No hard feelings."

"You're breaking my heart, Mort."

"Get a new lawyer, Paul. I don't need this anymore."

"Mort, I can't allow that."

Feldman turned and began to walk away. "I'll put my resignation in writing."

Moretti raised his voice. "I can't allow you to leave."

Feldman stopped and turned to face Moretti.

"It's not over, Mort. Not till I say so. And another thing. You're not leaving my home until I'm safely down in Arizona."

Feldman stood frozen in horror. "Are you serious?"

"You're not leaving this estate until I say so."

"Are you saying I'm a prisoner?"

Moretti gave a rueful smile. "Don't be so dramatic. Relax. I've got a lovely cottage on the grounds. It'll be great."

Fifty-Six

It was dark when Reznick finally caught sight of home.

He was mentally exhausted and physically drained. He had ridden north from Manhattan and dumped the bike at a salvage yard on the outskirts of Boston. Then he burned the documents he was going to hand over to Don Lieberman, showing Paul Moretti as an FBI informant. The last thing he did was dismantle the burner phone and drop the parts down a storm drain.

Reznick caught a train from Boston to Brunswick. And then caught the last bus back to Rockland.

He stepped off the bus in the middle of his hometown and headed up the dirt road leading to his home.

Reznick saw three SUVs and a cop car. He saw what looked like a phalanx of Feds waiting for him. He walked toward them and smiled. "What's all this?"

A senior Fed with an expensive-looking suit stepped forward. "Assistant Director Meyerstein is waiting inside. You've got some explaining to do."

Reznick eyeballed the special agent. "And who the fuck are you?"

The Fed stepped aside, shaking his head.

Reznick brushed past them and headed inside his home.

Meyerstein was standing in the hallway. "Hello, Jon," she said. "We've been looking for you."

"Well, here I am."

Reznick shut the front door and followed Meyerstein into the kitchen.

"You look like shit."

"Go easy on the compliments, Martha."

"Do you mind explaining where exactly you've been the last twenty-four hours?"

"I've been out."

"Out. Doing what?"

Reznick paused. "Walking around."

"Walking around, huh? Would you tell me where you were walking around?"

"Here and there. A few trails in the woods. Just trying to clear my head."

Meyerstein held up Reznick's cell phone. "Why in the world would you leave home without your cell phone?"

"I forgot it."

"Don't play me for a fool, Jon. I've had it up to here with you."

"Let me tell you something for nothing. I don't need lectures from the fucking FBI about criminality."

"What precisely does that mean?"

"It means they've been turning a blind eye to it for decades. You want to talk about the illegal wiretaps by Hoover and his goons?"

"That was a long time ago."

"Was it? Illegal mass surveillance of citizens. You want to talk about that?"

Meyerstein stuck her chin out.

"We all know it. Just as long as the end justifies the means. So, let's cut the bullshit hypocrisy. I know what this is about, by the way. The real story. And it's not pretty."

"What are you talking about?"

"You really want to go there?"

Meyerstein stared at him a second too long.

"A high-level confidential informant, huh? Have my actions encroached on that certain gentleman? Is that what this is really about?"

Meyerstein folded her arms.

"A top guy in the New York Mafia. One of the most feared men in the city. A killer. And you're doing deals with him?"

"There is a bigger picture."

"To hell with the bigger picture. Don't you dare have the audacity to tell me about my criminality."

"Have you accessed classified information? I could have you arrested. Is that what you want?"

Reznick stayed silent.

"We have an understanding. That understanding is reaching a breaking point."

"Are you talking in your capacity as an FBI assistant director or as Martha Meyerstein?"

"Both. I suspect you have been in touch with Trevelle Williams, who seems to have fled a grain store he had converted into a little high-tech palace."

Reznick scoffed. "He's helped you guys out many times. He's one of the good guys."

"He's breaking the law," Meyerstein said. "I want to know about your movements over the last twenty-four hours."

"Last time I checked, America wasn't a police state. Looks like I was wrong."

"What the hell has gotten into you? I'm asking you a question: Where were you?"

"Like I said, I've been out and about. Answer me this: Is the Mob boss safe as we speak?" Meyerstein said nothing. "I have not harmed him. I signed that contract."

"What have you been up to, Jon?"

"The day you start dealing with people like that, and turning a blind eye, is the day principles and the law go out the window. The law is the law is the law. Isn't that what you tell me?"

"The end never justifies the means, Jon."

"Are you sure about that?"

Meyerstein was quiet for a few moments. "Is this over? I need to report back to the Director. He gave me an ultimatum. And I need to give him an answer."

"What was the ultimatum?"

"'You either give up Reznick or resign.'"

"Seriously?"

Meyerstein nodded.

"So, what are you going to do?"

"That's the problem. I still don't know yet."

"Do what you have to do."

Meyerstein checked her watch. "I need to get back to DC. I have a meeting with the Director first thing in the morning."

Fifty-Seven

The craziness of the day before had lasted well into the night.

Reznick sat alone out on his deck, nursing a cold beer, staring at the sea. The conversation with Meyerstein was still ringing in his ears. The killing of Lieberman had thwarted Reznick's plan to leverage the Mob lawyer against Moretti. He felt waves of tiredness wash over him. He quickly showered, shaved, and collapsed onto his bed. He was out like a light.

When he awoke, the sun was streaming through his bedroom window. He checked his watch. It was nearly noon. He felt groggy, eyes heavy, muscles sore after hundreds of miles on the bike. He splashed cold water on his face to rouse himself. Then he got dressed and drove into town.

He bought some groceries and drove home, stocked up his fridge, freezer, and cupboards.

Reznick washed down a Dexedrine and drove to Bill Eastland's house. He imagined Eastland maybe trying to pull his gun. He thought Eastland would have put up a fight. A hell of a fight. But against a crew of hardened young psychopaths, Bill and Elspeth wouldn't have stood a chance.

It wouldn't be long until the house was a new family's home. It would be a knockdown price. The memories Reznick had of drinking at Eastland's would fade into the distance.

Reznick headed back into town. He stopped off at a flower shop. Then he went into a liquor store and picked up a bottle of Scotch. He drove to the cemetery. He walked over to Bill and Elspeth's graves and laid the fresh flowers on them. He touched the gravestones before pouring the booze into the earth.

"Rest in peace, friends."

He stood and read the inscriptions for a few minutes. His mind was replaying what Meyerstein had said.

Reznick knew she was at the end of her rope. The problem was, so was he.

Reznick's stomach grumbled. He drove back to Main Street. He stopped and picked up a copy of the *New York Times* from the newsstand. Then he drove the short distance to the Home Kitchen Café.

He sat down at his favorite table by the window so he could see what was going on.

A waitress ambled up, beaming broadly. "Afternoon, Jon. You had a late night at the Myrtle? You look rough."

"I've had worse, Catherine. No, I wasn't at the Myrtle last night. Just been busy."

"Glad to hear it. You hear about Bill Eastland?"

Reznick nodded. "I was at Bill's funeral."

"Goddamn shame. A good man like that. He helped my brother out when he was a kid running wild. You remember Lucas, right?"

Reznick knew Lucas from his school days. A complete delinquent. But he had seen him around many times since, and he seemed a bit more settled. "Yeah, how is he?"

"He got himself straightened out. He used to get into a lot of trouble."

"What happened?"

"Bill came to our house one night with Lucas. He'd caught him red-handed trying to break into the hardware shop on Main Street and came down hard on him. Bloodied his nose and everything. Hauled him in front of my father and mother, who knew nothing about what he was doing. He said if he ever caught Lucas again, he'd be going to jail."

"Interesting."

"My brother never got into trouble after that. And he had Bill to thank."

"Tough love, right?"

"Precisely. My father was always too soft with Lucas. But anyway, he's got a good job at the school as a caretaker, doing OK. And he's got a wife and three kids."

Reznick smiled.

"So, my family certainly has a lot to thank Bill for. If it had been any other cop, my brother would have been thrown in jail. And who knows where he would have ended up?"

"We all need to catch a break now and again."

Catherine tilted her head back. "Anyway, what can I get you?"

Reznick ordered a hearty all-American breakfast of eggs, bacon, and toast and a cup of black coffee.

"You got it. Nice to see you again. I'll be over shortly."

Reznick opened up the paper. And sure enough, there it was: the front-page headline was "Mob Lawyer Slain in Manhattan." He searched the picture of Don Lieberman, taken at a Midtown restaurant the day before he was gunned down. Beside the photo, taken nearly twenty-four hours later, another one—a stark color picture of a body under a sheet outside the office. The same thing Reznick had witnessed up close.

He read the article. A senior police source, according to the paper, speculated that Lieberman had fallen out with one of the New York families. The source also claimed he feared a Mafia war could "break out at any time." He said that Lieberman couldn't account for several offshore accounts, and one of the families had put out a contract on him. An FBI source claimed Lieberman might have been targeted for money laundering. But the article also speculated that the focus of the investigation was "changing by the minute" as information poured in. A former Mafia captain told the *Times* that Lieberman was an "FBI informer" and had been "whacked for breaking the Mafia code of silence."

Reznick realized he was inadvertently caught up in a potential war between the crime families of New York. He wanted no part of it. It wasn't his fight. But in a way, it was. He wanted Moretti to pay. He wondered if his failed escapade yesterday was a portent of things to come.

He finished the rest of the long article. If Lieberman was an informer, why would Moretti—and not someone from the families Lieberman worked for—kill him? None of it made any sense. Surely the FBI couldn't turn a blind eye after a hit on an alleged FBI informant. Then again, was it more plausible that the FBI was in the dark as to who ordered the killing?

He looked out the window. A sheriff's car was approaching. He spotted Tom Cain pulling up.

Reznick folded the paper before Cain sauntered in. The cop looked tired, as if he hadn't had much sleep. Cain sat down opposite him.

"Afternoon, Tom. Don't tell me you're having breakfast this late too?"

Cain gave a rueful smile. "Jon, you're killing me."

"What's wrong? A man's allowed to have a late breakfast in a café, right?"

Cain nodded. He ordered a latte and pancakes. "You OK if I sit here? Just thought it would give us a chance to catch up."

"Free country, man. Or so they keep telling me."

Cain smiled. They made small talk for a few minutes.

Catherine the waitress returned with the breakfasts and coffees. "Enjoy your meal, guys." She cocked her head toward the serving station. "If there's anything you need, I'll be right over there."

Reznick nodded. "Thank you."

Cain waited until she was out of earshot. He leaned closer. "Here's the thing, Jon. I didn't want to go onto your property."

"Tom, relax. You had to do that. I'm sure the sheriff's department got a court order. It's not a problem. We're good."

Cain sighed. "The whole thing is fucked up."

"You don't have to tell me. I know what the Feds are like, trust me."

"I was a bit surprised you weren't at home."

"I was clearing my head, Tom. After everything that's happened. Bill and I were very tight."

"Going to miss him. The whole town is going to miss him."

"So true."

"I want to give you a heads-up. With regard to the search of your home yesterday. I want you to know what I saw."

"What did you see?"

"Three Feds arrived shortly after I gained entry."

Reznick thought through where Cain was going with this.

"One of the three guys had flown in from Washington. They said he was from the Tactical Operations Section."

Reznick whistled. "Interesting."

"Wait till you hear this. The TacOps agent placed electronic listening devices in your TV, the radio in the kitchen, and your Sonos speaker in the living room. Those are the ones I know about. There might be more."

Reznick took a few moments to process that information.

"I didn't ask them why they were placing them. They just said they had a full warrant."

Reznick set his fork to the side, placed his hands on the table.

"Jon, this didn't come from me. I just wanted you to know that they're listening in on whatever you're saying to whoever you're saying it to. At least in your home."

"Tom, I owe you, man. You're a good friend."

Cain finished his coffee and stared out the window at the parking lot. "I felt sick. I couldn't sleep when I got home. Can't believe the American government is bugging people like you."

"It's good to know, Tom. Forewarned is forearmed."

Fifty-Eight

Reznick hung around the café for an hour, filling up on fresh coffee. Maybe he shouldn't have been as surprised as he was. It was the FBI, after all.

He wondered what Meyerstein really knew about the bugging of his home.

The reality was, Moretti was far more valuable than Reznick. No matter what Reznick had done for the country. No matter how he had helped the FBI in difficult investigations. The betrayal nevertheless stuck in his throat.

Reznick left a fifty-dollar bill on the table and walked out of the diner and back toward his vehicle. He acted as if he was being watched at that very moment. He got to his truck and sat for a while.

He was sure he had a fail-safe way to get to Moretti. He really thought he had a plan in place. It had been so carefully thought out. But the murder of Lieberman had put an end to that.

Reznick was at a crossroads. A little voice in his head was urging caution. *Do nothing. Move on.* But the more Reznick considered walking away, the more he felt himself being drawn back. He still wanted to kill Moretti. The only problem was that he hadn't figured out how he was going to do it.

Reznick started up his truck and pulled slowly away, headed down to the nearby harborside. A line of vehicles queuing up for the ferry. He drove past them and parked beside the pay phone. He got out of his vehicle and called Trevelle. He wasn't done with Moretti. It rang for nearly a minute.

"Hey," Trevelle said, "what the hell went down?"

"I was hoping you could answer that."

"The cops are still scratching their heads. They don't know who whacked the lawyer."

"I read in the *Times* that Lieberman might have been an informant for the Feds."

"That would be enough to get you iced, no question. The bigger question is: Who ordered the hit? It could have been the four families. Real possibility if they found out about that."

"Then again," Reznick posited, "can we exclude Moretti?"

"I don't know. Surely the Feds wouldn't have given a free pass for Moretti's men to kill Lieberman."

"Who knows how these guys think? Moretti is capable of anything."

Trevelle asked, "So, what're you thinking?"

"Just got word from a cop in Rockland. Feds have bugged my house, apparently."

"Bullshit."

"That's what he said."

"That's unbelievable. Seriously?"

"Tough one to swallow."

"So, let's back up. Your plan to pass on the information to Lieberman was thwarted. What now?"

Reznick thought on it. "I don't know. Feel like I've hit a brick wall."

"You want some advice?"

"Shoot."

"I think sometimes it's best to just move on. You got the guys who pulled the trigger. And you nearly got the main man. You couldn't do any more. Time to cut your losses."

"I feel like I could do more."

"Yeah, but listen: it would mean putting yourself at serious risk. You're not going up against some psycho hillbillies from Texas. This would be a suicide mission. You're talking a Mafia boss with dozens in his crew. And his compound, man. I mean, layers of security."

Trevelle was right. The odds were stacked against him. "Can you do me a favor?"

"What do you want, my friend?"

"My head is not in a good place right now. I need time and space to think. But what I would like from you, once I figure out what I'm going to do, if anything, is to get me the architectural plans for Moretti's home."

"That isn't going to end well. Moretti will be gone in two days."

"Maybe. Maybe not. Can you do that for me?"

"Let me see what I can do. I can't make any promises. When do you want it?"

"Can you have them sent to me by the end of the day? And I want full detailed plans. The works."

Fifty-Nine

Feldman remained a prisoner of Paul Moretti, in the two-bedroom cottage adjacent to the main house. He saw Moretti, his client, talking on a cell phone, laughing as if he didn't have a care in the world. A few of the armed goons perched not far away, trying to blend in.

Feldman considered whether Moretti was going to have him killed. His cell phone had been confiscated. He had no way of letting his kids know where he was. Even his ex-wife. That was the worst part.

Moretti ended the call and spoke to one of his bodyguards, who was toting what looked like a submachine gun. It was terrifying.

Feldman needed to speak to Moretti again. He had to gauge his mood. Hopefully his rational approach could win Moretti over from what appeared to be paranoid behavior.

Moretti had told Feldman that Lieberman had been an FBI informer. And that Feldman's conversations were being bugged by Lieberman. It was clear Moretti was not only highly dangerous but was also worryingly unpredictable.

Feldman left the cottage and walked aimlessly toward Moretti. He smiled at his client. "Hey, Paul, you have a minute?"

Moretti wrapped his huge arms around Feldman's shoulder. "Mort, for you, anything. What's on your mind?"

"Paul, I'm going to level with you. I always did my utmost for you. I never discussed your business. I operated by the highest ethical standards. I hope you'll agree."

"I've always liked you, Mort. And you've always been straight with me."

"Paul, I'm scared. I feel very uneasy being confined on your estate like this."

Moretti headed toward the water. "Let's walk and talk."

Feldman followed Moretti as they strolled the estate. "Let me go to New York, Paul. This is not how I conduct business."

"And I appreciate that. But this is a critical juncture for not only me, but my business and my family's future. It will all change in two days."

"Are you confirming that I'm confined to your house until this is over?"

"It is what it is, Mort. Let me ask you a question. Do you think you'll be safer outside or inside this compound?"

"I feel safe either way, Paul. But I don't like this. I don't want to stay somewhere against my will. It's worrying."

"Mort, the tragic killing of your friend Lieberman . . . It changes everything. I'm worried for your safety on the streets of New York."

"I've been in business more than a quarter of a century. I never encountered any problems. Ever."

Moretti turned and pointed to a bodyguard lurking under a shade tree, rifle slung over his shoulder. "You're safe here. I'll make sure no one harms you. A couple of days, Mort. And then I'm out of here, and you're free to go."

Sixty

The headlights of a truck appeared on the dirt road. Reznick sat on the front porch, drinking a cup of coffee, watching the approaching FedEx van.

The driver hopped out and handed over the cylinder-shaped parcel. "Hey, buddy, last on my list."

Reznick tipped the guy twenty bucks. "Appreciate it, man."

The driver got back in his van and headed off.

Reznick went inside, packed a bag of essentials, picked up the parcel, and put all of it into the back of his truck. He took out his cell phone and logged on to the Airbnb website, scanning nearby properties. A colonial house in Camden, overlooking the water, caught his eye. He booked it and drove over to the house.

He received a keycode from the building's owner and headed inside, switched on the lamps, and looked around. He began to check out the premises, room by room.

He made himself at home. He switched on a classical radio station, music playing low. He checked out the huge fridge and freezer.

Reznick took out a bottle of Bud Light and sat down. He liked the place he had booked on such short notice. An hour after he had booked it, he was sitting down, enjoying a beer in a beautiful house by the water. It reminded him a little of the ambience of his cabin up in the north Maine woods. Not as isolated. But with a relaxed vibe about it.

Reznick opened the cylindrical parcel, which was sitting in the corner. He rolled out the tube inside. It contained the architectural plans for Paul Moretti's waterfront estate in Connecticut. He cleared the books off the coffee table. He spread out the huge plans, using place mats to hold down the corners.

Reznick took a few minutes to scan the floor plans. He noted elevations. The construction material. The subbasement plans, schematics showing how the wiring and pipes and ventilation ducts flowed. Structural layouts, internal elevation drawings, the size of the lumber used, and on and on, down to the smallest detail. The Brazilian hardwood flooring. He looked over the myriad rooms. The place was massive, with twenty-five bedrooms, elevators all the way down to the subbasement, thirty bathrooms, five room-size clothes closets, Olympic-size indoor and outdoor pools, a squash court, an outdoor tennis court, a wine cellar, a basketball court, and a private lake. He despised a man who needed such excess space.

How many bathrooms was too many?

He surveyed the plans for the estate grounds. Two guesthouses. A pool house. And a small house on the periphery of the two-hundred-acre estate. A huge wall, twenty feet high. And on the other side, only woods and dirt roads. He checked the scale drawings and estimated the small house was maybe a mile from the main residence. If this was a panic room, which was what it looked like, judging by the size, it would have fireproof doors. But a panic room was usually found in the main residence, in a basement or subbasement. Yet panic rooms were ordinarily in basements or subbasements.

Reznick pondered the location of the small house at the very outer edge of the estate. He couldn't see the sense in the panic room being detached from the main home. The purpose was that if intruders broke in, the homeowners could get in the panic room, call the cops, and stay safe until help arrived.

He looked over the plans one more time. He checked the sub-basement plans. Then he saw it: a door at the far end of the huge wine cellar. A door marked "Emergency Exit." Behind the door was a tunnel. It consisted of ventilation shafts. And it headed straight for the house at the other end of the estate. Except the tunnel, after the exit to the panic room, continued under the estate's perimeter wall and finished ten yards on the other side.

He looked closer.

"You sly old fucker."

Reznick could see that the exit from the tunnel on the other side of the perimeter wall—outside Moretti's estate—was via a vertical shaft accessed by ladder to the surface. A manhole cover deep within the surrounding woods.

He considered potential scenarios Moretti might face. He figured if Moretti saw gunmen bursting through the main security gates, it would give him time to get to the wine cellar and head down the tunnel to the panic room. Maybe he would head straight down the tunnel and up the vertical shaft under the manhole cover in the woods. After climbing out, he would shut the manhole cover, lock it, and flee to safety.

It showed smarts.

Reznick researched whether he could access the property via the manhole. It shouldn't be too difficult to open up. An oxyacetylene torch could cut it open.

His problem would then be gaining access to the wine cellar subbasement. That would probably be a different set of keys. Again, he could cut it open with a torch. But that would take vital time. The element of surprise would be lost. Maybe the tunnels would be under surveillance by anything from thermal sensors to cameras.

The more he thought of a possible assault on the compound, the more problems he saw. It was hard to know where to start. He would be alone. He would have Trevelle for technical backup, but it was the very definition of a suicide mission. He wouldn't make it out alive.

The chances of getting near Moretti were slim. The master bedroom was on the third floor at the north side of the house. Farthest from his entry point—and what if he was somewhere else on the estate?

Reznick's cell phone pinged. He had an encrypted email from Trevelle. *Call me now. Urgent.*

He got in his truck and drove to the nearby gas station.

It rang two times before Trevelle answered. "Yeah, sorry to disturb you."

"What's the problem?"

"The software I use I developed when I was at NSA. It can extract specific words from conversations, and that includes police channels."

"What have you heard?"

"Your daughter's name came up."

"Lauren?"

"The FBI is trying to locate her. As a matter of urgency."

"Christ . . ."

"I put in a call direct to Martha, making sure she couldn't track me."

"What did she say?"

"She asked me to pass on a message to you."

"What kind of message?"

"The FBI is aware of the threat. She says to pass it on to you that they have credible evidence Moretti got your name. Somehow, some way, he got your name. And he sent a team to kill her."

Reznick felt himself slipping his moorings. "Why don't they take her to a safe house?"

"That's the problem."

"What the hell do you mean?"

"I mean the FBI can't find her anywhere."

Sixty-One

Meyerstein paced the SIOC as she adjusted her headphones.

"Someone must know where she is! What's her location? Why can't we find her? And where the hell is Andrew Collins? Get him on the phone!"

A young National Security Agency encryption and IT specialist looked up from her screen. "Ma'am, I've got a visual on Lauren Reznick."

"Where?"

"Midtown Manhattan. She's on the subway. Reception is terrible at the best of times. But she's one block from Times Square. The A train. She's headed east."

"And you've got a visual?"

"Copy that."

Meyerstein pointed at the young woman. "Get on it. Find her. Get NYPD on it too!"

Her headphones buzzed. "Martha, it's Andrew. I've been tied up trying to get to the bottom of where Lauren is."

Meyerstein adjusted the microphone. "We just located her. On the subway, one block from Times Square."

"I've got a team en route. They'll get her."

"Make sure they do. Now, what the hell happened? I got a message from the New York field office saying we had a potential threat to one of our agents. What do you know?"

"I just got up to speed myself. This is a shitshow."

"Tell me!"

"It all started when our confidential informant's coordinator, based in Manhattan, called me. He had a meeting with a mid-level Mafia informant out on Staten Island."

"And?"

"This informant, he's a longtime Moretti associate. He's not a made man. But he knows what's going on."

"I'm listening."

"This morning, during a discussion—it's a monthly sit-down between them—he said that the word was out: find a young FBI special agent and kill her. One hundred thousand dollars."

"And he gave the name Lauren Reznick?"

"He gave the name. And he had an address."

Meyerstein closed her eyes for a moment as she felt a wave of tension wash over her. "You did the right thing, Andrew. I'm glad you saw how this could go."

"We have a safe house for her. It's all set. We've got a team there waiting for her."

Meyerstein took off the headphones and left SIOC, going straight to the seventh floor. She was already late for the meeting of senior FBI executives discussing the imminent move of Moretti.

She took her seat. "Apologies for being so late. I was overseeing the situation in New York."

Franklin looked up from his papers. "Have they found her yet?"

"They've located her position. We're hopeful we'll have her in the next few minutes."

"Thank God. What a mess."

Crabtree cleared her throat. "I'm glad that's figured out. So, we can move on."

"Not so fast, Rachel. Paul Moretti, who we are making final preparations to designate our highest-level confidential informant and get moved to a safe house, has put out a hit on an FBI agent. I'm quite clear on this. We need to rip up the agreement. And arrest him. I've seen enough."

Franklin blinked fast before he cleared his throat. He seemed taken aback. "This is quite extraordinary, Martha. This isn't like you to be so impetuous."

"Enough is enough!"

Crabtree gave her best condescending smile. "I know how much this has affected you, Martha. We know how close you are to Lauren. You're like a mentor. I get it. But it's also your close relationship with Jon Reznick which has put us all in a tight spot."

"I'm only interested in Lauren Reznick getting to a safe house. She's one of us. A special agent. But the issue of Moretti and his flagrant lawbreaking is beyond the pale. It is simply not tenable to continue with him as a high-level informant, no matter what he brings to the table."

Franklin shook his head. "The FBI is well aware of Paul Moretti's criminality. And I know this breaches our protocol on high-level informants. But this is bigger than Lauren Reznick, Jon Reznick, me, you, or anyone. This is the big picture. We are going to gain unlimited and unprecedented access to intel that will save countless lives down the line."

The pay phone rang, and Reznick picked up. "Any news?"

"Your daughter is safe."

Reznick breathed a sigh of relief. "Are you sure?"

"Just had confirmation. One hundred percent safe."

"Any indication of why she might have been targeted?"

"They have your name. That's why."

"How did they get my name in the first place?"

"Very good question. It's a clear security breach. Maybe FBI. Maybe . . . maybe other agencies. But someone passed on your name."

"Maybe leaked it."

"I don't know. But it's clearly meant to be retaliation for your actions."

"They've crossed a fucking line once too often. They put a contract out on my daughter!"

"She's safe. That's all that matters."

"But for how long? Can anyone say for sure that this fuck or his crew won't target her again? They've got her name. They have my name. And they're being protected by the FBI. He went after my girl. My daughter. My flesh and blood. That's my red line. You come after my daughter, then as far as I'm concerned, all bets are off."

Reznick hung up. He realized he was breathing hard.

It was then, at that moment, that Reznick knew he had to fight. To the death.

Sixty-Two

Reznick picked up the pay phone again and called Ripley. "Sam, it's Jon."

"Everything OK, man?"

"Not really."

"What's the problem?"

Reznick related the chain of events, leading up to the contract being put on his daughter's life. "I've reached the end of my rope. I figure I could use some help. I want to kill the fucker."

"How can I help? Man, I'm in."

"Sam, this is a highly dangerous mission. I need someone who can fly a chopper."

"I'm the best there is."

"I know that. But you need to know what it entails. Sam, you could die."

"We're all going to die. Fuck it, this bastard needs to be put down."

Reznick gathered his thoughts again. He was beginning to formulate a fresh plan. "So, I need you to fly a chopper. You need to have access to a chopper too. It must have night vision."

"I've got one."

"Yeah, I know you fly helicopters and Black Hawks, Sam, but I mean you need to be able to take one out and fly it. Like, tomorrow night."

"Short notice, Jon."

"Can you do it?"

"I can do it."

"How?"

"My dad is a veteran."

"I remember. You told me."

"He was a pilot in Vietnam. He's the one who taught me how to fly. He bought a secondhand Huey five years back."

"The old Bell military chopper?"

"That's right. He takes out photographers for aerial photographs across Cape Cod, especially in the summer. Sometimes does chopper tours."

"So, why isn't he using it now?"

"He's in the hospital, recovering from a motorcycle accident. He's going to be fine."

Reznick smiled. "A motorcycle accident? How old is your dad, anyway?"

"He's eighty, man."

"Won't he mind?"

"It's for one night?"

"One night. And into the early hours. Back at sunup on September fourth. And you'll be flying as low as the treetops at sixty feet."

"I can help you, Jon."

"Right. Where is this Huey?"

"Out at my place on Cape Cod. I've got a hangar for it."

"I need you to paint it."

"What the hell for?"

297

"I want you to repaint it the same colors as the Coast Guard. The same markings."

"OK, I got that. It'll take a little while."

"Can it be done in time?"

"Sure, but it'll be tight."

"One last time, Sam. There's no shame in it. You're a good friend. But I need you to give me your definitive answer right now. Are you in or are you out?"

"Are you serious? I'm in. Fuck it. Let's go get the bastard."

Reznick hung up. The next person he called was Tom Hewson.

"Yeah, Tommy speaking."

"It's Reznick."

"Jon, how's the bike?"

"Very good, thanks," he lied. "Listen, I'm not going to sugar-coat it. I have to do something. You have the skills. And you've worked as a merc. So, I'm going to need that skill set. It's a one-off. And it happens in the early hours of September fourth."

Silence on the other end of the line. "I'm already there. Just like you were there in Ramadi. Remember, some of our corps got cut off. But you bastards choppered in and mowed the fuckers down. And you got me the hell out of there."

"You'll be in a chopper. All you have to do is drop flash-bangs across the property. Then you're out of there."

"Diversionary?"

"Correct."

"That's it?"

"That's it. But listen, this is a one-off. You tell no one. You in?"

"Fuckin' A, man."

"You got a pen and paper?"

"Sure."

"Write this down." Reznick gave him directions to the cabin in Camden. "You got that?"

Hewson repeated the address. "When?"

"I'll see you there in an hour."

"What do I bring?"

"I'm assuming you have some flash-bangs, rifles, and flares? That sort of shit?"

"And a whole lot more."

"Bring that kit. And an overnight bag. Also a mask and any tactical gear you want."

"Who you gonna kill?"

"I'll tell you in sixty minutes."

Sixty-Three

The hours that followed were like a flashback to the old days for Reznick. Planning, focus, and developing the hit. The problem was he didn't have weeks or months to prepare. He had one night and one day. Then it would begin at midnight. Twenty-six hours away.

Reznick pinned the architectural plans on the wall.

Hewson stood beside him as he studied the plans. "So, the chopper comes in from the east, right?"

Reznick nodded. "You got it." He pointed at the front elevation of the house, which faced the water. "You come in over Long Island Sound, and it'll be real fucking low, Tom. I mean skirting the treetops."

"What about power lines?"

"I've checked that. You're fine coming in from the east or the northeast side. The far side of the estate, there are wires. So, stay clear."

Hewson pointed on the map to the subbasement tunnel. "I'm going to drop all sorts of shit on the main house to fire the place up. And he will, we're assuming, head down the tunnel. Just say he doesn't?"

"It's a possibility. But I know the guy is there."

"How do you know?"

"The technical support guy I have is listening in to a lawyer's cell phone, which is being held at the gatehouse. It's switched off. But he's activated the microphone. So, we're getting a situational awareness update. We have full access to the comings and goings at the gatehouse too."

Hewson smiled. "You're crazy, you know that?"

"We're going to smoke him out. I also want you firing tear gas and whatever stuff you carry. But here's the problem. The glass that covers the east side of the house, facing the sea—according to the specs, it's bullet resistant. Level 6."

"Fuck. So, what the hell does level 6 mean?"

"The glass is designed to stand up to at least five 9mm rounds at a minimum velocity of 1,400 feet per second. What will penetrate that?"

Hewson grinned. "I know what will. A light fifty."

"You got your hands on a Barrett M107?"

"The latest version."

"Fucking hell, Tom."

"I got whatever it takes. And enough 0.50 ammo to last a month."

Reznick patted Hewson on the back. "Now we're talking. You need to bring all of that—and whatever else you might need—and be back here at dawn. We need to have firepower."

Hewson surveyed the plans. "This is a big fucking house. What about dropping some Tovex and C-4 on the house?"

"You have that?"

"I got a lot of stuff stashed away, Jon. This country is going to fuck. And I for one am going to be ready for anything. Now, whose house is this? Who are we after?"

"He's a Mob boss. His name is Paul Moretti. And he had Bill Eastland and his wife killed."

"The Mob killed old Bill?"

"Moretti gave the order. He didn't pull the trigger, but he ordered the hit. Bill had a huge gambling tab, and he was running his mouth. Threats to have a Mafia joint shut down. Death threats too. And they ran out of patience."

Hewson went quiet for a few moments. "Tell me about the pilot."

"He's the best there is. Black Hawk. Numerous classified missions for Delta, Marines, SEAL Team 6. I know him well. I vouch for him."

"That'll do for me."

"Go home. And get to work. I want your weapons stripped and cleaned to perfection. I don't want rifles getting jammed or some bullshit. Everything works. Right?"

"That's a given, man."

"You have one job. You're going to scare the shit out of this guy. You're going to punch a hole in that bullet-resistant glass. Tear gas. Flash-bangs. Then out of there. Moretti will be so freaked out he won't know what hit him. Then he'll head down to the subbasement and into the tunnel."

Hewson traced his finger along the tunnel until it reached the vertical hatch.

"He will emerge," Reznick said. "And I'll neutralize."

"You figured this all out yourself?"

"It doesn't mean a thing unless the execution is perfect. You in?"

"I love you, Reznick. You're a real crazy dude. But I love you. Fuck it, I'm in."

Sixty-Four

The following morning, Feldman sat at Moretti's kitchen table with a latte, a Doberman slobbering at his feet. He had a deep fear of dogs. All dogs. But especially dogs like this Doberman. It was unbearable.

Moretti laughed at Feldman's unease. "Relax, Mort, she likes you."

"How do you live surrounded by fucking dogs day and night?"

"That's how I sleep so well. Great security, isolated estate, and dogs. Man's best friend."

Feldman stared out the floor-to-ceiling windows across the huge front lawn to the choppy waters of Long Island Sound. "I want to go home, Paul. I can't sleep. I'm a mess. You need to get a new lawyer. I've had enough."

"Bullshit. You're still a sharp operator."

"Paul, please, I'm begging you. For my family—they need me home. I'm sure they've been trying to contact me."

"Relax."

"Can I at least have my cell phone? I'm a lawyer. I need to speak to people."

Moretti grimaced. "Not now, Mort. I swear, I'm out of here tomorrow morning, first light. Six a.m. motorcade straight to the

Westchester airport. I'll drop you off there. Can't get fairer than that."

Feldman shook his head. "My ulcer is killing me. I need to see my doctor."

"Take a Zantac. We have plenty."

"My high blood pressure, it's not good. None of this is helping me."

Moretti patted Feldman on the cheek. "Know your problem?"

"I'm being kept here against my will."

"Funny guy. No, you worry too much. Look at it another way. You're enjoying some downtime. A time to relax."

Feldman saw the Doberman looking at him. "How can I unwind when your dog is ready to attack?"

"Don't say that word."

"Why not?"

"If you say it twice, she will rip out your throat."

"Seriously?"

Moretti kneeled down and hugged the Doberman. "This time tomorrow, I'm going to be flying down to Arizona, sipping Dom Perignon. Ready to start a new life. And you? You can get back to being a lawyer in Manhattan again."

Feldman stared through the windows. Truth be told, he was scared to death. He feared Moretti was going to kill him before he boarded the chopper. Feldman knew it all. He knew all Moretti's secrets, from bank accounts to crimes he had committed. "I want to leave today. I think it's outrageous, Paul, that I'm being kept against my will."

"No one leaves until I say so. This is my call. One more day."

"What if the FBI is trying to contact me? What if they want to talk? I deal with dozens of people every week, mostly on the phone, about your businesses."

Moretti's eyes seemed to darken as he pointed at Feldman. "You need to learn to let it go. You're starting to bug me. You hear me? I've got a lot on my fucking mind. The last thing I want is my lawyer moaning in my ear."

"I'm not your lawyer anymore, Paul. Don't you remember? I quit."

"No one ever quits me. No one leaves until I say so."

"I'm not your fucking lawyer. Get over it."

"Mort, if you were anyone else, I would have had you taken outside and had a bullet put in your head."

Feldman cringed, frozen rigid by terror. "Why did you say that? What was the purpose of you saying that?"

Feldman looked at Moretti's eyes, never more dark and empty. A sense of foreboding gripped him as he realized what fate awaited him.

Sixty-Five

Late in the afternoon, Reznick was putting the finishing touches on his plan to kill Moretti. He drove to the gas station in Camden. A trucker climbed into his eighteen-wheeler and pulled away.

Reznick waited for that noise to subside before he walked over to the pay phone and called Trevelle one final time.

It rang for nearly a minute. Trevelle was breathing hard when he answered. "Man, sorry, I've been freaking out wondering when you were going to call."

"What is it? You sound stressed."

"Everything is fucked up. Moretti is fucked up. He's a psychopath."

"Tell me something I don't know."

"I've been recording everything that his lawyer's cell phone picks up."

"What've you heard?"

"A matter of minutes ago, Moretti had his lawyer killed. At the estate."

"What? In the house?"

"The guy at the gatehouse was talking to a bodyguard who had stopped by and was asking about visitors. And the bodyguard mentioned that Feldman's body was going to be taken to an incineration plant in Jersey."

Reznick felt sick. "And you have a copy of the conversation?"

"I've been recording the whole time. We need to go to the Feds."

"And say what? Moretti is a savage killer. They made a deal with him. And they're not going to back out at the eleventh hour."

Trevelle sighed long and hard. "It doesn't end there."

"What?"

"The guard says Moretti has changed his plans. He's moving earlier."

"How much earlier?"

"He's leaving his house in the dark. In the early hours of the fourth. Three a.m. precisely. 0300 hours. It was originally scheduled for six a.m."

Reznick realized he was going to have to move faster than he thought.

"Moretti's car is reinforced and bulletproof. It will be accompanied by three cars."

"Are you kidding me?"

"Negative. That's the conversation I picked up in the gatehouse."

"And Moretti moved the whole thing up?"

"Affirmative. They're leaving in the middle of the night. Four cars will be leaving the main gatehouse at three a.m. That's all I know."

Sixty-Six

Reznick stood beside the pay phone, trying to wrap his head around the eleventh-hour switch. "Fuck." His two-stage plan to have a chopper move in under the cover of darkness and kill Moretti when he emerged in the woods had sunk. The element of surprise would be gone. The bodyguards would all be in and around the main house and spread out across the grounds.

The bodyguards would fire at the chopper as soon as they saw it approach the house. Moretti wouldn't have to head down to the tunnel. But if he did, he wouldn't need to disappear into the woods. Moretti might stay in the panic room on the far side of the sprawling estate until the matter was resolved.

Reznick might be waiting in the woods for a Mob boss who wouldn't turn up. He needed another plan. It was the fourth quarter. And the clock was ticking.

It was only a matter of hours until Moretti left.

The first thing he did was call Ripley in Cape Cod.

"Sam, change of plan," Reznick said.

"I'm repainting the chopper."

"I'm still going to need you."

"Good."

"There's a chopper landing area adjacent to a minor league baseball field south of Camden. I want you to pick me and Tom up, along with a motorcycle we will be using, and take us to a drop-off point, five miles north of the target's estate."

Ripley was taking notes. "Got it. When?"

"Midnight."

"Then what?"

"You get us into position. Then head back to Cape Cod. And probably repaint your chopper tomorrow. Do you copy?"

"Copy that. This is a green light?"

"Damn right. Green light, Sam. Don't let me down."

Reznick ended the call. He felt bad making things any harder for his good friend Ripley. But he was glad that Sam was still on board. He had a crucial part to play if they were going to get down to Connecticut before Moretti left.

His mind switched quickly to what else he needed to do.

He picked up the phone and called Tom Hewson.

"Tom, you got a minute?"

"Sure, man. I was just packing up a few essentials."

"Change of plan, Tom."

"Man, seriously?"

"Yup. The target is leaving earlier than expected. A matter of hours. The original plan is not going to cut it."

Hewson remained silent.

"Here's where I'm at. I'm going to plan B."

"What's plan B?"

Reznick said, "That's the problem. I don't know. But I'm trying to figure it out. If you want out, I'll understand."

"Negative, man. I'm not cutting and running. That's not me. You know that. I'm in to the death."

"Sam will pick us up at midnight outside Camden."

"This really happening? Tonight?"

"Damn right it is."

"What do you need me to bring?"

"Bring everything you can get your hands on that can do damage."

"Tovex and C-4?"

"Exactly. Real damage. We're going to need stuff that will wake the dead. And bring your Kawasaki."

"It's got fake plates and all."

"That's perfect."

"What the hell you got in mind, man?"

"I want you over at my place in Camden. Bring all your gear, and let's run through some options. We haven't got long."

Sixty-Seven

It was nearly dark when Reznick saw the headlights of Hewson's motorcycle. He showed the ex-Marine inside. Hewson carried a huge backpack, bulging at the seams.

Reznick poured him a strong cup of coffee while Hewson unpacked his gear. It included a 9mm Glock, a sawn-off shotgun, boxes of ammo, and sticks of Tovex and C-4. "Wow. You really did it."

"Be careful. I have enough to level the neighborhood."

Reznick shook his head. "You're prepared. I'll give you that."

"That's who I am."

Reznick walked over to the architectural plans he had pinned on the wall. He pointed at the main house. "Moretti's main residence, OK?"

Hewson again studied the plans greedily, eyes darting back and forth as if devouring as much information as he could.

Reznick pointed to the main security gate. "Intel shows that he will be leaving here as part of a four-vehicle convoy. He will be in the middle. And before you ask, I have it on good authority that the car windows are bulletproof."

"Fuck," Hewson said.

"So, this is not going to be easy. We have to get in close to have a realistic chance of taking this guy out. Real close."

Hewson nodded. "We get close, and then what?"

"We're going to attach a magnetic explosive device to the vehicle while we ride past on your bike."

Hewson sat down. "Fucking hell, Jon. That's how we're going to kill a Mob boss?"

"Have you got a problem with that?"

"Shit, I don't know." Hewson looked pale, color drained from his brow.

Reznick was surprised by the reaction. "Tom . . . I don't understand. I thought I explained what this was all about."

"I know . . . but this is pretty far out."

"I'm not disputing that."

"The odds are not exactly stacked in our favor."

Reznick sensed his friend wanted out.

"What if . . ."

Reznick felt sick. He had thought the veteran, an acquaintance he had known for years, was on board. He hadn't imagined Tom getting cold feet.

"I don't know if I can do this without some more firepower alongside me. I'm out of my comfort zone a bit."

"Listen, if you're having second thoughts, that's perfectly understandable. But I need you to give me a straight answer. Are you in or are you out?"

"Jon, my line of work involves killing people. But usually it's with a team of six or seven, and breaking into their home to kill them. But this is . . . this is really off-the-charts crazy, I don't know. Too many complications."

Reznick put his mug of coffee down on the table in front of him and stood. "If you're having doubts, you need to bail."

Hewson bowed his head as if ashamed. "I don't know, Jon. I don't know if I'm losing my nerve."

"It's OK to be scared, Tom. We've all been there. And listen: this is my thing. I don't take it personal."

"I wish I had let you know earlier. I think I just got carried away. I thought it would all be fine on the chopper, firing off all that shit from up there. But on the bike at speed? I don't know."

"Tom, it's fine. I got this."

Hewson reached into his pockets and brought out a couple of old two-way radios, magnets, duct tape, a rudimentary circuit board, a small empty cigar box, and batteries. He placed it on the table.

Reznick knew what it was for.

Hewson got up from his seat. "Sticky bomb to the side of the car—the ingredients I have for you."

"Appreciate that, thanks."

"The Tovex and C-4 I brought is just a tiny amount. But it's all you'll need. Portable two-way radios. So, you've got a transmitter and receiver. And you can take the bike and the helmet."

Reznick hugged Hewson tight. "Take my truck home. I'll pick it up when I'm finished."

"I love you, man. But I can't do this."

"Don't worry. I got this."

Sixty-Eight

Reznick was going to have to do it alone. He had to get to work. And fast. The first thing he did was carefully assemble the magnetic bomb. It was something he had been taught when he joined Delta. He honed his skills when he was assigned to the CIA. He was meticulous as he made sure the components were painstakingly put together. When he was finished, the "sticky" with the Tovex and C-4 had been stuffed into a cigar box. The two-way radio was duct-taped to the lid of the cigar box, the magnet at the bottom to attach it to the vehicle.

He held the device carefully in his hands. The sticky was the weapon of choice for the Taliban in Afghanistan and Sunni groups in Iraq. He had seen how they could be used to devastating effect, time after time. Insurgents used kids on motorcycles to attach a sticky. And it would invariably kill and destroy whoever was on the other side of the metal.

The effect on morale for both civilians and American troops was debilitating. Reznick would hear of groups attacking Humvees or armored cars. Sometimes as they cruised past markets. The carnage was awful.

The hours dragged as Reznick contemplated how he was going to approach Moretti's vehicle on the motorcycle. He didn't know if

Moretti was going to be sitting in the back left, behind the driver, or on the back right, behind the passenger. That was a major problem.

He eventually decided that Moretti would sit behind the driver on the rear left of his vehicle. He figured one bodyguard would sit in the front passenger seat. And another bodyguard in the rear right, beside Moretti.

Reznick needed to have superquick access to the sticky. Ordinarily he would have a backpack over his chest, take out the device as he approached, and attach it to the target vehicle. But as the sole person on the bike, he had his work cut out for him.

One man to attach the bomb while operating the Kawasaki.

Reznick realized that if he approached from the rear left, he would need his right hand free to attach the device to the moving car. So, he would keep the device inside the left-hand side of his jacket.

But that didn't feel right.

Reznick had a leather messenger bag his daughter had given him as a present. He tested its weight as he slung it over his shoulder. Could he access the side compartment with his right hand?

It was a risk. But if he was honest, the whole thing was a monumental risk.

Reznick gathered everything together. Finally, he packed two 9mm handguns—a Beretta and a Glock—with extra ammo.

He was going to do this, come what may.

Sixty-Nine

Three minutes after midnight, the lights of a chopper cut through the dark sky.

Ripley's chopper approached and landed, the downdraft kicking up sand and dirt and grass.

Reznick screwed up his eyes as he hauled the Kawasaki into the rear of the helicopter. He buckled up and put on his headset, messenger bag strapped across his chest.

Ripley turned around and gave the thumbs-up. "You OK?"

"I'm good. Let's do this."

The chopper turned over the water, banked steeply, and headed south.

Ripley said, "What happened to Tom?"

"I decided I could do it alone."

"When do you want me to do the extraction?"

"Drop me off by the beach. Extraction could be anywhere between 0400 hours and 0500 hours, realistically."

"Copy that. I'll sit tight on the beach."

"If I'm not there by five, get the hell out of there."

"Copy that."

It was a one-hour chopper ride to the drop-off destination—a parking lot adjacent to Weed Beach, on the outskirts of Darien, Connecticut.

"Meet you here by five at the latest, Jon!"

"Copy that." Reznick checked the luminous dial of his watch and gave the thumbs-up sign. He took off his headset, hauled the bike off the chopper. He started up the bike and rode it away from the beach, taking narrow roads. Then he rode south for a few miles.

He was only minutes from the estate of Paul Moretti. Closer and closer. Nearer to his prey and his crew.

A million crazy thoughts were running through his head. He imagined the convoy emerging. He would be waiting in the darkness.

Reznick felt his heart rate hike up. Suddenly, he saw a private road fringing the estate. He slowed down and pulled up. He switched his lights off. And waited.

Seventy

The lights of the four-car convoy edged through the iron gates of Moretti's estate at 0303 hours. Zero day had arrived.

Reznick was sitting astride the motorcycle in a wooded area just off the road, cloaked in darkness, messenger bag across his chest. His lights were off. His heart was beating hard. A rush of adrenaline surged through his veins. He thought back to what Meyerstein had said. She told him he wasn't acting rationally. It was at that moment, all alone, he realized she was right. What he was going to do was the very definition of irrational. But just then, waiting in the darkness, he was way past caring. Fuck the FBI. Fuck rules and regulations. Fuck law and order. He felt himself being consumed by a raging inferno inside.

He waited until the convoy was out of earshot. Then he started up the motorcycle, lights still off. He adjusted the unzipped messenger bag on his chest.

He kicked the bike into gear and pulled away down the dirt road that wove around the trees, before he got back on the asphalt.

Reznick rode faster. He switched on his lights and pulled away. He turned right and headed down a few beach roads until he spotted the convoy up ahead.

He accelerated hard. He approached the rear car fast. He rode past and glanced inside. A driver and a thickset goon. Then he got to the next car, the bulletproof car. He pulled alongside the vehicle and looked inside.

Reznick's heart jolted hard. He struggled to take it in. No one in the back seat or passenger seat. Just a driver. He accelerated to the front two cars and checked if Moretti was sitting in either of them. He turned and looked inside. Just a driver in both cars.

Fuck! What the hell had happened?

Reznick wondered why they were transporting some of the team to the airport but not Moretti. The intel from the gatehouse had been very clear. He pulled over to the side of the road and waited until the convoy whizzed past.

He flipped up his visor and called Trevelle.

"What the hell? Moretti wasn't in any of the vehicles."

"What?"

"I'm telling you, I just passed them. Nothing."

"That doesn't make sense."

"Unless the bastard pulled a fast one. Trying to keep his team on their toes. And if there was anyone compromised on his crew, maybe thinking of switching allegiance, they would be in the dark."

"Maybe he's in the trunk of the car."

"Maybe, I don't know."

The sound of tapping on a keyboard. "Hang on, wait. I'm looking over the footage again from the surveillance camera at the gatehouse. It looks fine. Four-car convoy passing just like we thought . . . Hang on, I'm going to fast-forward the footage and see if there's anything else going on."

Reznick revved up the motorcycle. "Talk to me. Don't leave me hanging!"

"Wow!"

"What?"

"Four minutes and thirty seconds after the four cars left, a black BMW SUV left. One driver."

"Moretti?"

"No idea. Tinted windows."

"So, we have no idea if it's him?"

"That's correct."

"So, where the hell did he go?"

"I'm in the dark on that. No cameras outside that estate for miles. What are you going to do?"

"I think he would've headed off in a different direction."

"Then again, maybe not."

Reznick revved up the bike hard. "I think the convoy is a ruse to throw anyone off the scent."

"Maybe."

He turned the bike around and headed away from the outskirts of suburban Greenwich. "Where am I?"

"You're on Brookside."

The lights of Reznick's bike illuminated the dark road lined by woods either side. He turned a bend, then another, not a car in sight. Faster and faster. He accelerated harder. He felt the adrenaline surging through his body.

He had no idea if he was headed in the right direction. He feared he was going to lose him, that he'd been outfoxed by Moretti. But he kept on going, hoping and praying he was on Moretti's tail. He had to move faster. But he was already doing seventy on narrow rural roads. He might be wrong. Hopelessly wrong. But he guessed Moretti had taken this quiet route. He sensed Moretti wasn't far away.

Reznick rode on, mile after mile, taking the sharp country bends in the dead of night. Then he turned a sweeping corner.

The lights of a solitary car up ahead.

Reznick accelerated hard, the power of the bike coursing through his body. He was closing. Within one hundred yards. Then fifty yards. Closing.

He saw the license plate. It was a black BMW, a silhouetted figure up front driving.

Reznick felt his blood pumping. He edged closer. He overtook the vehicle on the driver's side. He turned.

And there he was!

Moretti was staring straight ahead as if lost in his thoughts.

Reznick reached into his messenger bag and gripped the sticky. Then as he controlled the bike with one hand, he attached the magnetic bomb to the driver's door. Moretti spun around.

But Reznick accelerated, doing ninety, one hundred, one hundred and ten miles per hour! The trees and houses whizzed past! He turned the throttle to the max.

The seconds felt like hours.

Suddenly, an earth-shattering explosion.

Reznick braked hard and turned around. The car was engulfed in flames, lying on its side in a ditch. Flames licked the black sky, incinerating the trees in a nearby field.

Moretti was dead.

Seventy-One

It was just over an hour later when Reznick, lashed with sweat, loaded the Kawasaki onto the chopper. It was 0433 hours. He strapped himself in and put on his headset.

"You OK, buddy?" Ripley said. "You got him?"

Reznick nodded, shaken up. He was wired. "It's done."

"We need to get out of here."

"Copy that. Head right out onto the Sound; I want to dump the bike in the water."

"Got it!"

The chopper took off and rose across the water, then it banked sharply as they headed north.

"Sam, appreciate this. Above and beyond, man."

"It is what is, Jon. The target dead, I assume?"

"Burned to a fucking crisp, I would imagine."

Reznick waited until they were far out over the dark waters of Long Island Sound, where he pushed out the bike and the helmet. He strapped himself back into his seat. He sat in silence for the rest of the flight back to Cape Cod.

The chopper landed.

Reznick followed Ripley into his home. He showered. He watched the sunrise over Cape Cod Bay. He and Ripley headed to a local diner for an early breakfast. He was famished. He popped a couple of Dexedrine.

"You need to go easy on that stuff, Jon," Ripley said. "It's only for short-term use."

"Yeah, I know."

"You don't need it, man."

"Maybe I don't."

Ripley stifled a yawn. "I'm exhausted."

"Want some amphetamines?"

Ripley laughed. "You're crazy, Jon. It's official: you're fucking crazy."

Reznick closed his eyes for a few moments. "Know what the funny thing is—ever since Eastland was killed, I've hardly slept."

"Jon, you need to take a break. And kick back for a few weeks. Maybe months."

"Maybe you're right."

"You want to rest up here? Plenty of room."

Reznick shook his head. "Not now, Sam. Maybe sometime. Right now, I just want to go home."

Seventy-Two

It was late that night when Reznick decided to go out for a celebratory drink. He walked to the Rockland Tavern. He enjoyed the cold craft beers, listening to a raucous live blues band. The TV behind the bar was showing CNN.

The bartender, Simon, was wiping down the bar. "Bill used to sit right there," he said, gesturing to the wooden stool beside Reznick.

"I know. That was his stool. He was a creature of habit. As am I."

"You want another, man?"

"Set it up." Reznick pointed to his glass.

Simon poured another fresh craft lager. Reznick handed him a twenty-dollar bill. "Keep the change."

"That's too much."

"Take it while you can, son."

Simon grinned. "Thanks, man."

"Always nice to have a few bucks in your back pocket."

"Damn straight."

Reznick's eyes were on the TV. A breaking-news flash came up on the screen.

New York Mob boss killed after car bomb attack.

He took a long gulp. He didn't take any satisfaction from that. Truth be told, he felt numb.

Reznick watched the footage for a few minutes. He finished his beer and got off his stool.

"You calling it a night, Jon?"

"I'm done. Make sure no one takes Bill's stool. Not tonight."

"Not a problem."

Reznick left the bar and headed back down Main Street. A few minutes later, he got on the dirt road that led to his home. He walked on, guided by the pale moonlight. The sound of the trees stirred as the wind got up.

He felt the need to escape. To get away again. To a place no one could find him. Not a soul.

Reznick arrived at home, packed his trusty Nosler long gun and the rest of his hunting gear, then loaded up supplies in the back of his truck. He went out onto the deck and sat down, staring out over the waters of Penobscot Bay. The same waters his father had stared out over. The same waters his daughter had stared out over. The same waters he had gazed at since he was a child.

He fell asleep, the sound of the water crashing onto the cove below.

The following morning, after a hearty breakfast, Reznick cleaned up and prepared to set off for his cabin in the north Maine woods. A long, long drive ahead. But it was his place of refuge. A place of solitude. A place to forget.

Just as he was placing the luggage into the truck, his cell phone rang. "Reznick speaking."

"Jon, where the hell have you been?" The voice of Meyerstein.

Reznick wasn't in the mood for tense discussions. "Around."

"I've been trying to contact you. Did you see the news?"

"I don't watch the news," he lied.

"Moretti is dead. You didn't know?"

"No, I didn't. What happened?"

"A car bomb. Forensics is working on it."

Reznick stayed silent.

"You don't have anything to say?"

"What do you mean?"

"I mean, I thought you'd be pleased."

"I'm not pleased. That doesn't please me."

"Jon, the FBI will want to know your whereabouts when Moretti was killed."

"Whatever."

"You don't sound bothered."

"Martha, I'm kinda tired. I was planning to head up to my cabin in the north Maine woods. I need some time to think things over."

"I think we both need some space at the moment." Reznick pressed the cell phone tight to his ear. "I hope you reflect on our relationship. Where we're going."

Reznick closed his eyes for a moment, realizing how out of control he had been. "Martha, I'm sorry."

"For what?"

"For everything. For giving you so much grief. I think maybe I lost my bearings."

"Taking some time is sensible. For both of us."

Reznick felt the warm morning sun on his skin. It felt good to be alive.

"When you get back, let's talk. About us. About where we go from here."

Reznick shielded his eyes from the glare of the sun.

"Did you hear what I said?"

"I hear you. We'll talk when I get back."

"Stay out of trouble, tough guy. Is that too much to ask?"

"I'll see what I can do."

"You're not going to change, are you?"

Reznick smiled. "You sound like my daughter. She looks up to you so much, Martha."

"She's a smart young woman. I'll do whatever I can to look out for her."

"I know you will."

"So, when you leaving?"

Reznick closed his eyes. "I'm leaving now. I've got a long, long journey ahead of me."

Acknowledgements

I would like to thank my editor, Victoria Haslam, and everyone at Amazon Publishing for their enthusiasm, hard work, and belief in the Jon Reznick thriller series. I would also like to thank my loyal readers. Thanks also to Faith Black Ross for her terrific work on this book, and Randall Klein, who looked over an early draft. Special thanks to my agent, Mitch Hoffman of the Aaron M. Priest Literary Agency, New York.

Last but by no means least, my family and friends for their encouragement and support. None more so than my wife, Susan.

About the Author

J. B. Turner is a former journalist and the author of the Jon Reznick series of action thrillers (*Hard Road*, *Hard Kill*, *Hard Wired*, *Hard Way*, *Hard Fall*, *Hard Hit*, *Hard Shot*, *Hard Target*, and *Hard Vengeance*), the American Ghost series of black-ops thrillers (*Rogue*, *Reckoning*, and *Requiem*), and the Deborah Jones political thrillers (*Miami Requiem* and *Dark Waters*). He has a keen interest in geopolitics. He lives in Scotland with his wife and two children.